The Cowboy Cookie Challenge

The heavy wooden door creaked open, bringing a blast of chilly December air. Jazzy turned to watch a lanky cowboy mosey in.

Charlie sat up straighter and readjusted the maroon beret that matched his scrubs. "Mmm, who do we have here?"

The cowboy navigated his way to the to-go counter and Charlie slumped back against his chair, disappointment tugging his mouth down. "Oh, it's just Roan Sullivan. I thought we had a fresh face in town."

Roan Sullivan. The father of Jazzy's four-year-old tonsillectomy patient, Trinity. The guy who'd almost fainted.

"You know him?" she asked.

Handsome, lean, and muscular in the wiry way of men who performed physical labor for a living, Roan was drool worthy. Dark, thick hair and soulful brown eyes.

Just her type.

The Cowboy Cookie Challenge

A TWILIGHT, TEXAS NOVEL

LORI WILDE

AVONBOOKS

An Imprint of HarperCollins*Publishers*

Excerpt from *The Wedding at Moonglow Bay* copyright © 2023 by Laurie Vanzura.

THE COWBOY COOKIE CHALLENGE. Copyright © 2022 by Laurie Vanzura. All rights reserved. Printed in the United States of America. No part of this book may be used or reproduced in any manner whatsoever without written permission except in the case of brief quotations embodied in critical articles and reviews. For information, address HarperCollins Publishers, 195 Broadway, New York, NY 10007.

First Avon Books mass market printing: October 2022

Print Edition ISBN: 978-0-06-313806-3
Digital Edition ISBN: 978-0-06-313804-9

Cover illustration by Reginald Polynice
Cover image © James Hackland/Alamy Stock Photo (lamp posts); © Getty Images; © Shutterstock; © Hum3D

Avon, Avon & logo, and Avon Books & logo are registered trademarks of HarperCollins Publishers in the United States of America and other countries.

HarperCollins is a registered trademark of HarperCollins Publishers in the United States of America and other countries.

FIRST EDITION

22 23 24 25 26   BVGM   10 9 8 7 6 5 4 3 2 1

To Carol Hoefs—Thank you so much for your enduring support over the years. I feel blessed to have you in my life.

The
Cowboy Cookie
Challenge

CHAPTER 1

Jazzy Walker watched her best friend, Charlie Cheek, trot across the barroom in an adroit Fred Astaire two-step, dodging tipsy patrons on his way to their bistro table in the far corner, balancing two candy cane martinis without sloshing a drop.

Medical personnel from Twilight General Hospital across the road patronized the Recovery Room Bar and Grill, and at seven thirty on a Friday night, the seven A.M. to seven P.M. shift workers had descended on the watering hole en masse.

"You look thirsty, Lambchop," Charlie hollered over the rowdy crowd and the jukebox blasting "Santa Claus Wants Some Loving."

"Parched." Jazzy reached for her drink, offering him a winning smile in thanks.

"Ready to blow off some steam?"

"You betcha! Karaoke '70s contest here we come!"

"My little ray of sunshine."

"It's as easy to smile as frown." Jazzy giggled.

"Good Lord don't embroider that on a pillow."

Charlie raised his glass. "Cheers. Candy cane martinis ought to fix us right up for 'Bohemian Rhapsody.'"

They clinked glasses and grinned with the ease of childhood friendship.

"So how was your week?" Charlie fished a plump cranberry from his drink and popped the tart fruit into his mouth.

"Pretty good."

"Is this true or just generalized Jazzy optimism?" he asked.

"Pediatric admissions are down. That's always something to celebrate. The only new admit I had today was a tonsillectomy."

Charlie raised his eyebrows. "They admitted a tonsillectomy case?"

"Minor complications. No biggie. Doc Freeman will send her home tomorrow, but the excitement came when her father almost fainted. I caught Dad just in the nick of time. One second later and *boom*, he would've pancaked the floor."

"Look at you, shero." Charlie held up a palm.

Jazzy slapped him a high five and sipped her drink. The peppermint set her tongue tingling. She wasn't a big drinker, and the martini packed a punch. If she wanted to sing a song as complicated as "Bohemian Rhapsody," she needed to slow down. She ran her fingers over the glass stem, wiping away condensation.

"FYI," Charlie said. "I ordered all-the-way nachos, so don't be afraid to drink up. Gooey cheese will soak up any liquor."

"Yay! Thanks. I'm starving. We were shorthanded and slammed, and I skipped lunch." Slammed because she'd been tending the light-headed single dad of her tonsillectomy case; a gorgeous single dad, just to be clear. Not that she noticed. Much.

"Now the big question." Charlie placed both palms flat. "Have you heard from Traveling Nurses? How did the second interview go?"

Jazzy crossed her fingers. "No news is good news, right? I don't expect a call until after the New Year. Holidays get in the way."

"You'll get it."

"Here's hoping." She crossed her fingers. "They were very encouraging."

"Doubts?"

"A little. I've never lived outside of Twilight."

"More reason to hightail it out of town. It's your big chance to see the world. I'm jealous."

"Don't be. I wouldn't leave if not for . . ." She gulped. "Well . . . we won't get into that. I'm going to miss everyone. You most of all."

"I remember when we were kids, and you collected travel brochures and we spent hours in your hospital room poring over them and spinning Eiffel Tower fantasies."

Yes, and until her high school sweetheart got engaged to her former childhood friend, Andi Browning, Jazzy had clung to hope that she and Danny would reunite, despite their incompatibility. When they were dating, people—Charlie chief among them—used to teasingly say, "Here comes Darkness and Light." Once, she thought that meant she and Danny dovetailed. Now she understood that opposites had simply attracted. Not always a healthy combo.

Ahh, believing in fairy tales, legends, and myths. The downside to living in a tourist town that exploited its romantic history. Magical thinking. She'd cut her teeth on stories of "one true love" and reunited high school sweethearts. Such fables were pure bunk, and she'd stayed too long in a relationship that had run its course, because of a ridiculous belief in happily-ever-after.

"I should have left before now."

"You weren't ready. But the time *has* come." Charlie hummed a few bars of "Time Has Come Today" and drummed the table.

It sounded ominous.

The heavy wooden door creaked open, bringing a blast of chilly December air. Jazzy turned to watch a lanky cowboy mosey in.

Charlie sat up straighter and readjusted the maroon beret that matched his scrubs. "Mmm, who do we have here?"

The cowboy navigated his way to the to-go counter and Charlie slumped back against his chair, disappointment tugging his mouth down. "Oh, it's just Roan Sullivan. I thought we had a fresh face in town."

Roan Sullivan. The father of Jazzy's four-year-old tonsillectomy patient, Trinity. The guy who'd almost fainted.

"You know him?" she asked.

Handsome, lean, and muscular in the wiry way

of men who performed physical labor for a living, Roan was drool worthy. Dark, thick hair and soulful brown eyes.

Just her type.

Jazzy recognized his sexiness when she'd taken his elbow and eased him down into the waiting room chair that morning. He smelled nice too, like pumpkin spice and sandalwood soap. She didn't lust after her patients' parents, but something about Roan stoked her interest.

And her empathy.

He's a single father raising a daughter. You identify with him because of you and your dad.

Roan Sullivan appeared worn and frazzled. Her heartstrings tugged anew, and her nurturing instincts flared. She ached to tell him Trinity would be fine. He had nothing to worry about.

Charlie planted his elbows on the table and leaned forward. "Roan's a cutting horse rancher and he owns a small spread halfway between Twilight and Jubilee, but he's also an accomplished cowboy chef. Two years ago, he won a campfire cook-off competition on the Food Network and set the town buzzing."

"Oh yeah." Jazzy crinkled her nose. "I remember hearing something about a local man winning a national cooking challenge."

"It was so sad."

"Winning the competition?"

Charlie clicked his tongue. "No. While Roan was out of town competing, his wife scheduled a minor surgical procedure and she ended up dying on the operating table. A reaction to the anesthesia, I believe. Not at Twilight General though, thank heavens. She was in a Fort Worth hospital."

"Oh my goodness, the poor man." An icy chill passed through her and she rubbed her arms.

She studied Roan from across the room. His back was against the wooden shiplap wall, his muscular arms folded across his chest, a distracted furrow creased his brow. His Wranglers fit him like a second skin, showing off muscular thighs.

"*Jazzy.*" Charlie drew out her name. "What's going on in that noodle of yours?"

"Nothing. Why?"

"You've got that I-need-to-fix-somebody light in your eyes."

"I do?"

Charlie nodded. "It's the same look you got when we were fourteen and you tried to kiss me before I'd come out to you."

Jazzy's cheeks pinkened. "That was stupid of me. I didn't understand. I thought you were cute and needed a girlfriend."

"I know. And I realize you know there was nothing in me to 'fix.'" He reached across the table and laid his hand on hers. "But remember, not everyone needs fixing and even if they do, you're not in charge of the cure."

"My fatal flaw." She sighed. "Wishing everyone a safe and happy life."

"Being ever ready to help is an endearing quality." He chucked her under the chin. "But you can't control other people."

Yes, yes, she'd learned that lesson the hard way

with Danny. Disconcerted, Jazzy slipped off the barstool.

"Where are you going?"

"I'll just be a sec."

"Jazzy . . ."

Before she reached Roan, the bartender leaned over to hand him a white paper to-go bag branded with the golden Recovery Room logo.

Roan grabbed the sack and headed for the door.

Jazzy popped into his path, blocking his exit. "Hi!"

Roan stepped back, blinking like Rip Van Winkle. "Oh," he said. "It's *you*."

She'd caught him off guard. She should have listened to Charlie and kept her butt parked on the barstool. "Hey."

"Hello, Nurse Walker."

His eyes were soft and kind, and she was glad she'd come over. "I noticed you standing over here by yourself."

"Got a burger. The hospital cafeteria was already closed."

"How's Trinity?"

"She seems okay. I didn't want to leave her, but my mom dropped by to check on us and insisted I take a break."

"Smart mother." Jazzy waved at Charlie, who motioned her back to their table. "Would you like to join me and my friend for a drink?"

"I appreciate the invite." Roan shifted his weight and shook his head. "I don't like leaving Trinity for too long."

"Her grandmother is with her."

"I better not, but thank you for taking such good care of her." He paused. "And me when I got light-headed after talking to Dr. Freeman. Sorry I was such a wimp."

"Just doing my job, Mr. Sullivan, and you weren't a wimp. You had a stressful morning. Normal reaction."

"Please," he said. "Call me Roan."

"Only if you call me Jazzy." *What are you doing? Stop this.*

"I've watched you with Trinity. I'm bowled over at how gentle you are with your patients. More so than the other nurses. Although, everyone's been great. You're just *more*."

She heard gratitude in his voice and saw it in his chocolate brown eyes. This was the praise she lived for. The reason she'd become a nurse, to help sick children and their families.

Roan wore a red plaid shearling coat over a green Western-style shirt. He looked like Christmas itself. The smell of juicy cheeseburger wafted between them and when his eyes latched on to hers, it seemed everything around them halted and it was just the two of them in the bar.

Goose bumps sprang up on her arms, and her pulse kicked.

Roan was in his early thirties, at least ten years older than her own twenty-three years, and he possessed an air of steady responsibility she seldom found in men her own age. This cowboy knew his worth and made no excuses for who he was. Those qualities appealed to her. Jazzy liked him, this single dad who knew how to cook over a campfire.

Flirting isn't an option. He's the parent of your patient. Just don't.

A patient on tomorrow's discharge list. She had him alone. This was her chance to ask him out. How could she let the opportunity slip away?

"My friend tells me you're a professional camp-fire cook." She pointed toward Charlie with her thumb.

Charlie was still waving her back to the table, an exasperated but loving expression on his face that said, *Leave that poor man alone, you hussy.*

"That's true," Roan murmured.

"I'm sorry about your wife. That must have been so hard."

"Small town folks love gossip."

"I hate that you had to go through that." Jazzy was itching to touch his forearm as a gesture of comfort, but his stiff body language warned her off. *Boundaries, Jasmine.*

He shrugged. "It's been two years since we lost Claire. Trinity and I are still getting used to being alone."

"Your daughter seems happy and well-adjusted. She's a bright little girl."

Roan gave a rueful sigh. "I don't think Trinity remembers her mother at all. Which is sad. I do the best I can to keep her mom's memory alive. Tell my daughter stories, keep photos of her mom around, and show Trinity that I love and cherish her. I pray it's enough."

"Your love *is* enough," Jazzy said, thinking about how she and her dad had formed an un-breakable bond after her mother, Crystal, had abandoned them. Her situation wasn't the same as Trinity's, but there was more than one way to lose a mother. "It must be challenging to raise a four-year-old on your own."

"Oh, I've got lots of help," he said. "Claire's mom is a gem, and my mother and sister, Rio, are always ready to pitch in. Sure, we've had bumps in the road like any other family, but I consider myself a lucky man."

"That's a healthy attitude," she said. "I'm glad you're able to see things that way. Not everyone is so resilient."

"Why thank you, Ms. Jazzy. I appreciate you saying so." He moved as if to tip his cowboy hat, then looked embarrassed when he realized he wasn't wearing one and dropped his hand. "I better be getting back."

"Yes. Well . . ." Jazzy stuck out her hand. "Nice seeing you."

He stared at her hand.

Ninny. Quickly, she retracted her palm at the same time he shifted the paper bag to his left arm and extended his right.

She rushed to take it, but in the meantime, he pulled back.

Their gazes met, and they laughed, and then they shared an awkward handshake. "It's Beginning to Look a Lot Like Christmas" oozed from the jukebox.

"I have an extra ticket to the annual Twilight Christmas pageant," Jazzy blurted. She'd bought the ticket for her mom, so they could do a mother-daughter thing, but Crystal had announced last minute she was spending Christmas in Aspen skiing with her new husband and couldn't use the ticket. "I'd love for you to be my guest at the Christmas Eve performance."

What in the heck are you doing? Shut up!

"Er . . . my family has plans for Christmas Eve."

"Oh yes. Right." Her laugh sounded ridiculously forced, and her stomach churned. "Of course, you already have plans. Forget I asked. It was a half-baked idea . . ."

"Did you ask me out because you feel sorry for me?"

"No, no," she denied.

"It's okay." He shrugged again. "I'm used to it. Whenever women find out that I'm a widower with a young child, they pity me. It's not a good feeling, but it is what it is."

"I do apologize," she said, uncertain how to respond.

"It's not romantic," he said. "And I'm not sure why women think a widowed dad is romantic."

"I don't think that."

He cocked his head, his gaze drilling into her hard. "Thank you for the generous invitation, Ms. Walker. I'm so grateful to you for taking good care of my daughter. But I'm just not into pity dates. I hope you understand."

"Good night, Mr. Sullivan." She wriggled her fingers and hurried back to the table to find that Charlie had eaten all the nachos.

Her friend took one look at her chiding face and

deadpanned, "Hey, you left me alone with a plate of all-the-way nachos, Lambchop. It's your fault for trotting off and trying to fix a broken man."

Jazzy opened her mouth to deny it, but her best friend dialed up his grin and said, *"Again."*

CHAPTER 2

Roan left the Recovery Room with a wide smile on his face. It was the first time he'd smiled since Trinity's surgery. Even the biggest grinch in Hood County couldn't resist grinning at Jazzy Walker.

Jazzy was cute as a speckled pup, but she was too young for him. She had wild oats to sow, and he was a widower with a four-year-old. He wouldn't let himself admire how her golden blond ponytail bounced above her slender neck when she bobbed her head, or how the blue scrubs enhanced the color of her eyes. Or how her bright smile lit up an entire room.

C'mon, he wasn't fooling himself. Jazzy held him spellbound. But it was ridiculous to personalize her kindness. He spent the day watching her with other patients and parents. She gifted every one of them with the same inviting charm and warm sentiments. He was nothing special to her, and it was silly to believe otherwise.

Thinking about Jazzy, and the memory of her hand on his arm when she'd kept him from passing

out in the surgical waiting room, had him breathless again. She had seen him at his worst, weak and
vulnerable.

He hated that.

Then she'd asked him out and from the oh-you-
poor-widower look on her face, he'd known she'd
pitied him. Had he been too harsh? Worried about
his reaction, Roan felt his smile slip away, and by
the time he reached Trinity's room, he was his serious self.

He pushed open the door. His mom sat next to
the bed, reading a book. Ava Sullivan looked up
with a soft smile.

Trinity lay sound asleep, her soft red curls stark
against the white pillowcase. On the bedside table
rested an empty container of orange sherbet, his
daughter's favorite. Sherbet that Jazzy had brought
Trinity after she'd roused from the anesthesia.

At the sweet sight of his slumbering child, Roan's
heart pushed into his throat. An IV tubing snaked
from her little hand to the bag attached to an IV
pump on a wheeled pole. His daughter looked so
tiny, so vulnerable.

He'd fight hand-to-hand combat with a grizzly
bear for her. No one meant as much to him as Trinity. His love for her leaked from every pore.

His mother tucked an errant strand of strawberry
blond hair behind one ear. Trinity had gotten her
peaches and cream coloring from Mom. "You're
back already."

"Grabbed a cheeseburger from across the street."
He held up the paper bag.

"Why didn't you stay for a beer?"

"I need to have my wits about me. Trinity comes first, *always*."

His mother slipped a bookmark into her book and closed it. "You're a wonderful dad, Roan, and far be it from me to criticize your parenting, but there's a reason they tell you to put your oxygen mask on first during an airplane emergency before assisting your children."

"I'm fine, Mom."

Yawning, his mother stood and stretched for the ceiling. "Let me stay the night with her. You go home and get some sleep."

"You've raised your kids," he said. "My turn."

"I respect you, son. You've been through a lot. Losing Claire, yet still putting one foot in front of the other and keeping things going. I'm proud of you."

"Thanks, Mom."

He didn't need her validation, but he wouldn't lie. It felt nice to know his mother approved of how he was handling solo parenthood. The road was rocky, and he couldn't do it without the help of his family.

"She'll be okay," his mother said, nodding at Trinity. "History won't repeat itself."

"I know. This time I'm here."

"What happened with Claire wasn't your fault, son."

Roan swallowed. "If only I'd—"

"She still would have died."

"But I could have held her hand before she'd gone into surgery. Given her one last kiss . . ." He broke off, the lump in his throat so big he couldn't swallow.

His mom came over and hugged him. "Claire knew you loved her. She never doubted it for a second."

"She was all alone."

"No, she wasn't. Your father and I were there, her family was there—"

"And I was halfway across the country winning some lame-ass cast-iron cooking contest."

"Claire was proud of your culinary skills. She'd hate that you stopped competing because of her."

That was true, but Roan couldn't separate Claire's death from his campfire cook-off victory. He'd been on a sound set, showing off with his trophy as Claire lay dying. Now the idea of competing turned his stomach.

"Mom, I don't have time for foolish pursuits. Trinity is all that matters."

"One day, Trinity will grow up, and where will that leave you?"

"Knowing I did everything I could for my child after she lost her mother."

"You're not ready to bake again. I get it. Too bad though because this year's Twilight Christmas Cookie Challenge is cowboy-themed. The contestants must use campfire cooking in their recipes. You'd be a shoo-in."

"I have no desire to compete in an amateur contest. It'd be pure ego on my part to take the win away from aspiring bakers."

"It'd be good for Trinity to see you as a well-rounded person. You don't want her thinking you sacrificed your own life because of her. That's a big burden for a child to carry."

THE COWBOY COOKIE CHALLENGE   17

"Mom—"

"I get it, I do. I'm butting out and minding my business." His mother fished in her handbag and took out a blue piece of paper and settled it onto the table beside the sherbet carton. "I'll put the flyer about the baking contest right here, on the off chance you'll change your mind."

He crossed his arms over his chest. "I won't."

"Stubborn as your father." She smiled tenderly.

"Good night, Mom."

"Are you leaving, Grammy?" Trinity asked in a croaky voice.

Roan's gaze shifted to his child, who was rubbing her sleepy eyes.

"Yes, I'm heading home, Doodlebug, but your daddy will stay right here all night."

Trinity propped herself up in the bed, pushing her hair from her face, yawning big. "Where's Jazzy?"

"Her shift ended and there's a night nurse on duty," Mom said. "Jazzy will be back in the morning. Do you need me to help you to the bathroom?"

Trinity nodded.

"I can help her." Roan moved toward the bed.

"I want Grammy."

Sidelined. Roan grunted.

While his mother took Trinity to the restroom, pushing the wheeled IV pole along with them, Roan straightened Trinity's covers and plumped her pillow. The acrid smell of anesthesia clung to the linens. He stepped back and his gaze fell on the flyer.

He picked up the paper, crumpled it into a ball, and tossed it in the trash. There, temptation gone.

His mother and Trinity returned from the bathroom, Trinity chattering away as Mom guided her to the bed. "Jazzy is so nice, and she smells like cotton candy. She told me she stayed at the hospital a bunch when she was a little girl and her daddy took care of her all by hisself, just like me and my daddy."

"That's true," Mom said. "I knew Jazzy when she was not much older than you."

"You did?" Trinity's eyes got big. "How?"

"I taught at her school before I retired." His mother helped Trinity crawl between the covers.

"You taught Jazzy?" Roan folded his arms. While his mother had taught school in Twilight, Roan and his sister, Rio, had gone to school in Jubilee because they'd lived on the east side of the Hood-Parker county line.

"I wasn't her teacher," Mom said. "But I knew about her situation and despite everything she'd been through, that child was so full of joy. She's irrepressible. No one can keep her down for long. Not even her lifelong rival, Andi Browning."

"Jazzy and Andi have a rivalry?" Roan had trained a cutting horse for Andi Browning, and while the woman was a bit full of herself, she was also an excellent horsewoman.

"You haven't heard? Everyone in town knows about Jazzy and Andi."

"Mom, I'm not into gossip."

"Learning about your neighbors isn't gossip, it's called taking an interest. In fourth grade, Andi beat Jazzy out for the school Christmas pageant.

Although she was a fan-favorite, because of her asthma, Jazzy couldn't handle the long-winded monologues and she lost the part. Then there was the whole Girl Scout cookie kerfuffle."

He didn't want to indulge his mother's tendency to spread stories, but damn if he wasn't intrigued. "What happened?"

Mom waved a hand. "I don't know the exact details, but Jazzy and Andi were neck and neck in cookie sales, with Jazzy pulling ahead in the final few days, and then out of the blue, Andi gets a bulk sale that sunk Jazzy's chances. Rumor has it Andi's mom bought a big batch to ensure her daughter's win."

Roan shifted his weight. "Jazzy doesn't seem the type to let petty childhood rivalries get to her."

"Jazzy is more competitive than you'd think. The rivalry didn't stop with plays and Girl Scout cookies. When Andi and Jazzy were in nursing school together, Andi slept with Jazzy's boyfriend, Danny Garza. Danny broke off his four-year relationship with Jazzy to be with Andi. I've heard Jazzy hasn't dated since . . ." Mom tapped her chin with an index finger and looked lost in thought. "My goodness, that was almost two years ago. Not too long after you lost Claire."

"This conversation is making me uncomfortable. I don't enjoy talking about people behind their backs."

His mother looked hurt. "I wasn't trying to bad-mouth Andi or Danny."

"No?"

"Don't look at me like that. In my book, Jazzy and Danny were never a good match. I was just telling you what happened."

Roan angled his head at Trinity. "Little pitchers. We don't want her thinking we make a sport of judging other people."

"You're right. Guilty as charged. What can I say? I'm team Jazzy, especially after the excellent care she's given our Trinity, and I got carried away."

"Let's make amends by not discussing Jazzy, or anyone else for that matter, when they're not present," Roan said.

"You get your sense of honor from your dad. I'm ashamed of myself."

"I don't mean to judge you either, Mom."

Kinda hypocritical, Sullivan. Don't pretend you aren't curious about Jazzy.

Okay, fine. He was human and wondering why his mother thought Danny and Jazzy hadn't been a good match. Or why Jazzy gave up on love.

Damn, man, are you shooting for the hypocrite trifecta?

Because he hadn't dated either. Not since Claire died. And until tonight, when he'd stared into Jazzy's big blue eyes at the Recovery Room and she asked him to the Christmas pageant, he'd thought his love life was over.

At least until Trinity was grown.

But now, he couldn't stop himself from wondering, *what if?*

CHAPTER 3

Jazzy was on her second candy cane martini gearing up for the karaoke contest. Normally, she was a one-drink-on-a-Friday-or-Saturday-night kind of gal, but Andi and Danny had just walked into the bar and she was distracting herself. She'd wanted to bolt, but Charlie wouldn't let her.

"Don't give them the satisfaction."

She angled a glance at the couple. Andi was showing off her engagement ring to an adoring entourage. Once upon a time, Jazzy had been part of Andi's coterie. Danny sat next to his fiancée, perusing the karaoke menu.

A stab of jealousy went through her, sharp as a new knife. She didn't like this feeling. Not one bit. By nature, Jazzy was built to choose joy. She brought smiles to faces and positive vibes to the world and that was her essence. But whenever she saw Andi and Danny together, her honorable intentions took a hike and Petty Jazzy reared her tacky head.

"Whoa," Charlie said. "What's with the rictus grin?"

"They're entering the karaoke contest," Jazzy said.

"We'll beat them. Danny can't carry a tune in a titanium bucket."

"No. But Andi's got an amazing voice. Her pipes will cancel out his."

"You have a great singing voice too, Lambchop."

She met his gaze. "Not as good as yours. We're gonna smoke 'em like a beehive."

Charlie leaned away from her. "You're scary when you get competitive."

"Hey, we were here first."

"I agree. The witch stole your boyfriend, and she deserves no sympathy, but they do have a right to be here. We can just go—"

Now he wanted to leave? She pounded her fist on the table. "No! We're winning this damn contest."

Charlie's eyes widened. "Wait . . . is Petty Jazzy in the house?"

"Maybe," she mumbled.

"Hello, Petty Jazzy. Haven't seen you in a while. Welcome."

She stuck out her tongue at Charlie.

"Oh, P.J., I've missed you." Her friend winked. "You add spark to any contest."

"I don't enjoy being this way," Jazzy grumbled.

"Wanna talk about it?"

"Nothing new to say."

It had been twenty months since Danny had chosen Andi over her. She should be well over him. And, she was. In her heart of hearts, she knew they weren't a good match. In retrospect, their breakup was inevitable.

But dang. Did he have to ask Andi to marry

him? The one woman who always bested Jazzy in everything?

"You know why you never win to her, right?" Charlie read her mind.

"You have insight?"

"You're not cutthroat enough. Whenever the finish line is in sight and you are about to win, Andi pulls the victim card, and your tenderheartedness won't allow Petty Jazzy to plow her over."

"You think?"

"Just my opinion."

Jazzy mulled over his input as she watched the excited group gathered around Andi, oohing and aahing over her ring. Andi had announced her engagement to Danny two weeks ago on the Pediatric Ward where both she and Andi worked. Danny was an EMT at Twilight General as well. The next day, Jazzy had applied to Traveling Nurses, to pursue her long-held dream of seeing the world. She couldn't stick around and watch her former love marry her frenemy.

"Hello!" The contest emcee, Nan Highsmith, was a retired nurse who now owned the bar. She was barely five feet tall and loved neon colors. Tonight, Nan wore a lime green tunic over fluorescent orange leggings and bespoke cowgirl boots. "Y'all folks ready to get your karaoke on?"

The audience cheered and clapped.

"Maybe we shouldn't sing 'Bohemian Rhapsody,'" Jazzy said to Charlie. "Something simpler perhaps?"

"But we're so good at Queen. And changing songs midstream could throw off our rhythm."

"If you're new to our friendly Friday night competition, it's not too late to enter." Nan pointed to the whiteboard mounted near the bar. "You have ten minutes before we close the sign-up."

A few customers went to write their names on the whiteboard.

Jazzy's and Charlie's names were first on the list. Danny and Andi were fifth. The pair had chosen a number from the musical, *Grease*. "You're the One That I Want."

Nauseated, Jazzy pushed the half-empty martini glass away.

Nan explained the rules for the uninitiated, then waved in their direction. "Jazzy and Charlie, you're up first."

Jazzy blew out her breath.

"You wanna back out?" Charlie asked.

"No way. Let's bring down the house."

Charlie put out his hand, and she slapped her palm into his. They climbed onstage as the TV mounted over the bar switched to the karaoke screen. A photograph of Queen and the "Bohemian Rhapsody" logo appeared as Nan cued up the song.

Charlie and Jazzy picked up their microphones.

They'd sung this karaoke number so many times that Jazzy could sing it with her eyes closed, but tonight, she wanted to show up Andi and Danny. She would give this performance one hundred and ten percent.

Or rather, Petty Jazzy would. She was itching to compete.

Charlie started off the song, singing the intro solo. Jazzy joined in on the chorus. After that, they went back and forth, alternating between the two of them and miming Freddie Mercury's movements.

The audience egged them on, applauding and cheering and stomping their feet. She and Charlie sang their hearts out. Six minutes later, they were perspiring and breathless and awaiting their scores.

The judges awarded them 9.6.

"That's our best score ever." Charlie lifted his hand for a high five. "We've got this in the bag, babe."

Jazzy slapped his palm and peeked over at Andi and Danny.

Danny smiled and gave her a thumbs-up.

Jazzy's heart fluttered.

Andi scowled and whispered something in Danny's ear. His smile faded.

The second pair of contestants took the stage and sang "Proud Mary."

"No competition there," Charlie muttered.

Jazzy shot another glance across the bar. Danny and Andi were smooching. Jazzy's cheeks burned.

"Stop staring at them. Concentrate on what song we're going to sing for the final round. More Queen?"

"Sure. We're on a roll."

"Which song? 'We Will Rock You' or 'We Are the Champions'?"

"How about 'Crazy Little Thing Called Love'?"

Charlie cleared his throat. "You're playing with fire."

"Fine. 'Somebody to Love'?"

"We haven't practiced that one as much. Besides,

do you really want to let Andi know you're still hurting?"

"It's thematic."

Charlie rolled his eyes. "Let it go, woman. It's been almost two years. Yes, I know they just got engaged, and it's pushed you back into a dark headspace, but I'm pulling rank. 'We Are the Champions.' It's always a crowd-pleaser."

The "Proud Mary" couple finished to tepid applause and a score of 7.2. Two more couples sang duets. Both passable, but neither came close to Jazzy and Charlie's score.

Jazzy grew more agitated. She couldn't stop watching Danny and Andi, who couldn't seem to stop kissing. Didn't they ever have to breathe?

Charlie waved his palm in front of Jazzy's face. "Woman, what's gotten into you?"

"Andi is kissing him in public just to provoke me." Jazzy couldn't look away. Oh wow, she was losing it as feelings of jealousy, betrayal, hurt, and anger tangled up in her throat.

"Grab your purse." Charlie slipped his arm through hers. "We're outta here. Forget the contest. You need an intervention."

But she couldn't move. Her butt stayed welded to the chair. Her attention glued on her ex. Danny must have felt her stare, because he pulled away from Andi and raised his head. His gaze met Jazzy's. In his eyes, she saw pity.

For her.

Danny felt sorry for *her*.

Blistering humiliation blinded her, and her ears

burned hot. Had Roan Sullivan felt this way when she'd pitied him?

"Next contestants," Nan called from the stage. "Andi Browning and Danny Garza."

Charlie got up and tugged on Jazzy's arm. "Giddyup, Walker. Let's go."

"We're not leaving."

"Oh-*kay*," Charlie mumbled and plunked back down. "I see we've chosen masochism over common sense."

Hand in hand, Andi and Danny walked to the stage. Jazzy couldn't take her eyes off them, no matter how much she wanted to. Andi stuck combs in her curly dishwater blond hair, arranging it into an Olivia-Newton-John-as-Sandy hairdo. She donned the black leather jacket that she'd been carrying. Danny took out a comb and slicked back his dark curls, and then put on a letterman sweater in imitation of Danny Zuko.

"They brought props," Charlie said. "We should've brought props."

"What? Freddie Mercury armbands and ballet shoes?"

"Props could put them over the top," Charlie said. "You've got to give 'em credit. They came to play."

Jazzy wished she'd known that. She shouldn't have come to the Recovery Room tonight.

Andi and Danny were singing and prancing onstage as they peered into each other's eyes in a near-perfect rendition of Sandy and Danny from *Grease*.

When Jazzy was dating Danny, she couldn't get him to sing karaoke to save her life. Tonight, he was acting as if he were competing on *America's Got Talent*. Had he been taking singing lessons?

For Andi?

Jazzy gritted her teeth. "I've gotta pee."

"We can still leave," Charlie called after her.

In the bathroom, Jazzy couldn't shake her jealousy. Not that she wanted Danny back. Far too much water under that bridge. She just didn't want Andi to have him.

No, no, she retracted that. She'd loved Danny once, and she wanted the best for him. If Andi made him happy, okay.

In the meantime, she had a karaoke competition to win.

Jazzy splashed some cold water on her face as the bathroom walls vibrated with the fading notes of the *Grease* song and she reapplied her makeup. Feeling more in control of her emotions, she ran a brush through her hair and smiled at her reflection.

"You're fine. A-okay. So what if Danny and Andi are fantastic together? It's got nothing to do with you."

From the speakers in the bar, she could hear Nan announcing Andi and Danny had also scored 9.6, the same as she and Charlie.

"We'll take a brief break and then we'll finish the elimination round, followed by the final round as our two highest scoring couples return for the sing-off," Nan said.

Jazzy walked out of the bathroom door and ran

smack into Danny's chest. They leaped back in unison.

"Sorry," Danny mumbled.

Andi was behind him. "Watch where you're going, Walker."

"It was an accident," Jazzy said, terrified that she sounded defensive.

Red-faced, Danny merged with the wood paneling.

"He's *my* man." Andi flashed her engagement ring under Jazzy's nose.

"Yeah, I can see that. Congrats."

"You had your chance, and you blew it."

"Life's one big learning curve."

"I bet you're regretting that happier-than-thou attitude now." Andi tossed her head, still sporting the Sandy combs.

Floored, Jazzy stared. "Wh-what are you talking about?"

"If you weren't so toxic with your positivity, Danny wouldn't have dumped you. But you are and he did . . . and *ta-da*." Andi wriggled her ring finger in Jazzy's face again. "So, thank you."

Toxic positivity.

She remembered all too well when Danny had thrown those words at her. Her mind slipped back almost two years. Danny's boss had passed him over for a big promotion. When she'd tried to give him a pep talk, he'd turned on her and said the phrase that had cut her to the core.

Your positivity is toxic, Jazzy. Not everyone likes to pretend life is a bowl of cherries. Some of us prefer reality.

That hurtful fight had led to them taking a break from their relationship, as Danny moved out of their shared apartment. During that time, Danny rebounded into Andi's waiting arms.

The betrayal hurt, but she wouldn't show her feelings, or stop having an upbeat personality. Jazzy was an optimist, but even so, she had to ask herself if she was a Pollyanna?

It wasn't the first time someone called her on the carpet for excessive perkiness. She felt ashamed again.

Jazzy met Andi's stare head-on. "I wish only the very best for you both."

Her attention shifted to Danny, who'd jammed his hands into his pockets and was studying his sneakers. How had she ever believed he was the love of her life; this guy who couldn't meet her eyes?

Danny darted a quick glance in her general direction. "We didn't know you and Charlie would be here for karaoke, Jazzy. Otherwise, we'd've gone to the Horny Toad Tavern."

"It's fine, Danny. You and I ran out of steam years ago." She offered him a forgiving smile. "I'm thankful for what we shared and I'm happy you've found the love of your life."

Danny looked relieved. "You mean it?"

"I do."

"Aww, Jazz." For a split second Danny looked like someone who'd bet big at the Vegas craps table and lost. "You're the best."

Andi pasted up a forced grin and wrapped her arm around Danny's waist. "But she's not wearing your ring, is she?"

"I'm gonna go get us a couple of beers before the second round starts," Danny said and wandered off to the bar.

"Listen," Andi said to Jazzy once Danny had left. "No need to keep up the happy, happy, joy, joy facade. Our engagement upsets you. Admit it."

She wouldn't let Andi rattle her, not for all the karaoke wins in the world. "I'm not upset."

"Uh-huh." Andi toyed with the engagement ring, spinning it around on her finger.

Charlie came over, watching the exchange between them. "No supply for you here, Browning." He made shooing motions. "Get on your broom and fly away."

Ignoring him, Andi stepped closer to Jazzy. "Well, I'm happy that you're happy."

"Jazzy is a happy person," Charlie said. "You can't ruin that."

Andi screwed up her face, as if searching for a way to disprove Charlie's claim. "Danny and I are going to win this karaoke sing-off."

"We'll see about that." Charlie narrowed his eyes.

"Yes, we will." Andi bared her teeth.

"You're going down, Browning," Jazzy said, startling herself with her vehemence. "Count on it."

"Ha!" Andi said, but her forehead wrinkled slightly.

"We'll hash this out on the karaoke stage." Charlie glowered at Andi.

"I'm looking forward to it." Andi flounced off.

"Ready to get out of here now?" Charlie's tone pled.

"Not on your life. The party is just getting started."

"Oh boy." Charlie beseeched the ceiling. "What did I get myself into?"

Her exchange with Andi strengthened Jazzy's resolve. By gosh, come hell or high water, she and Charlie were winning this competition.

Ten minutes later, Jazzy had polished off her second martini while Andi was back to sticking her tongue down Danny's throat.

Nan was onstage at the microphone again. "I can feel the energy heating up at this rivalry, can't y'all. You folks ready for an old-fashioned knockdown, drag out competition? In case y'all don't know, Andi and Danny just got engaged." Nan applauded, and the crowd joined in. "And Danny used to be Jazzy's boyfriend, so you know that's some hot kindling on the fire of this sizzling sing-off."

"Good grief," Charlie said. "She's overselling this. Gee thanks, Nanny Goat, for fanning the flames."

"We *have to* beat them," Jazzy said. "We must pull out all the stops."

"Got your back, Lambchop. Let's go."

Nan waved them onstage for their second number. *Gotta win, gotta win, gotta win.* The chant launched Jazzy up the steps, Charlie hurrying to catch up. Looking out across the audience, she spotted Andi running her palm up the inside of Danny's shirt.

The crowd glanced from Jazzy to Andi and back again.

"Slow down," Charlie hissed through clenched teeth. "You're too amped. You'll crash and burn."

Jazzy's brain heard him, but her jealousy ignored

caution. She grabbed the microphone and started off on the wrong foot, singing too fast.

Charlie did his best to make up for the misstep. She couldn't fault him for anything except playing defense.

Defense wouldn't cut it. If they wanted to win, they had to go big and play offense. No holds barred.

Fueled by the cheering crowd—and Andi groping Danny at the back of the room—Jazzy put everything she had into the performance, leaving nothing on the table. She was in this to win it.

In an enthusiastic homage to Freddie Mercury, she picked up the mike stand, flipped it upside down to belt out the lyrics, spun wildly around . . .

And whacked Charlie in the face with the base of the stand.

CHAPTER 4

Charlie sat on the edge of the stage with his shirt covered in blood and a package of frozen peas held against his nose.

Jazzy crouched at his eye level, her hands clutched to her chest, feeling wretched. "I am so, so sorry. I didn't mean to hit you."

"I tried to warn you," Charlie said, but because of his staunched nose, it came out, "I twied to warn ew."

Several people had gathered around them, including Danny. Nan, who'd supplied the frozen peas, watched from across the bar, head cocked, eyes assessing.

"Jazzy smacked me pretty good like that once," Danny said. "We were at a Black Friday sale and she was lusting after the last Xbox for her half brother, Justice. The crowd trapped her and when I tried to pull her out, she thought I was someone trying to steal the Xbox from her. She jerked away hard, and her elbow clipped my eye. I sported a shiner for two weeks."

Oops. Jazzy had forgotten all about that incident. "It was an accident."

"Which time?" Danny and Charlie asked in unison.

"Both!"

"She's accident-prone," Danny told Charlie. "A little clumsy."

Clumsy? Gee thanks, Danny.

"She's competition-prone is what she is," Charlie grumbled, and fingered his nose. "She'll do anything to win."

"Not *anything*." Jazzy's cheeks heated.

"She'll never win against Andi," Danny said. "Andi takes no prisoners. Jazzy's just too nice."

"Why are you over here?" Jazzy asked her ex.

"Andi sent me to see if you're conceding the contest."

"No, we are not—"

"Yes," Charlie interrupted. "Yes, we are. I'm a bloody pulp. You and Andi win. Hip-hip-hooray."

"Yay!" Danny said, raising his arms in the air like goalposts, and called across the bar. "We win, babe. They're quitting."

"Woot!" Andi ran toward Danny and he grabbed her in his arms and whirled her as she raised her hands overhead and sang at an earsplitting decibel, "We Are the Champions."

"You're throwing in the towel?" Jazzy asked Charlie, struggling not to sound disappointed.

"You threw it in for me." Charlie lifted the peas so Jazzy could see how swollen his nose was. "I'm lucky my schnoz isn't busted."

Ouch. She winced. "I am *so* sorry."

"Don't be sorry. Just stop being so obsessed with beating Andi."

"But look at her." Jazzy indicated Andi, who'd mounted Danny's shoulders. He was piggybacking her around the bar as Andi unfurled the karaoke banner and waved it behind her like a flag as her fiancé toted her from table to table.

"You've got a serious problem," Charlie said. "Why can't you accept all the wonderful things about *you*? Why are you always comparing yourself to Andi? You do you, Lambchop. Folks love you just as you are."

It killed her soul that she'd injured her best friend. "You're right. I screwed up and I'm sorry. Please, forgive me?"

"Sorry enough to stop this silly rivalry?" Charlie asked.

"Hey, Walker," hollered Andi, from Danny's shoulders. "We win. You lose. Suck it."

Jazzy arched her eyebrows. "Tell her that."

Charlie shook his head and put the peas to his nose again.

"Hey, Walker, what say you go against me in the cowboy cookie challenge? Let me thrash you again?" Andi tweaked Danny's ear to get him to turn toward the bulletin board beside the bar where the locals posted flyers announcing babysitting services, puppies for sale, and events in town.

Andi plucked the baking contest flyer off the board and waved that along with the banner. "I'll win this year's Christmas baking contest again. I'd just love if you'd enter so I could give you another thrashing."

"She *is* super annoying," Charlie said. "How was it again that she stole Danny away from you?"

"I'm too happy, remember?"

"You don't look very happy right now."

Touché.

"There is absolutely no competition in this one-horse town," Andi complained. "You're all so lame."

Danny, red-faced and huffing, stopped so Andi could slide from his shoulders to the ground right in front of Jazzy and Charlie.

Do not rise to the bait. Do not! Jazzy coached herself. *Do not enter that contest.*

"There's Roan Sullivan," Charlie pointed out. "He's won a national baking championship. I'd say he could provide you with stiff competition."

"That guy? He's old as dirt and a single father," Andi scoffed. "No way that dude would enter our cookie contest. Besides, he cooks campfire food. I'm the reigning cookie queen! I could take him."

"Someone should dethrone you. If I could bake, I'd do it," Charlie said.

Andi rolled her eyes and tossed over her shoulder as she walked away, "As if!"

"Okay," Charlie said to Jazzy. "I see why you're so hung up on beating her. She's begging to be taken down a peg or two."

"I guess you didn't see the theme for this year's contest?" Jazzy called to Andi, speaking when she shouldn't have.

"What?" Andi whipped her head around.

Charlie stretched his lean body long and snatched the flyer from Andi's hand. "Look closer.

It's campfire baking. They're holding the event at the marina pavilion."

"Oh." Eyes widening, Andi blinked. "Well, no matter. I'll still win."

"You know," Jazzy mused. "I just might enter this year."

"You?" Andi hooted. "Don't be ridiculous. I was only joshing. You don't know how to bake. How do you suppose you'd win? Face it, Walker, in competing against *me*, you'll always come up second best and I really hate trouncing you, it's so embarrassing. Wait, what am I talking about? I *love* trouncing you. Do it. Enter."

"The point isn't to win," Jazzy said. "The entry fees go to charity. That's why I would enter. To raise money for Holly's House."

"Not about winning?" Andi said. "Yeah, that's what all the losers say." Rubbing salt into the wound, Andi made the letter *L* with her hand and held it against her forehead.

Behind Jazzy, Charlie growled.

Jazzy smiled. "So, you're familiar with campfire baking?"

Andi fluffed her hair. "No, but I'll still win. I do my best work under pressure and I'm a quick study."

"I admire your belief in your own greatness," Jazzy said, meaning every word. Andi's self-confidence had been the draw when Jazzy walked into Miss Avery's third grade class and spied Andi sitting cocksure in the front row. They'd been friends back then. "It's inspiring."

"What's that supposed to mean?" Andi narrowed her eyes.

"I'm jealous of the way you can stomp over other people in your relentless drive to the top and not give it a second thought."

"Stop it," Andi snapped.

"Stop what?"

"Being nice. I'm trying to insult you, Walker."

Jazzy smiled. "I know and you're great at that too."

"You're at it again with your toxic positivity."

"And you're entitled to your opinion."

"Hmph." Andi snapped her fingers. "Danny, come on, we're leaving." To Jazzy, she said, "I've got better things to do. Like taking *my* fiancé to bed."

With a toss of her head, Andi grabbed Danny's arm and shuttled him out the door.

"Wow," Charlie said after they'd left. "You dodged a bullet with Danny. Good thing Andi stole him from you."

"Please, Charlie." Jazzy pressed her palms together and brought her joined thumbs to her sternum. "I know you're trying to help, but let's not put Danny down. He meant a lot to me once and if Andi makes him happy, then I'm happy for him."

Charlie snorted and eyed her. "You mean it?"

"I do." Danny had been her first kiss, her first love, her first *everything*. He would forever hold a special place in her heart, but most importantly, he'd taught her what she didn't want from a life partner.

"I've said it a million times before, but I'm saying it again. You're a far better person than I am, Jazzy."

"I'm not. I'm petty and small."

"In what universe?"

Jazzy tapped the flyer. "The universe where I enter the cookie contest and beat the pants off Andi."

Charlie raised his eyebrows. "You sure about that? Beating Andi in a baking contest won't be easy. She's a darn good baker."

"Maybe it won't be easy," Jazzy said, "but I have a secret weapon."

"What's that?" Charlie tossed the bag of peas in the trash can near the stage. "I'm intrigued. What's up your sleeve?"

"I'm going to convince Roan Sullivan to teach me how to bake."

"Santa Claus is coming to town," Jazzy sang as she swept past the empty bed of the semiprivate room and over to the corner bed where Trinity rested.

Jazzy wore a smile as bright as Christmas, jingle bells pinned to her scrub top and her blond hair pulled back into a jaunty ponytail that swished when she walked.

Charmed, Roan couldn't help returning the animated nurse's grin.

Trinity responded like a daisy turning toward the sun. In a voice that was much stronger than yesterday, his daughter cried, "Nurse Jazzy!"

"He's making a list." Jazzy settled the tray on the overbed table. "Checking it twice . . ."

From where Roan reclined, he'd been trying to get some shut-eye. He sat up straight and swung his legs around, jamming his feet into his well-worn cowboy boots. He felt defenseless without footwear. Give him a horse or a cast-iron Dutch oven, and Roan was in his element, but he was out of his league in a hospital.

Or near Jazzy Walker.

"How are you this morning?" Jazzy asked as she slipped an electronic blood pressure cuff around Trinity's little arm.

"Better!" Trinity said.

"And how is Daddy?"

"He keeps yawning," Trinity tattled and giggled.

"Hard to sleep in those chairs, right, Dad?" Jazzy asked.

"Right," he agreed. "We're ready to go home and get some real rest."

"Gotcha. A hospital is a busy place. As soon as Trinity eats some breakfast and keeps it down for a couple of hours, I'll start processing her discharge papers."

Good news. Roan wanted out of here. Even though he hired trusted ranch hands, he'd been away from the Slope Ridge Ranch for well over twenty-four hours, and that made him antsy.

Jazzy finished taking Trinity's vital signs. "Everything's perfect, Doodlebug. How's your throat?"

Doodlebug.

Claire's term of endearment for Trinity that Roan and his family continued to use. Jazzy must have heard him call Trinity that. The pretty nurse's familiarity both flattered and bothered him. It didn't seem fair that some other woman was calling his daughter by the nickname his wife had given her.

Trinity put a hand to her throat. "It hurts a little."

"The night nurse used some medicated spray on her throat during the night," Roan said. "To numb the pain."

"Does it hurt too much to eat breakfast?" Jazzy asked. She elevated the head of the bed with the remote control and then whisked the metal dome off the food dish.

Trinity leaned forward to investigate the breakfast offerings: cream of wheat, a carton of plain Greek yogurt, and applesauce. His daughter wrinkled her nose. "No ice cream?"

"I guess the dietary staff didn't think ice cream was a good breakfast choice."

Trinity angled her head down and peeked up at Jazzy, giving her a look that was as manipulative as it was adorable. "Canna have some ice cream, please?"

"I sort of promised her ice cream after the tonsillectomy," Roan said, feeling sheepish. "Could she get some ice cream?"

"You betcha. We keep ice cream on the floor. She's not the first to ask for ice cream for breakfast. We have three flavors. Chocolate, strawberry, and vanilla."

"'Nilla!" Trinity clapped her hands.

"Hang on. I'll be right back. While I'm gone, try a bite of applesauce or cream of wheat, please."

"Thanks," Roan said. "I appreciate you making a special trip."

"No problem. All part of the job." Jazzy waved

off his thanks. She held his gaze for a second too long and then lowered her lashes.

Roan couldn't help watching the sway of her shapely hips as she strolled off. Heaven help him. Why was he thinking like this? Jazzy was his daughter's nurse.

Not after Trinity goes home.

He had no time for romance.

You make time for what's important.

He had more baggage than a jetliner's cargo hold.

Okay. He had no comeback for that.

Roan got up to shut the door Jazzy had left ajar, heard murmuring voices in the hallway, and he peeked out.

Christmas decorations that the staff put up yesterday, replacing Thanksgiving turkeys and cornucopias with Christmas trees and North Pole villages, festooned the corridor. Soft Christmas music played from the nurses' station. They'd done their best to make the ward festive for their young charges.

Jazzy stood at the nurses' station. Another nurse came up beside her. Roan recognized the woman as Andi Browning.

Andi looked smug. Jazzy's back was to Roan, so he couldn't see her face, but he saw tension stiffen her shoulders. The two women's body language confirmed the gossip his mother had shared.

None of your business, Sullivan. He closed the door and went to coax Trinity into eating some applesauce.

A few minutes later, Jazzy returned with the vanilla ice cream and a sweet smile. "Here you go."

Trinity abandoned the applesauce and reached with both hands for the ice cream. The night nurse had removed her IV and put a Snoopy bandage over the spot.

"Hang on." Jazzy chuckled. "Let me pull the top off."

She peeled the lid from the ice cream, gave the small cup to Trinity, then leaned over to drop the paper lid into the trash can. As she bent over, Roan noticed the way her scrubs stretched across her bottom.

Staring seemed rude and he glanced away. He refused to objectify Jazzy. Ever since he'd become the father of a daughter, he'd noticed how some men thought it was their right to ogle women.

"Hey," Jazzy said, straightening. She'd fished the crumpled flyer from the trash can where he'd tossed it last night. "Are you thinking of entering this contest?"

"No," Roan said, gentling his tone. Fear set up a bake shop in his belly. "I gave up competing."

"Oh, too bad. This one is right up your alley. Campfire baking."

"I'm not interested."

"I see." She dropped the flyer back in the trash can and stepped to the sink to wash her hands. Once she finished, she turned back to him. "I might enter."

"You bake?"

"I'm a horrible baker."

"Then why would you enter?"

"Andi Browning." Jazzy sighed. "She beats me at everything." She told him about her rivalry with

Andi, and what had transpired at the bar last night, confirming his mother's gossip. "And now, she's engaged to my ex-boyfriend."

"That's gotta hurt."

"I wish them well. I'm happy they're happy . . ." She paused.

"Just once you'd like to win?"

Jazzy pointed at him. "You get it."

For some crazy reason, that little finger pointing sucked him right in. She looked at him like he was something special.

"Baking might not be a winning ticket for you, Jazzy," he murmured. "It takes time to perfect baking techniques and even longer to perfect cooking over a campfire."

"I know. I just wanted to give it a shot."

"The competition takes place over the course of the two days before Christmas Eve. That's just under three weeks. To stand a ghost of a chance, you'd have to spend hours a day baking."

"I'm off for a three-week vacation starting tomorrow. I'm using up all my vacation time and paid days off before I take a job as a traveling nurse."

"No kidding." So, she was leaving town. Too bad about that.

"I'm excited for this opportunity, but I want to beat Andi before I go. It'll give me courage as I face the big wide world."

"How good is Andi at baking?"

"She won the cookie challenge the last two years in a row."

Roan made a face. "I'm afraid you're setting yourself up for a tall order."

Jazzy cleared her throat. "But I'm an optimist at heart. Does that count for anything at all?"

"I'm a realist and I hate to burst your bubble, but the odds are against you."

"Do you know anyone in the area who gives campfire baking lessons?" she asked.

"Nope."

"Have you ever considered teaching the skill yourself?"

Roan grunted. He liked Jazzy a lot, but he was not coming out of retirement to teach her how to bake. "I just don't have the time."

"Oh." She looked disappointed.

He felt cruddy for saying no. She seemed like a sweet person, but it was important to have boundaries. He didn't want to bake. He wouldn't bake. It reminded him too much of all he'd lost.

"Why do you want this," he asked, "knowing you'll most likely lose to Andi again?"

"It's not just about beating Andi," Jazzy said. "I enjoy challenging myself and gaining new skills. Plus, the entry fee money goes to Holly's House."

"Holly's House helped me pay for a play therapist for Trinity after Claire died," Roan said. "Because I'm self-employed, I have a high insurance deductible and the monthly payments are so expensive that Claire's social security money for Trinity wouldn't cover even her half of my insurance policy."

"That's got to be difficult."

"I can't complain. I make a good living on my ranch. Too good to qualify for other aid. But that's what's so great about Holly's House. They help people who fall between the health care cracks."

"It's good Trinity had therapy. Holly's House is an excellent resource for Hood County families in need," Jazzy agreed. "They did so much for me and my dad when I was suffering from childhood asthma."

"Agreed. Anytime Holly's House has a fundraiser, I'm there."

"Except this time."

"Except this time," he echoed. "It's nothing personal, Jazzy. Baking's just not something I care to do anymore. Not even to teach."

"I get it." Her warm smile returned, and he couldn't resist smiling back.

"All gone!" Trinity announced and held out her empty ice cream container.

"Look at you, Doodlebug. Keep that down and you'll be busting out of here today." Jazzy tousled Trinity's hair. To Roan, she said, "I'll get her discharge plan and go over it with you."

"Thanks," he said. He couldn't wait to get Trinity home and put some distance between Jazzy's understanding eyes and him.

"BRB." Jazzy picked up the breakfast tray.

"Wait," Roan said as she reached the door.

Jazzy paused and turned back to him. "Yes?"

"While I can't teach you to bake, my wife and I used to have a YouTube channel where we featured campfire cooking tutorials. I could reactivate the account."

Gratitude lit up Jazzy's entire face. "You would do that for me?"

"Give me your phone number. I'll text you when they're re-uploaded."

"Oh, Roan. Thank you so very much. You're the best."

And everything was just peachy in Roan Sullivan's world until Trinity barfed vanilla ice cream all over him.

CHAPTER 5

Monday, December 5, was the first day of Jazzy's three-week vacation and the day after Trinity was released from the hospital. That morning, she received a three-word text from Roan along with a link.

Up on YouTube.

Aflutter, she marched to the Twilight Chamber of Commerce and submitted her entry in person. She was doing this thing. No backing out now.

The move turned out to be a big mistake.

She should've watched the YouTube videos of Roan and his wife before committing. She sat down with her gray tabby, Sabrina, in her lap and two recordings into their series, the *Basics of Campfire Cooking*, Jazzy was ready to throw in the towel. The only thing preventing her from calling up the Chamber of Commerce and forfeiting her nonrefundable $125 entry fee was Charlie.

Before she'd ventured into the third video, sub-titled "Cast Iron Baking," she sent him an urgent text.

Help!

Charlie also had the day off. He texted back right away. B there in 2 shakes of a Lambchop's tail.

She felt better. The cavalry was coming. Although Charlie wasn't a baker either, it felt good to have support. While she waited for him, she put on the kettle to make pumpkin spice tea and gathered the supplies listed in the video description.

Ten minutes later, after a cursory knock at the door, Charlie strolled into Jazzy's neo-retro 1950s kitchen. She'd painted the cabinets and drawers sea foam green and installed black granite counter-tops along with white appliances. The chrome and pink table and chairs had come from Rinky-Tink's, an old soda fountain shop that had gone out of business, and Jazzy had refurbished them her-self. Framed black-and-white photographs on the walls featured her travel dreams—Paris, Amster-dam, London, Madrid. She might not be a baker, but thanks to her dad, she knew her way around power tools.

"Never fear, Charlie's here." He bent to scratch Sabrina, who was eeling around his legs and gaz-ing at him with rapt eyes. "Whatcha gonna do with Miss Priss here when you're trotting the globe with Traveling Nurses?"

"Dad and my stepmom, Sarah, promised to look

after her," Jazzy said wistfully. Leaving Sabrina wouldn't be easy. "*If* I get the job."

"If you *take* the job."

Jazzy thrust out her chin. "Oh, I'm taking it."

"Doubts?"

"Pfft." She flipped her wrist over her opposite shoulder and swiveled her head toward him. "Yes. How's your nose?"

"It's fine. A little sore. The swelling is gone. Not broken."

"So fine?"

"It's miserable."

"I am so sorry about hitting you with the mike stand." Jazzy clasped her hands to her chest. "How can I make it up to you?"

"Forget about it." He came to peer over her shoulder where she stood at her laptop and pressed his chin against the top of her head the way he used to do when they were kids.

"What do you want in the way of amends? I'll pay any penalty."

Charlie slanted his head. "Honestly?"

"No, lie to me."

"Reattach my towel rack with your power tools."

"All you need is a screwdriver."

"See. You're perfect. You know things like that. Fix my towel rack and all is forgiven."

"You've got it."

"So." He leaned in closer for a better look at the computer screen. "What's cookin', good-lookin'?"

"Nothing," Jazzy said. "That's the problem. I'm completely lost."

He eyed her laptop. "In?"

"Oh right, I haven't told you yet. I bit the bullet and entered the cookie contest."

He studied her. "Jazzy, I'm not sure this competitiveness you have with Andi is healthy."

"Because I keep losing?"

"Well . . ." He pulled a rueful face. "Yeah. You *never* win. I hate to see you keep pitting yourself against her. You're Wile E. Coyote and she's the Road Runner."

"Odds are I'll have to win *sometime*, right?"

"Maybe, but I don't think campfire baking is your arena. Something less smoky, perhaps?"

"I can do this. I just need to focus."

He held up his phone with her Help! text. "Why the SOS?"

"Two heads are better than one?" She offered him a beguiling smile. "I could fix your towel rack today. After this."

"All right, all right." He chuckled. "What's this all about?"

She filled him in on the videos. "I have to jump in with both feet. The first day of the baking challenge is on the twenty-second. That gives me seventeen days to perfect my skills and that's counting today but because of my vacation, I can devote hours a day to this project."

"Burning the candle at both ends, Lambchop." The teakettle whistled, and Charlie's face lit up. "Are you making pumpkin spice for me?"

"Of course. Anything for my cohort."

"All right," he said. "I'm in."

"You're so easy." She grinned and took two cups

from the mug hooks underneath the cabinet. Sabrina jumped onto the windowsill to groom herself and watch them through slitted eyes.

"Honey, I never claimed to be hard to get." Charlie rubbed his palms together. "Where do we begin?"

"Let's watch the baking video first. Afterward, we'll head to the backyard pit to start a fire."

"Okay, I'll try to channel my inner mountain man."

"That might be interesting to watch."

Jazzy pulled up a chair for him and parked herself at the computer. When Charlie took the seat next to her, she hit "play" on the video and Roan's wife appeared in her kitchen.

"Welcome back, campfire cooking enthusiasts," Claire Sullivan said with a twinkle in her hazel eyes and a sultry tone in her cultured voice. She wore snug-fitting boot-cut dark-wash jeans, a crisp white shirt, red cowboy boots, and understated turquoise jewelry. Her thick brunette mane was pulled back with a pearl clip. "If you're enjoying the series, please like and subscribe."

"She's gorg!" Charlie murmured.

Yeah, Jazzy noticed. "She's so animated and lively. Hard to believe she's dead."

"Such a shame." Charlie clicked his tongue.

"It's clear she's the driving force behind the videos and Roan was the chef," Jazzy said, feeling sad for the couple.

Roan appeared on-screen carrying an armful of baking supplies identical to the ones Jazzy had assembled on her kitchen counter per the recipe's instructions—flour, salt, butter, eggs, vanilla, sugar, cinnamon, and leavening agents.

As Roan lined up the ingredients, the camera panned in. They could hear him voice over the video. "You'll need a cast-iron Dutch oven for campfire baking. If you don't have one yet, check the link below for a twenty percent discount on the Pit Boss from Tractor Supply."

The video was three years old. Jazzy wondered if the discount still applied. Wouldn't hurt to try.

"You'll also want to invest in a lid lifter." The camera panned back to Claire, who showed the tool for lifting the lid off a Dutch oven.

"And don't forget the heat-resistant gloves." Roan, wearing a pair of red grilling gloves, appeared in the shot with Claire. "No burned fingers, campfire cooks."

Claire looked at Roan with such deep affection that Jazzy felt Roan's loss keenly. The poor man. No wonder he no longer wanted to bake. Claire had been the heart and soul of the endeavor. Even if he'd been the real chef.

"They are too adorbs." Charlie clutched his heart. "So sad she's gone. Life sucks the big one sometimes."

"Indeed."

Charlie rested a hand on her shoulder. "Don't absorb their pain, my empathic friend. It's not your burden to carry."

He knew her so well. She smiled. "Thank you for the reminder."

They finished watching the video. In the end, the cookies Roan and Claire baked in the Dutch oven, smothered in campfire embers, turned out crisp and golden. They made it seem so easy. After much oohing and aahing, Claire and Roan leaned in for a cinnamon-sprinkled kiss, waved at the camera, and invited viewers back for the next video in the series.

Feeling blue, Jazzy turned it off. "They had it all. They were the perfect couple, and *poof!* Gone in an instant."

"Want my take?" Charlie asked.

"Always."

"You're starting off too ambitious. Break it into steps. First, learn how to bake cookies. Then transfer those skills to campfire cooking."

"Agreed."

"So, no outdoor fire today. Instead, let's start with baking basics. Have you ever made cookies from scratch?"

"Not by myself, no," Jazzy admitted. "Have you?"

"Sure, plenty of times with Emma and Lauren," he said, referring to his stepmom and much younger stepsister. "First up, let's find a simple basic cookie recipe and bake that."

"I'll never beat Andi with a simple recipe. I need something that'll knock the judges' socks off."

Charlie cleared his throat and angled her a look.

"What?"

"Baby steps. They didn't build Rome in a day." He turned the computer around and studied the basic cookie recipe. "I'll read off the instructions and you do the baking. Preheat the oven to 350."

"On it." Jazzy turned on the oven. "What's next?"

"Music," he said. "And more tea."

"You find the tunes. I'll pour the brew."

Charlie cued up a Christmas playlist on his phone and soon he was two-stepping her around the kitchen to "Skater's Waltz." Laughing, they sank against the kitchen table to catch their breaths.

"At this rate, we'll never get those cookies baked," she said.

"Aww, who cares? We're having fun."

"I should withdraw from the competition," Jazzy said. "I'm deluding myself, thinking I can beat Andi. What do I need? A boulder to fall on my head?"

"Chin up. You're still reeling from news of their engagement. You were doing fine until that happened. I know you don't want Danny back, but it still hurts."

"You're a good friend. Thank you."

Charlie sniffed the air. "What's that smell?"

Jazzy sniffed too. Something was burning. She jumped up and whirled around. Smoke seeped through the oven door. "Oh my goodness! I forgot the wildflowers I was drying for flower hair crowns to celebrate Sarah's launch party."

Sarah wrote children's books, and she'd just released a new story called *The Magic Flower Crown*, and Sarah was having an arts and crafts session with the kids at Ye Old Book Nook in the town square this week to launch her new release.

Grabbing a tea towel, Jazzy yanked open the oven to an acrid blast of burnt flowers roasting on the cookie sheet. She'd dried them the night before but stuck them back in the oven when she'd set out the ingredients for cookies, thinking she'd be baking outside over a campfire. When she preheated the oven, the flowers had slipped her mind.

Now the flowers were on fire. The pan much too hot for the doubled-up tea towel. She could feel the heat radiating from her fingers.

The smoke alarm went off, emitting a relentless high-pitched shriek. Sabrina yowled and fled the room.

Charlie went for the fire extinguisher she kept mounted on the wall beside the fridge and fumbled to remove the plastic clip.

"Hot! Hot!" Jazzy yelped and dropped the flaming flowers into the sink.

Charlie jumped into action, spraying the fire with the extinguisher, and dousing it in white, foamy stuff.

Jazzy ran the cold water and stuck her singed fingers underneath the faucet. "Ouch, ouch."

The smoke detector screamed at them.

Charlie grabbed a broom and poked the detector with a handle until he'd dislodged the battery and it fell silent. He stared at Jazzy, wide-eyed. "Well, that was dramatic."

"I should have checked the oven before I turned on the preheat."

"Always a wise policy."

"You were a quick draw with that fire extinguisher."

"I dated a firefighter once. He made me learn how to use them. I'm glad he did."

"Bryan, right?"

"Yes." Charlie sighed. "It smells like him in here now, charred and smoky."

"I thought you hated the way his job made him smell."

"You know how nostalgic I can get." Charlie grinned at her. "Scents trigger memories and I'm remembering what it felt like to have Bryan toss me over his shoulder and carry me upstairs. Remind me again why I broke up with him?"

"You had nothing in common beyond the great sex."

"Oh yeah. Why was I so picky?"

Jazzy playfully swatted his shoulder. "Back to the present, Cheek. We got a major mess here."

"Minor setback. Let's get this place cleaned."

Once they'd thrown out the burnt flowers, wiped away the fire extinguisher spray, and reinstalled batteries in the smoke detector, they turned their attention back to cookie baking. This time without the music. They needed full focus on baking.

Jazzy didn't own a mixer, so they stirred the batter by hand.

"After this, I can skip the gym today. My arm is about to fall off," Charlie complained good-naturedly.

"Since when do you hit the gym?" Jazzy asked.

"Well, I'm not starting today. Here." He gave her the mixing bowl and wooden spoon. "Your turn to build biceps."

"Do you think this is how Roan bulked up? High-intensity baking?"

"Honey, no. That man wrangles horses for a

living. His physique is from manual labor. But I'm impressed you noticed his biceps. It's been far too long since you've dated. Glad to see it. I worried you were still pining for Danny."

"No, no, not at all." Jazzy finished mixing the ingredients and moved to spooning the batter onto the cookie sheet. "I promise."

"Whew!" He pantomimed wiping massive sweat from his forehead.

Laughing, Jazzy put the cookies into the oven and set the timer. Ten minutes later, she took them from the oven and Charlie edged over to investigate.

"They look yummy. We got off to a rocky start, but we've rebounded. Well done, Walker."

She beamed at him. "Thanks."

Charlie took a spatula and scooped a cookie onto a plate. "I'm impressed. Crisp on the outside but soft in the middle. Perfect cookie in my book. Just gonna let it cool a minute . . ." He paused, waiting, and then picked up the warm cookie and popped the entire thing into his mouth.

He took one chew. His mouth dropped open, and he spewed the cookie back onto the plate. "Gak! Good Lord, woman! You trying to kill me?"

"What's wrong?"

"Tastes like ocean. How much salt is in the batter?"

"What the recipe called for."

"No, you did*n't*. I'm out! You're not baker material." Charlie threw his hands in the air.

"Wait. You can't abandon me!"

"I do like a spectacle, girlfriend. But this?" He shook his head. "This wild escapade is too much, even for Good Time Charlie. Sorry, Lambchop, teaching you to bake is beyond my skill set."

"It can't be that bad." Jazzy picked up a cookie and took a nibble. Pure salt. She tossed it in the trash can. "How did that happen?"

"You tell me."

She turned to the plain white canisters, sorted by size, opened the lid, and dipped her finger in, and touched her tongue to her finger. "Yuck. It's salt."

"No sugar, Sherlock. What happened?"

Jazzy smacked her palm against her forehead. "I was helping Justice make a salt map for geography class a couple of months ago and I told him to pour the box of salt into the canister," she said. "He must have put the salt in the sugar canister."

"Why aren't the canisters labeled?" Charlie asked.

"They came without labels."

"I should go get my label maker. If you're planning on becoming a baker for real, it's a must-have."

"You're right."

"Question for you." Charlie scooped up the cookie sheet and marched over to dump them into the garbage can. "Seeing as how your stepmom's family originated the whole Christmas cookie town legend, and she wrote *The Magic Christmas Cookie*, how is it you never learned to bake? I thought cookie baking was ubiquitous in your house."

He was referring to the prevailing Twilight myth that if you baked kismet cookies and slept with them under your pillow on Christmas Eve, you'd dream of your one true love.

"They were. I think that's the problem. I got cookied-out."

Charlie gasped and planted a palm against his chest. "Blasphemy!"

Jazzy shrugged. "What can I say? I'm the cookie renegade in the family."

"Tsk, tsk." Charlie slid the empty cookie sheet into the sink. "Next you'll be telling me you never slept with a kismet cookie under your pillow."

Jazzy hung her head. "I didn't."

"For real! I can't believe it!"

"It seemed corny," she said. "And messy."

"Afraid that if you did, you wouldn't dream of Danny?" Charlie said.

"No. Maybe. Yes," she admitted.

"Maybe some small part of you recognized that you and Danny were too different. High school sweetheart love is fine in high school, but beyond that? Not so much."

"Danny is a good guy," Jazzy said. "He just got mixed up with Andi."

"Danny's ancient history. Let's not discuss him." Charlie flapped a hand.

"Did you ever sleep with a kismet cookie underneath your pillow on Christmas Eve?" Jazzy asked.

"I'm a die-hard romantic. What do you think?"

"I'm assuming you didn't dream of—"

"No one. I dreamed of nothing. No one. It was depressing. I never tried again. What if the cookie prophesy is true? What if I never find my beloved?" he mourned.

"It's just a cookie, Charlie."

"Will we ever find love?"

"We're not even twenty-four yet. We've got plenty of time to find love," Jazzy reassured him and herself.

"Maybe," he said. "But you've only got seventeen days to learn how to bake."

"Sixteen," she corrected. "I'm throwing in the towel for today. C'mon. Let's go install your towel rack."

CHAPTER 6

The next morning, Jazzy doubled down instead of withdrawing from the contest. She wasn't a quitter. She would see this through.

After her morning coffee and a romp session with Sabrina, she was off to buy a cast-iron Dutch oven and take another run at campfire baking.

It was midmorning when she walked into Tractor Supply with the coupon code she'd gotten from Roan's video. Would it work? She didn't know, but it wouldn't hurt to try.

She didn't shop at the farm store, so it took a minute to find the cooking section.

When she rounded the corner, she spied Andi in the middle of the aisle, standing in front of the cast-iron cookware.

Gak! Instinct had her backpedaling.

Too late.

Andi spotted her. "Morning, Walker."

If Jazzy fled now, it would look like she was avoiding her. Pulling in a deep breath, and putting a big smile on her face, she strolled over. "Hi!"

"Heard through the grapevine that you went ahead and entered the cowboy cookie challenge." Andi eyed her up and down. "Gotta hand it to you, you're a glutton for punishment."

"Danny's not with you?" Jazzy asked.

"He's meeting with Pastor Luther," she said. "Reserving a spot for our wedding for next Christmas."

Ouch. She'd once imagined she'd be the one marrying Danny at the Presbyterian church. "How come you're not with him?"

"Danny has his list of prewedding chores and I have a cast-iron cookie recipe to perfect."

"Me too."

Andi snorted. "You gotta know how to bake before you can perfect your technique."

"How do you know I haven't already perfected my baking skills?"

"Have you?" Andi arched her eyebrows and looked superior.

"I'm working on it," Jazzy said, hearing the defensiveness in her voice.

Andi said, reaching for the most expensive Dutch oven, "I'm getting this one. It's Roan Sullivan approved."

It was the same brand, but the next model up. The label sporting Roan's name. Jazzy couldn't believe she'd been so unaware of Roan's high standing in the campfire cooking community.

"I have a discount code for twenty percent off," Jazzy said. "Do you want me to text it to you?"

Andi eyed her. "Why?"

"Why what?"

"Why would you help me?"

"Why not?"

"I'm your competitor."

"Helping you save twenty percent won't hurt me in the contest." Jazzy took out her phone and texted the digital coupon to Andi.

"Ahh," Andi said. "That explains it."

"Explains what?"

"The reason you're such a loser. You don't know how to take care of yourself in this dog-eat-dog world."

Jazzy shook her head. "That is just sad."

"What is?" Andi narrowed her eyes.

"Your cutthroat view of the world."

"I think your lollipops and gumdrops attitude is the stupid one."

"I never said your viewpoint was stupid."

Andi glowered, grabbed the Dutch oven, and stormed off.

"You're welcome for the discount code," Jazzy called after her.

Andi lifted a middle finger above her head.

"Nice, Browning. Real nice," Jazzy mumbled and turned to see that Andi had taken the last of the Roan Sullivan–branded Dutch ovens. Oh well, the cheaper version should do just as well. Although it didn't qualify for the twenty percent discount, so it ended up costing more.

"Jazzy!" a clear little voice rang out in Tractor Supply.

With the heavy Dutch oven clutched in her arms, Jazzy glanced up to see Roan coming toward her, pushing Trinity in a shopping cart. All six foot three inches of hot masculine body. His eyes met hers and he smiled big. He'd been through hell and back, but he still had the capacity for joy.

Jazzy's heart warmed at the sight of them. "Hi there, Sullivans!"

"Your vacation has started?" Roan asked, wearing an outfit almost identical to what he'd worn at the hospital—Wranglers, boots, jeans, a Stetson. The cowboy's uniform. And he looked sexy as sin in it.

"Yep." Jazzy couldn't stop smiling. "How is this dumpling doing?"

"Fine!" Trinity announced.

"No sore throat?"

Trinity waggled her little head. "All better."

"After she cleaned me out of ice cream and popsicles." Roan chuckled.

"That's wonderful news." Jazzy beamed at them.

"You're doing some shopping?" Roan nodded at the Dutch oven.

"I was going to buy the one you recommended on your YouTube channel, but Andi Browning took the last one."

"I saw her at the register," he said. "But you don't need to buy one. You're welcome to use mine."

"You won't need it?"

"Nah, I'm done with campfire cooking."

"That's a generous offer. I'd love to have your Dutch oven if you're sure you won't ever use it."

"I've got an extra one," he said. "I was just browsing the aisles while I wait for them to load my truck with horse feed. If you're not pressed for time, you can follow me back to my ranch and pick up the Dutch oven."

"Mr. Sullivan," a voice broadcast over the public address system. "Your order is complete."

"That's us," Roan said.

Jazzy put the Dutch oven back on the shelf and followed Roan. He parked the cart and took Trinity out. The little girl slipped her arms around her father's neck. The two of them looked so adorable.

"This way," Roan said with a crook of his finger. "I've already paid for my purchases."

She walked beside him to where his truck, now loaded with bags of horse feed, sat parked right beside her trusty Toyota Corolla.

Roan loaded Trinity into her car seat, then turned to Jazzy. He assessed her with that steady, brown-eyed gaze of his. A look that sent goose bumps prickling her skin. "You look nice. It's fun seeing you out of scrubs."

"Thanks." She ducked her head. She had on yoga pants and a long-sleeved, dark green top.

"Did that sound risqué? I didn't mean it that way."

"I understand." She chuckled. "I get that a lot, actually. People who know me only from the hospital often don't recognize when they see me in street clothes. Out of context I guess."

Suddenly, things felt awkward.

"Guess we better . . ." He pointed a thumb at his truck.

"Roll?"

"Yeah," he said. "That."

It was a fifteen-minute drive to Slope Ridge Ranch and on the way they crossed from Hood County into Parker. Parker County was the cutting horse capital of the world and anyone who was someone in the cutting horse industry in Texas lived there.

Jazzy felt weird about following him to his home. It seemed like a boundary violation. She had to ask herself, was her vain attempt at trying to best Andi worth it?

Then she remembered how sexy Roan looked in blue jeans and the sweet compliment he'd given her and decided, yes, yes it was.

Roan watched Jazzy in his rearview mirror. Her right front tire looked low. He'd check it for her when they got to the ranch.

Hey, not your place to take her under your wing.

Maybe not, but she'd done so much for him and Trinity. He wasn't about to let her drive around with a bad tire. Yet, if he hadn't offered to give her a Dutch oven, her tire wouldn't be his problem. But how could he not help her when he'd overheard that cocky Andi Browning taunting her?

So, you just had to ride to her rescue, huh, cowboy? It was Claire's voice he heard in his head, sweet and teasing. His wife had often poked fun at what she called his "cowboy code of honor."

Sighing, Roan blew out his breath. He needed to stay out of the past. Nothing but ghosts there.

Trinity was strapped into her booster seat, crooning the alphabet song. He and his mom had been working on teaching her the alphabet. Smiling, he joined in.

His daughter sang, "Now I've learned my ABCs. Tell me what you think of me!"

"I think you are the smartest girl on this ranch," Roan announced.

"Daddy! I'm the *only* girl on this ranch."

"See, you are the smartest. You figured that out all by yourself."

Her childish giggles warmed him from the inside out. It thrilled him that Trinity had quickly bounced back from the tonsillectomy. He'd been pretty worried in the hospital, but she had no problems since they'd been home. The surgery should put an end to her frequent ear and throat infections. He hoped it would. Seeing her sick killed his soul.

He parked his pickup truck beside the barn to make unloading the horse feed easier for his hands, got out, and went around to help Trinity from the pickup.

Jazzy pulled up beside them. She rolled down her window. "Where should I park?"

He waved her to a spot in front of the garage.

"Got it." Jazzy smiled so big Roan felt as if she'd wrapped him in rainbows. She was so bright and fun. Jazzy was the perfect name for her. She parked and got out of her car.

"Your right front tire looks low," he said.

"Does it? Oh my." She twirled to peer at her tire, her long blond hair arcing through the air as she moved her head. In the hospital, she wore her lush locks pulled back into a ponytail. While he enjoyed watching that ponytail bounce, her hair flowing like silk over her shoulders mesmerized him.

She straightened with her bottom lip caught up

between her teeth. "It does look a little low. Do you think it'll get me back to Twilight?"

"I'm not letting you get back on the road with a low tire. I'll check the pressure and add some air. Then we'll head into the house and get the Dutch oven and feed Trinity her lunch, and by then we should be able to tell if the tire will hold air."

"Thank you," she said. "I'm so glad you noticed."

"No problem," he said.

"Lunch!" Trinity hollered. "PBJ sammy!"

"She eats PB&Js every day," Roan explained.

"With Ruffles!" Trinity spun around her with her little arms outstretched wide. "Ruffles have ridges."

"It's so good to see you doing so well, Doodle-bug." Jazzy laughed.

"Do you like PB&J?" Roan asked. "We have grape, strawberry, and blueberry jelly."

"I love PB&J."

"Then you've come to the right house."

"Daddy adds honey to the peanut butter," Trinity whispered as if sharing a secret. "It's extra 'licious."

"Sounds like it."

Trinity reached over and took Jazzy's hand. "C'mon. I'll show you my Barbies."

And with that, his daughter dragged their guest into the house.

Roan turned his attention to her car. It was a trusty compact. The type of car he'd buy for Trinity when she started driving. The inside was vacuumed clean. A kitschy pink flamingo hung from her rearview mirror and a medical bag sat in the back seat. A *Simpsons*-themed thermos rested in the cup holder and the floor mats were custom-order Van Gogh's *Starry Night*. Before she'd pocketed her keys, he'd noticed she had a kitty cat key chain. He liked her fun, effervescent sense of style. Even the inside of her car made him smile.

He checked the tire pressure. It was low. He took the air compressor from the garage and went to fill the tire.

The cool December breeze shifted, and he smelled burning leaves. Was one of his neighbors using a controlled burn to ready their fields for spring? To Roan's way of thinking, it wasn't the best timing. They weren't in an official burn ban, but it hadn't rained since mid-October.

Filling the tire, Roan checked to see if he could find any reason for a leak. No punctures he could see. The tires were new, so it wasn't a tread issue. Perhaps the valve stem had been loose. He tightened it when he finished airing it up. Fingers crossed that it would hold. He put away the air compressor and ambled into the house.

In the kitchen, he found Jazzy and Trinity munching on PB&J sandwiches with the crusts cut off and a third sandwich waiting for him on a paper plate. At the sight of the sandwich, he felt touched by the effort she'd made.

"Hey thanks," he said, sweeping off his cowboy hat and hanging it on a hook by the door.

"Least I could do," she said. "Since you were looking after my tire and giving me a Dutch oven. I hope you don't mind that I made myself at home."

Did he mind? No doubt it felt odd knowing she'd been bustling around his kitchen, opening cabinets and drawers. But not in a bad way. Just unfamiliar.

Trinity seemed comfortable, perched on the barstool beside Jazzy. Roan wondered where he should sit. After washing up at the sink, he elected for standing at the counter in front of them to eat his sandwich.

"Aired your tire," he said. "We'll give it fifteen or twenty minutes to see if it's gonna hold enough to get you back to town where you can get your mechanic to double-check it."

"I appreciate it so much," Jazzy said.

"No problem." Roan took a bite of the sandwich. "Wow. I think that might be the best PB&J I ever ate."

"Jazzy used all the jellies," Trinity said. "And honey too."

Roan met Jazzy's dazzling blue-eyed gaze and arched an eyebrow.

"She couldn't decide which flavor she wanted. We went for the more-is-more school of thought." Jazzy laughed.

Gosh, she had the best laugh. It could lift a man's soul right up to the roof.

"You haven't decorated for Christmas," she said.

"Not yet. I took boxes down from the attic, but with Trinity in the hospital . . ."

Jazzy studied him, and he wondered what she was thinking. He hoped she wasn't feeling sorry for him again.

"Let's get that Dutch oven." Roan dusted crumbs from his fingertips.

"Yes." For the first time, her smile did not reach her eyes. She pushed back from the barstool and got up.

Trinity hopped down too.

"I put the Dutch oven in storage," Roan said. "In the garage. It'll take me a minute to find it."

"You know, if this is difficult for you, I can just buy a Dutch oven."

"No, you've come all this way. Please take it."

She moved closer to him. If she reached out her hand, she could touch him. She looked like she wanted to touch him, but she kept her hands at her sides. Or maybe it was just his wishful imagination.

"Roan?"

"Yeah?" Something in her tone gave him pause, and he studied her face. It was heart-shaped, he realized. Her chin small and pointed a little at the end, with a widow's peak at her forehead.

"The YouTube recordings are great, so helpful. Thank you for putting them up again just for me, but are you sure that you can't tutor me in campfire cooking?"

Roan blew out his breath. "I—"

"I'm willing to pay the going rate for lessons." Then she told him how she'd botched her first attempt at baking cookies with her friend Charlie.

He steeled his jaw to keep from grinning at her mix-up with the salt and sugar. He didn't want her to think he was making fun of her. "I'm sorry. I just don't bake anymore."

"I understand and again, I am grateful for the videos." Her smile faltered. "I hope I didn't offend you by pressing the issue."

"You?" That amused him. "No way could you offend me, Jazzy."

"You never know," she quipped. "I might chew with my mouth full."

"Just saw you eat. You don't." He paused. "It takes a lot to offend me."

They stared into each other's eyes and Roan didn't know what might have happened next, if the back door hadn't slammed open and his ranch hand Rowdy Keats hadn't run into the house hollering.

"Boss, the back forty is on fire!"

CHAPTER 7

"I called 911," the red-faced ranch hand gasped. "Leon and Polk are herding the livestock from the pasture. I came back for sandbags and shovels."

Open-mouthed, Jazzy stared at the harried man who smelled of smoke and paused to cough hard.

Roan grabbed his Stetson from the hat hook and turned back to Jazzy. "Can you stay with Trinity?"

"Sure, sure, yes, yes. Please, take care of your animals." The man had an emergency, she wasn't about to tell him she had a hair appointment for later that day. She'd reschedule.

"Trin," he said to his daughter. "You mind Jazzy, okay?"

"'Kay." The little girl nodded.

He swept his child into his arms and gave her a big kiss, then straightened and met Jazzy's gaze again. "I'll be back as soon as I can."

"No worries. Go, go." She waved him out the door behind the ranch hand, her pulse thudding in her throat.

He lifted his hand goodbye and was gone. Leaving Jazzy alone in a stranger's house with his four-year-old. Luckily, Jazzy loved entertaining kids. She'd even been accused of being a big kid herself at heart.

Jazzy sent up a prayer that Roan, his ranch hands, and his animals would come through this just fine. In the meantime, Trinity was her focus. "So, what would you like to do?"

"Go outside and swing!" Trinity raised her arms in the air.

"Um, maybe not. How about we put up the Christmas decorations?"

"Oh yay, yay!" Trinity hopped around on one foot. "But first I gotta pee-pee."

Jazzy took her girl to the bathroom, made sure she was okay, and then stepped outside in the hallway to give the child privacy. She folded her arms over her chest and looked at the wall lined with family photographs. Heartbreaking to see pictures of a smiling Claire Sullivan and Trinity as a baby. This family had suffered a great loss.

Feeling like a voyeur, Jazzy averted her gaze.

Trinity opened the bathroom as she pulled up her pants and Jazzy helped her wash her hands. In the hall, the child pointed at a particularly poignant photograph of Claire discreetly breastfeeding the baby.

"That's my mommy."

"She's very pretty."

Trinity tucked her hands into her armpits. "I don't 'member her."

Jazzy didn't know what to say so she gently

reached for Trinity's hand. "Let's go put up the Christmas tree."

"'Kay." With a four-year-old's attention span, she quickly dropped the topic of her mother.

Jazzy tried to remember what she was like at four. Crystal was long gone by then and it was pre-Sarah. For years, it had just been Jazzy and her dad. She'd never felt deprived in any way, until other kids poked fun at her for not having a mom. That had hurt, but she'd felt no big mother-shaped hole in her life because her dad, Travis, took care of her every need.

"Thanks, Dad," she murmured.

In the living room, it was clear Roan had not changed the decor since his wife's death. The place had a woman's touch. The color scheme was light-toned grays and soft pastels with plush pillows on the sofa and cozy throw blankets. There was plenty of greenery with pots of ivy, airplane plants, and ficus.

On the floor, she found boxes labeled with the contents in a lovely feminine script. *Nativity Scene. Christmas Village. Plastic Ornaments. Twinkle Lights.* She imagined the pretty woman from the photographs writing it, full of hope for future Christmases.

"Dang it, Claire, this should not have happened to you," she whispered.

"Huh?" Pushing her hair from her face, Trinity peered up at Jazz from where she crouched peeling the tape off a box.

"Oh look," Jazzy said, opening the box. "Angels!"

"Daddy says Mommy is an angel." Trinity stroked a finger over the ornament. An angel trio holding hands.

Jazzy didn't know what to say. In the distance she heard the wail of sirens.

Trinity's eyes widened. "What's that?"

"Fire trucks." The sirens rapidly grew louder.

"Canna see?" Trinity hopped up and ran to the back door.

"I know it sounds exciting, but we have to be careful," Jazzy explained. "There's a small fire in your daddy's pasture and they've come to put it out. We'll stay out of the way and let them do their job."

"Aww, man," Trinity said in such a cute voice that Jazzy couldn't resist chuckling.

The fire trucks screamed into the driveway. The sound was so deafening, Trinity plastered her palms over her ears, but she was grinning.

"Please canna see?"

"Okay," Jazzy said as the sirens halted and other sounds began—doors slamming, feet running, voices commanding. "We'll take a quick peek, but that's all."

"Yay!" Trinity clapped her hands.

To control the girl in case she decided she wanted to rush out to greet the firefighters, Jazzy scooped her into her arms, took her to the back door, and stepped out onto the wraparound porch.

Trinity swiveled in Jazzy's arms to stare agog at the firefighters in their turnout gear. The southerly breeze sent white smoke rolling in, wafting around the barns, and drifting toward the house.

Jazzy couldn't see the fire from where they were standing but she could hear sharp crackling noises as the fast-moving grass fire consumed the pasture. She spied Roan's Stetson on the opposite side of a firetruck, but she couldn't make out his face. The smoke was too thick.

The firefighters scurried efficiently about their business. Their presence calmed her, but she had a desperate urge to stick Trinity in her car and drive away for her safety. Jazzy might even have done it if the firetrucks hadn't blocked her exit.

The firefighters piled back onto their trucks and lumbered through the gate Roan opened for them, heading for the back pasture. She and Trinity watched until they disappeared from sight.

Trinity coughed and covered her mouth with her little palm.

"Let's get back in the house. It's too smoky out here."

"Bye-bye, firetrucks." Sweetly, Trinity waved to the departing emergency vehicles. Then she turned to look Jazzy in the eyes. "Is Daddy gonna be okay?"

"Yes, he'll be just fine. The firefighters are with him now. They won't let anything bad happen. Everything is A-okay."

But a niggling voice inside her, the one she normally kept tightly under wraps, whispered, *What if it's not?*

Dadgummit, a pasture fire was the last thing he needed.

He guided the three volunteer firetrucks to the

back pasture where his ranch hands were doing their best to build a firebreak. It was just a grass fire and didn't even involve trees. The acreage would grow back greener and healthier for it, but the wind had picked up and shifted directions and was swiftly moving toward the house.

While that was concerning, he was confident the firefighters could handle it. The smoke blew into their faces. Roan pulled out the red bandana he kept tucked in his back pocket and fashioned a mask from it.

He hoped Jazzy wasn't unduly worried. She seemed an easygoing sort, not given to alarm. Claire, on the other hand, would have been beside herself with anxiety. His wife had needed a lot of emotional reassurance.

Scorched earth lay in front of him with widening rings of fire spreading outward in all directions. His nostrils burned with the acrid scent and it stung his eyes. Blinking repeatedly, he motioned for his ranch hands to get out of the way and let the firefighters do their jobs. He and his men gathered off to one side, watching as the firefighters rolled out their hoses and went to work.

"Do you know what started it?" he asked Rowdy, his foreman.

Rowdy shook his head. "Leon smelled smoke and came out to investigate."

"You've got the nose of a bloodhound," Roan told Leon. "Good work."

Leon, a rangy cowboy in his midfifties, simply nodded. He wasn't a big talker.

"All the horses accounted for?" The question was rhetorical. He knew if a horse was missing, they'd be out searching for it.

"Yep," Polk said. He and Leon were cousins, but where Leon was thin, Polk was plump and several years younger. "Cattle too."

"Thank you," Roan said. "I appreciate you."

"Just doing our jobs," Polk said.

Trinity was with Jazzy. The livestock were safe. The firefighters were dousing the fire. This emergency was minor. Roan felt tension ease from his shoulders.

Tempted to return to the house and let Jazzy be on her way, he stayed, not feeling right leaving while the fire was still burning. It felt odd to have a stranger in his home and he wondered if Jazzy was the type to snoop.

She's not a stranger. She was Trinity's nurse.

And his daughter adored her.

Heck, his mother adored Jazzy. Mom had gone on and on about what a great nurse Jazzy was and how she'd overcome so many obstacles in her life. In fact, Mom talked about her so much, Roan was beginning to wonder if his mother was trying to play matchmaker.

It was a ridiculous thought. Jazzy was too young for him.

Besides, Roan had zero interest in dating. Not because he was still grieving for Claire, but with all the responsibilities in his life, the idea of making the effort that dating took simply felt too overwhelming.

The fire chief, Captain Sherley, came over to talk to him.

"Any idea what started it?" Roan asked.

"Spark from somewhere." Captain Sherley eyed his ranch hands. "Any of you men smoke or vape?"

All three shook their heads.

"No untended campfires?"

"Nope," Rowdy said. "We did run the ATV to round up the cattle but that was after the fire started."

"There's a new firing range they built on the ranch next door," Polk offered. "I heard target shooting this morning. Could a spark have come from that?"

"It's possible." Captain Sherley planted both hands on his hips and widened his stance. "The county's been pretty dry. They've discussed a burn ban. I'll have a talk with your neighbor and make sure they steer clear of metal targets."

"Thanks," Roan said. "I appreciate it."

It took over an hour for the firefighters to completely drench the pasture and declare the fire extinguished. The grass still smoldered, but the smoke dissipated. The stench clung to his hair and clothes, clogged up his nose. He was ready for fresh air.

The ranch hands drifted back to the barns to tend the livestock and after Roan thanked the firefighters, shook their hands, and pledged a big donation to the volunteer fire department, he stood alone looking at the surface scarring. The pasture would look beautiful come spring, but so much for winter grazing. He'd have to put in an order for extra hay. That would take a hit from his Christmas budget.

Dirty with soot, he climbed into his pickup and drove back to the house, doing the mathematical calculation in his head. He wondered if Jazzy would mind staying while he took a shower and cleaned up. He hated to ask. He owed her as it was.

He climbed the back porch steps, scraping grime off his boots. Heard music seeping through the door. "Jingle Bells" played at an elevated volume, along with the heartwarming sounds of Jazzy and Trinity singing along.

The happy sound brought a smile to his face. The fire hadn't affected them one bit, thank heavens. Claire would have been wringing her hands and pacing the floor, in between frantic texts. Immediately, he felt disloyal for thinking about his late wife's negative traits. Heaven knows, he had his faults. Living with generalized anxiety disorder had been rough on Claire.

And from time to time, him too.

Shaking off those thoughts, Roan pushed open the back door. The house smelled as good as it sounded. Jazzy must have found the Christmas-scented candles because the fragrance of gingerbread and cinnamon crowded out the stench of his clothing. A weird ache stabbed him dead center in his chest. He must have breathed in too much smoke.

"Daddy!" Trinity came running into the mudroom, arms outstretched, face beaming. "Come see, come see!"

She slipped her little hand in his and started

dragging him toward the living room and a help-less grin spread across his face. There was nothing in the world he loved more than to see his daughter happy.

They rounded the corner and Roan couldn't believe his eyes. He halted, and dang if his mouth didn't drop open to see his living room transformed.

The eight-foot artificial Christmas tree was up and fully decorated. The Christmas village figu-rines that Claire had loved to collect were set up on the coffee table exactly the way his late wife used to display them. He was beginning to think Jazzy was a mind-reading psychic and then he remembered his wife had created a layout chart for her collection. He hadn't decorated last year. It had been too soon, his heart still too tender. He and Trinity had celebrated Christmas with his parents instead. Two stockings hung from the fireplace mantel, his and Trinity's. The middle of the mantel, where Claire's should have hung, was empty.

The weird ache in his chest sharpened.

"Look it, Daddy, look it." Trinity flitted around the room, her eyes wide and shiny. "Jazzy fixed *everything*."

Roan's gaze found Jazzy, who was on a step stool, leaning over to add the star to the top of the tree. She had indeed fixed everything. Why then did he feel a rush of hot emotions pumping through his veins? Fear, irritation, and something else.

Something he couldn't put his finger on.

She finished, then straightened and glanced over

s quick. It was spontaneous. It was inno-
st a hug. That's all.

ragrance intoxicated him. Roan wrapped
s around her and held on for just a second
.

ulled back, blue eyes dazed, let out a long
and said, "I guess I'll see you tomorrow."

at him. "Did I do it right? Is this how it usually
looks?"

"Isn't it bootiful, Daddy?" Trinity clutched her
hands together and lifted them to her chin in a gesture so adorable, his anger instantly deflated.

"Yes," he said, finding Jazzy's gaze again. "Very
beautiful."

And that was the problem, wasn't it? Jazzy
had slipped right in and taken over. It had been a
kind gesture. As generous and caring as the sweet
blonde standing in front of him.

Jazzy moved over to her phone on the coffee
table and silenced the music she'd been playing.
"How bad was the fire?" she asked.

"Scorched the back forty," he said. "No people
or animals hurt. Everything's fine."

"Thank heavens. I was worried about you."

"I can't believe you did all this." He waved at the
room. His voice came out gruffer than he intended.

"Should I not have?"

"No. It's fine, it's great, it's . . ." Roan searched
for the right words to express the tension in his
body.

"I crossed a boundary."

"No. Well, maybe." He pulled his mouth down-
ward. "A boundary I didn't even know I had."

"I get it," she murmured. "Decorating was
something you and your wife did together."

"Yeah."

"Thank you for your patience and understanding with my overexuberance. I just thought Trinity
needed a little Christmas magic."

"She does and it's not you. You didn't do anything wrong, Jazzy."

"Should I take the decorations down?"

"No!" Trinity cried. "I love them."

"Of course not," Roan said. "This is my issue. I'll sort myself out."

"Is there anything I can do?"

"I'll be fine. It's time to let you get on your way." Roan pulled his wallet from his pocket and took out three twenty-dollar bills.

"Oh no, no." Jazzy raised both palms and shook her head. "You're not paying me."

"You've been here almost two hours and you decorated my house. I'm most certainly paying you."

She kept shaking her head. "It was my pleasure. Seriously."

He reached for her hand to press the money into it, but she jerked back. "Please don't insult me."

"Dang it, Jazzy. I don't like owing people."

"You owe me nothing."

"But I do. It's been a long time since I've seen her like that." He nodded toward Trinity, who was staring raptly up at the tree. "Take the money."

"You're already going to give me the Dutch oven. That's payment enough."

He shook the bills at her. "*Please.*"

Jazzy pressed her lips together and locked her arms behind her back. "Do you really want to pay me back?"

"I do."

"Then give me campfire cooking lessons."

Roan let out a grunt. "I'd rather give you cash."

"And I'd rather have cooking lessons." She stood

her ground. She had helped him the living room looked festive an cent. Ju lift a finger to get it that way.

You owe her. Her

"Jazzy—" his arn

"Roan." too lor

"I don't bake anymore." She

"You don't have to bake. I'll dc laugh, just need your help. Without it, th me to beat Andi Browning."

"Why is winning the cookie co tant to you?"

"Because she took the man I onc said simply. "Because she beats me Just once, I'd like the upper hand."

"Revenge doesn't suit you."

"I don't want revenge," Jazzy said to prove I'm worthy, you know?"

"All right," he said.

She cocked her head and looked so he got that weird chest ping again.

"I'll give you campfire cooking les

"Really?" Her eyes lit up as if he fortune.

"I don't have a lot of time, so I endless help, but yeah."

"When do we start?"

"Tomorrow evening? After Trin Would eight be too late?"

"No, no, that would be perfect. pirouette, her gorgeous hair flari body. Then she did the darndest th herself at him for a big bear hug.

CHAPTER 8

Jazzy was beyond excited. She couldn't believe she'd coaxed Roan into giving her baking lessons.

On the following evening, by the time she parked her car in his driveway—the air he'd put into her tire had held—she was downright giddy. With Roan in her corner, she stood a halfway decent chance of winning the competition.

The air smelled of burning mesquite wood and if it hadn't been for the curl of smoke coming from the backyard, she would have supposed the odor had lingered from yesterday's fire. She rounded the side of the house to find Roan standing in front of the outdoor firepit.

He was feeding fresh wood into the fire and his back was to her. Snug-fitting Wranglers clung to his butt, which was very nicely shaped. He wore a long-sleeved, blue-plaid flannel work shirt, and cowboy boots. Her heart did this strange little bump and grind, knocking around in her chest.

She had a sudden urge to back out and if he hadn't

turned and spotted her at that exact moment, she might well have fled.

He raised a hand, smiled. "Right on time. The fire's perfect."

"Shouldn't you have waited to show me how to start the fire?" she asked.

"We can do that on your next lesson when we have more time. Tonight, I figured I'd give you a jump start."

"Thank you." She stepped down off the sidewalk and crossed into an area paved with gorgeous flagstone.

He came toward her to take the grocery sack filled with baking supplies and set it on the table next to the outdoor grill. It was a lavish setup, complete with a sink and minifridge. Like something from a fancy model home.

"We used to do all our entertaining out here," he explained.

"You don't entertain anymore?"

"Not since Claire died. She was the life of the party. Without her . . ." A wistful look came into his eyes.

"You miss her a lot."

"At first I missed her so much I couldn't breathe," he said, holding her gaze. "But it's been two years now and the hole in my heart is starting to heal."

"I am so sorry for your loss."

He gave a slight shrug. "Everyone has loss. I'm not special."

You are to me, she thought, startling herself. Without him, she couldn't finally put Andi in her place.

"Are you going to be warm enough out here?" Roan asked.

"My coat's warm."

"It'll get confining. I can turn on the propane heaters." He indicated the stoves set strategically around the deck. "Although to be honest, I don't know if there is any propane in them."

"I should be fine," she said, shrugging out of her puffy white ski jacket and draping it over the back of a patio chair.

"Let's see what you've got in here." Roan turned to the paper sack she'd brought and started taking out items. "Flour, check. Butter, check. Sugar, white and brown, check." He paused and raised his head to meet her eyes. "What cookie recipe are we using?"

"I thought the Toll House recipe on the back of the package."

"That's a decent recipe and it's great for a first-time effort, but you need to be thinking about something special for the bake-off."

"I know," she said. "Chocolate chip recipes are not allowed in the cookie contest. It's a long-standing thing in Twilight."

"Everyone and their sister will be using the kismet cookie recipe, so let's avoid that one as well."

"I had the same thought." She studied him in the glow from the festive outdoor string lights that cast a daisy yellow gleam over the outdoor kitchen.

His dark hair was slicked back off his forehead and he had a regal profile—thick brows, high cheekbones, strong jawline, firm chin. He smelled of something trustworthy and earthy. Solid, dependable. She couldn't help comparing him to Danny.

Beside a man like Roan, her former boyfriend came off looking like a kid.

"Do you play video games?" she asked, surprising herself with the question.

"No," he said. "I don't have time for that stuff."

Danny was an avid gamer. Jazzy didn't know why, but Roan's answer made her smile.

"Not that I mean to imply there's anything wrong with video games," he said. "Lots of people enjoy them. Do you play?"

"Not really."

"Look at us. We've got something in common." His smile moved all the way to his eyes.

"And now we have baking as well."

He chuckled and she really liked the sound of his laugh. "I guess we do."

Her awkwardness ebbed and she felt like her usual self again.

Rummaging around in the counter underneath the sink, Roan pulled out a large mixing bowl, a whisk, and a big wooden spoon. "There's a cookie sheet in the pan drawer to your right. We will use the cookie sheet to put the dough on to rest."

"Why not just put them directly in the Dutch oven?"

"Because the Dutch oven needs to be hot before you put the cookies in. Pro tip for getting crispy bottoms that don't burn as easily."

"Do you need to go check on Trinity before we start baking?" Jazzy asked, getting out the high-quality baking sheet. This man took his tools seriously.

He pulled his cell phone from his pocket and

showed her the feed from a camera installed in his daughter's bedroom. Jazzy peered over his arm for a better look. Trinity lay curled up in the middle of her bed with a stuffed animal, sound asleep.

"The miracle of modern technology," he said.

"She won't appreciate it when she's sixteen and sneaking out her window to meet a boyfriend."

Roan handed her measuring cups and spoons. "When she's old enough to need her privacy, I'll take the camera out."

"And put them up outside her window?"

Roan studied her. "Did you sneak out of your window when you were a teenager?"

"No way." Jazzy grinned and laid out the bag of chocolate chips so she could read the recipe on the back. "Not me. My dad and I had a really good relationship, and I didn't want to give him any reason not to trust me."

"Do you think your dad will give me parenting tips when Trinity and I reach that stage?" Roan arched an eyebrow. He looked especially debonair when he did that, playful and just the tiniest bit rakish.

"You're forming your relationship with her right now." Jazzy pulled medical scissors from the pocket of her jeans and cut open the sacks of flour and sugar. "I believe your relationship will be solid."

"Thanks for the vote of confidence," he said. "It's not easy being a single parent."

"I bet," she said. "I saw my dad go through it with me. And he struggled a lot until he met my stepmother, Sarah."

"We own a couple of your stepmom's books. I try to read Trinity to sleep every night."

"See, my dad read to me too." Jazzy's heartstrings tugged. "It's a sweet tradition I hope to pass onto my own kids."

"You want children?"

"Oh yes." Jazzy beamed just thinking about it. "At least three, although my personal motto is 'the more the merrier.'"

"Wow," he said. "Three kids are a lot."

"You don't want more children?"

"I gotta concentrate on the one I have. Trinity comes first. *Always*."

"I could see how that might cause problems if you remarried." She paused. "Working on a Pediatric Ward, I often see blended families that didn't really blend. People who refer to the stepkids as *his* or *her* children. I mean technically, they aren't related, but if you make a show of 'my' kids versus 'your' kids, how is a family supposed to solidify?"

"I have no plans to get remarried."

"Ever?"

"I'm just not interested. Claire was one in a million and lightning just doesn't strike twice."

"That's not true." Jazzy locked eyes with him.

"What?" He startled.

"There was a big old oak tree in my backyard when I was growing up and it got hit by lightning three times."

"Really?"

"Yep."

"Hmm." Roan turned to eye the ingredients she assembled. "Did you bring eggs?"

"Oh gosh." She smacked her forehead with her palm. "I left them sitting out on the counter at home."

"No worries," he said. "I have chickens. Fresh eggs are always in my fridge."

"Sounds nice."

"It is. Trinity's named all ten of ours after Disney princesses."

"How cute! I wish I could keep chickens. Alas, I live in the middle of town."

"You can always come here for fresh eggs," he offered. "Anytime you have a hankering."

Was "fresh eggs" code for something else? She darted a glance at him. He was smiling gently. Did she *want* it to be something else?

Sudden heat spread through her body, and she quickly dropped his gaze.

"I'll go get the eggs," he said.

Watching him walk into the house, Jazzy exhaled and sagged against the outdoor sink. Her revved body tensed in a sexy way. Dear heavens, she was hot for the man.

Very hot.

All wrong for you, whispered a niggling voice in the back of her head.

"Why?" she whispered, fingering her lips as she imagined what it would feel like to have his mouth on hers.

Three words, Jazz. Baggage, baggage, baggage. Clearly the man was still struggling with the loss of his wife. All those pictures of Claire on his walls.

So what if Roan was hotter than a west Texas summer? He was a decade older than her. But why was that a deal breaker? His age gave him a comforting maturity the guys her own age lacked. Whenever she was around Roan, which, granted, hadn't been more than a handful of times, she felt safe in a way she hadn't felt with any man other than her father.

In fact, his steadfastness reminded her of Dad. Was that weird? Or a good thing? After a childhood filled with unexpected challenges, she craved peace and stability. Just because Roan was peaceful and stable—*and hot, don't forget hot*—didn't mean he was boyfriend material.

She liked him, but she wasn't so sure he liked her. A relationship with a single dad had challenges. Was it really smart to entertain thoughts of hooking up with him?

No, no, it was not smart. Trinity would always come first, as he'd made abundantly clear, and Trinity's well-being should come first. She admired him so much for that attitude, but it meant she'd never be first place in his world.

Getting way ahead of yourself, Lambchop. Cool your jets. It was Charlie's voice in her head now. *You know your tendency to turn people into projects. Leave Mr. Rancher Man alone.*

Right. The Charlie in her head was one hundred percent correct.

She was here for one reason. To learn how to bake cookies over a campfire. That was it. Her sole goal. And that's what she would focus on. Anything else, she'd leave in her imagination. She did not have to act on a fantasy just because it popped into her head.

Boy, was Roan Sullivan ever a fantasy. Tall, dark, handsome, kind. And in her mind, extremely good in bed.

Okay, yes, she'd been dreaming about what it'd be like if he took her to bed. No harm in daydreaming. None at all.

But she would not act on it. Decision made.

Roan came out of the house with a carton of eggs in one hand and two long-necked beers caught between the fingers of his other hand. "Would you like a beer?"

"Sure."

He set down the eggs, twisted the tops off the beers, and handed her one.

The moon had started its climb up the sky amid a twinkling of stars. It was quiet out here far from town. Somewhere, a horse neighed. The fire in the pit crackled as flames licked at the aged wood. Far off in the distance she heard a coyote howl, but even that sound was strangely comforting.

Using kitchen scales, he helped her carefully measure out the ingredients for basic chocolate chip cookies, telling her the scientific reasons for the precise measurements, which she appreciated. Under his tutelage, she mixed the softened butter, sugars, and egg together, then Roan slowly poured in the dry ingredients as she continued stirring.

Once the dough was ready to go, he showed her how to carefully move coals from the fire to the side of the pit to create a cooking bed of embers. He demonstrated how to use the tools and gave her a thermal glove to wear during the process.

Following his guidance, she spooned dough

into the cast-iron Dutch oven, then used the lid-lifting tool to place it over the embers. After he positioned the cookware, Roan showed her how to distribute more hot coals over the lid. When everything was set, Roan stoked the main fire for warmth and they sat in front of it, sipping their beers.

"How do you keep coals from falling into the cookies when you lift the lid?" she asked.

"Very carefully. That's part of the challenge in campfire cooking competitions. Get ashes or soot in the food and you're disqualified."

"Yikes. Not only do I have to be a good baker, I also can't be klutzy and expect to win."

"You'll do fine. We'll practice this process enough times you'll get it down pat."

"How long will it take?"

"To be a pro at campfire baking? Months of dedicated effort. To be good enough to beat amateur campfire bakers like the ones you'll be up against?" Grinning, he shook his head. "I'd say forty hours give or take and you'll stand a great chance of beating your rival."

"Double yikes! There's just over two weeks until the baking challenge. Do we have forty hours?"

"Well, today will count for two hours. That leaves thirty-eight to master campfire baking."

"Good thing I'm on vacation. I could never do this otherwise. So, when can we do this again?"

"Tomorrow night? You could come earlier, and I'll make Dutch oven stew and we could try a snickerdoodle recipe for dessert."

"Perfect." Jazzy paused, recognizing that this

was the firepit Roan and his wife had used in their videos. Once upon a time, Claire had sat here with him sipping beers. That made her feel weird. She stared into the fire, the camaraderie they shared morphing into awkwardness.

"Time to check on the cookies," he said.

"But it's too early." She showed him her phone with the timer app she'd set. "It's only been seven minutes and the recipe instructions say ten to twelve."

"The recipe isn't for campfire cooking. We don't have as much control over the heat as we do in an oven. It may take much longer or shorter than what the recipe recommends. In campfire baking, you have to keep a closer eye on the product."

"Gotcha."

"You want to try taking the lid off with the lifter?"

"Why don't you demonstrate this first time and let me watch how a master does it. Then I can try my hand at it tomorrow."

"Okay," he said easily and with languid movements, stretched from the chair to the firepit.

Donning a glove, he lifted the Dutch oven from the fire and set it on the brick border surrounding the pit. The embers on the lid glowed red in the darkness. Another coyote howl echoed across the ranch and sent goose bump shivers up Jazzy's arms.

Cautiously, Roan raised the lid with the lifting tool, smoothly settling the cover to one side without missing a beat. Even from where she was sitting, Jazzy could feel the heat radiating off the Dutch oven.

"Want to peek?" Roan asked.

Nodding, she moved to crouch beside him and peered into the Dutch oven. The dough was melting and spreading in the pan, but it still looked raw on top. "Needs more time."

"I agree." He reversed the process he'd used to remove the Dutch oven from the coals, settling it back down again, then took his seat next to her.

"Another beer?" he asked as she polished off the first one.

"No. I need to drive home."

"I have two guest rooms," he said. "You're welcome to stay the night."

Oh wow. Did that invitation have some hidden meaning?

"I have to check on my cat. Sabrina is pretty self-sufficient, but if I don't give her enough attention, she'll get revenge-y and poop in my house shoes."

"Can't have that, can we?" he chuckled.

"No sirree. I just got out my Christmas slippers."

"Christmas slippers?"

"I have slippers for every major holiday," Jazzy explained. "Bunny for Easter, Uncle Sam for Fourth of July, witches for Halloween, turkeys for Thanksgiving, and Santa slippers for Christmas."

"No kidding?" He looked amused.

"I adore holidays."

"You're a kid at heart."

"Why do you think I work on the Pediatric Ward?" she asked.

"I thought it might be because you were sickly as a kid." He paused. "Or so my mom told me."

"That too. I had crazy bad asthma or so the doctors thought until they discovered the real cause and the nurses helped me so much," Jazzy said. "I wanted to give back to the profession that did so much for me."

"Admirable. Do you like nursing?"

"*Love* it. I mean it's really rough when I lose a patient, but thankfully that's very rare."

"You have a huge heart, Jazzy Walker."

His compliment brought a flush to her cheeks, although she told herself it was just the heat from the fire. She didn't want to want his approval.

Silence fell over them and she didn't feel any urge to chatter as she might normally have. By nature, she was a chatty person, but she could tell Roan was not. From a sheltering of oak trees across the pasture came the hoot of a barn owl. Farther off, another owl answered. *Who? Who?*

"It's tranquil out here."

"It is."

"How long have you lived on this ranch?" she asked.

"All my life. I was born here. My grandfather bought Slope Ridge in the 1940s, when he came home from World War II and he passed it onto my dad. After Pop had a heart attack it was too much for him to keep up with and he and Mom both decided to retire. Claire and I had just gotten married and were living in an apartment in Fort Worth. We jumped at the chance to take over the place."

"Wow, that's an impressive heritage." She wanted to ask him what Claire had done for a living before they started making campfire cooking videos. The woman was pretty enough to have been a model, but she didn't want to discuss his late wife. "Not many people have that kind of legacy."

"It is special," he said. "Knowing your roots run three generations deep and you're raising the fourth."

"Would you be disappointed if Trinity didn't want to take over the ranch?"

"I imagine a little," Roan said. "But I don't want her to ever feel she can't be who she wants to be."

"That's a healthy attitude." She paused, sniffing the air. "Does it smell like the cookies are burning to you?"

"Go ahead and check them."

"By myself?"

"Hands-on is the best way to learn."

"Okay," she said, feeling out of her element as she recalled how badly she'd screwed up the cookies she'd baked with Charlie.

Roan talked her through the steps. She was surprised by how difficult it was to lift the piping hot Dutch oven from the coals with the cast-iron lifting tool.

"I didn't realize I'd have to pump iron to be a campfire baker," she joked.

"It is heavy and unwieldy lifting it from the fire, but I bet a dollar to a doughnut that Andi will have the same struggles as you in that regard."

"That's comforting," Jazzy said and feeling rather wobbly, settled the Dutch oven onto the bricks the way Roan had earlier. "If she and I are on a level playing field with the campfire part, maybe I should focus on perfecting my baking skills."

"Good point." He got up and came to kneel beside her in front of the brick border. "And you'll need to create your own special recipe."

"That sounds daunting."

"You can do it," he said.

"You really think so?"

"With me in your corner? How can you fail?" His eyes twinkled in the firelight.

"You're going to help me create my own cookie recipe?" Excitement sped up her pulse.

"Sure . . . if you want my help with that."

"Oh yes, yes!"

"Do you want me to do the honors?" He nodded at the Dutch oven.

"No, you're right. I need to learn." Hauling in a deep breath, and clenching her jaw, she took the lid lifter and hooked it around the lid handle.

"Steady," Roan coached at her elbow.

Her arm trembled under the weight of the lid. One slip and it was coal cookies. Biting down on her bottom lip and gripping the lifter with both hands in thermal gloves, she eased the lid down onto the bricks beside the Dutch oven.

"Ta-da." Sweat beaded on her brow.

Roan applauded.

She stripped off the gloves and leaned over to peer at the cookies. The edges looked a little too brown, but the tops were golden. Roan handed her a metal spatula and a paper plate.

Mindful of the edges of the hot pan, she gingerly leaned forward to scoop out the cookies one by one. The last cookie flipped over in the process.

"Aww," she said. "The bottoms are burnt."

"Common mishap when first learning campfire cooking."

"I'm assuming points are counted against you for that."

"If you're lucky. Usually, in competitions you're disqualified if you burn something, but the coordinators of this contest might cut the contestants some slack since the money goes to charity."

"How do you keep the bottoms from burning?"

"That's a lesson for another night, but just because they're a little singed and inappropriate for competition, doesn't mean we can't enjoy them." Roan reached for the cookie that had flipped over.

Jazzy grabbed a cookie too. "Ow, ow, hot, hot."

Roan blew on his cookie to cool it. Jazzy juggled hers from hand to hand. The burnt smell curled into her nose. Other than slightly scorched, the cookie looked good. Crispy on the outside, soft in the middle, the chocolate chips completely melted into chocolatey goodness.

She popped the cookie into her mouth. It tasted pretty darn good except for the burnt parts.

"Congratulations," Roan said after he finished his cookie and dusted the crumbs from his fingers. "You've made your first campfire cookies."

"I couldn't have done it without you." She rocked back on her heels beside him and looked up to see his face.

"You've got some chocolate right there." He rubbed at his chin.

"Oh." Laughing, she dabbed her chin.

"Other side."

She scrubbed the other side.

"You're still missing it." He leaned in, cupped her jaw in his hand, and with the pad of his thumb, gently wiped away the chocolate smudge.

He was still touching her face. She could feel the warmth of his breath on her cheek, smell the scent of chocolate in the air, and for one glorious second, she thought he was going to kiss her.

"There," he murmured. "All gone."

"Thank you," she croaked and leaned into him. *Kiss me, kiss me, kiss me.*

His lips puckered and she held her breath.

"Jazzy?"

"Yes."

They stared at each other, spellbound, but then the back door opened and on the soft breeze came the sound of Trinity's sleepy little voice.

"Daddy," his daughter called out into the darkness. "Where are you? I had a bad dream and I'm scared."

CHAPTER 9

"Did you see Andi Browning's Insta?" Roan's younger sister, Rio, asked him on Friday, December 9, two days after he almost kissed Jazzy.

Two days during which they'd spent the evenings from five to nine P.M. stoking the firepit and baking various kinds of cookies. Two days they'd shared good food, laughter, and growing camaraderie. And two days he'd devoted to raking himself over the coals. He had no business lusting after a woman ten years his junior.

Yeah? So why are you still helping her?

Um, it was selfish motivation, but when he'd realized how quickly Jazzy's baking skills improved, his ego could see that golden cookie trophy in Jazzy's hands. She was a fast and eager learner. Her win could actually happen.

Living through her vicariously. Sad.

How could he pull out now? After hours of hands-on practice, Jazzy was on the verge of next-level campfire cooking. If he pulled the plug at this point, he doubted she'd have a chance of winning on her own. Plus, he owed her. She'd done so much for him and Trinity.

Sounds like excuses to me, pal.

"Roan?" Rio nudged.

A talented metal artist, his sister specialized in welded Western-themed sculptures. Because it was easier for her work, she kept her dark hair cropped short in a pixie cut. She wore black leggings that looked like leather, an avant-garde blouse with billowy sleeves and an asymmetrical hemline, silver rings on every finger and a pair of knee-high black boots. Dramatic Rio versus reserved Roan. They were night and day. Their mom said, with much motherly pride and affection, that whenever Rio was around you better take a good deep breath before she sucked up all the oxygen in the room, and with Roan, go ahead and leave your valuables out, he'd protect them for you.

He blinked at his sister, who'd come to babysit Trinity while he took Jazzy on the hunt for the perfect cookie recipe that could win her the bake-off.

"Huh?"

"Have you seen Andi Browning's Insta?" Rio repeated.

"You know I hate social media."

Rio took out her phone, scrolled through Andi's social media feed and handed the phone to him so he could see for himself.

The post tagged with #heputaringonit and there was a picture of Andi's ring finger sporting a glittering diamond.

"Yes," he said. "I know she's engaged to Danny Garza."

"Not that post," Rio said, leaning over to flick the post away with her finger, bringing in another.

This one was labeled #win@allcosts, #thegolden cookieismine, #kissmygritsjazzywalker, #goingfor trophynumberthree. Below the hashtags she'd posted a picture of herself with the previous year's golden cookie and photoshopped into another pane overlaid onto the first picture, was a caricature of Andi kicking Jazzy in the behind. The most disturbing thing? The picture had gotten over six hundred likes.

Anger surged through him. "What the hell?"

Rio raised her head and shot a sidelong glance at Trinity, who was sitting at the table munching cornflakes. "Andi has always been a mean girl and now she's a mean woman. She's actively trying to hurt Jazzy."

That comment erased any lingering doubts Roan harbored about helping Jazzy. He was her secret weapon and together they'd take down the unkind Ms. Browning.

"Thanks for sitting with Trinity," he said, grabbing his Stetson from the hook in the mudroom. "Hopefully, I'll be back by noon."

"Fingers crossed you find the perfect recipe," Rio said. "It's past time Andi's had her comeuppance."

"Thanks." Roan went to the table to give Trinity a goodbye hug. "I'm gonna try my best to help Jazzy win this."

Rio gave him a thumbs-up and all the way to Jazzy's house, Roan kept stewing over Andi's tacky posts. He should feel sorry for the woman's desperate need for attention, but she was gunning for Jazzy and that didn't sit well with him. Jazzy was the sweetest person. She didn't deserve Andi's ugliness.

It was ten thirty when he pulled into her driveway. Jazzy was waiting for him on the front porch of her modest little cottage not far from the town square. It was a whimsical house that made him think of *The Hobbit*. The stone home had a turret underneath a highly pitched roof, a cobblestone walkway, an overgrowth of shade trees, and a flowerbed filled with colorful chrysanthemums. She'd decorated for the holidays with garden gnomes in Santa caps, twinkle lights dripping from the eaves, and candy cane cutouts lining the drive. Through the bay window, he could see her Christmas tree, lit up and twirling, and a gray tabby cat grooming itself on the sill.

Just looking at the house made him feel as if he'd gotten a wholehearted, full-body hug from Jazzy. The cottage was precious to the core. No wonder Andi had it in for Jazzy. The woman possessed something Andi never would. A magical sense of style that radiated from who Jazzy was—a good and decent person.

He wondered what she'd do with the house when she started with Traveling Nurses. She might have trouble selling a place that so distinctly reflected her tastes. The thought of her leaving town stirred something murky inside him. A sense of melancholia.

Waving, Jazzy hurried down the steps before he'd

even parked his truck. She wore a pink car coat—
she called the color "mauve"—a white turtleneck
sweater, dark-wash denim jeans, and pointy-toed
black ankle boots. Her hair was down today, flowing over her shoulders in that curtain of golden silk.
She looked elegant as any princess and Roan drank
in the sight of her.

From the radio, tuned to the 1960s channel after Mom and Dad had borrowed his truck to haul
home a garage sale furniture find, Dean Martin
started singing "Ain't That a Kick in the Head."

Spellbound, Roan watched Jazzy leap lightly
over the small stone wall, not bothering with the
charming metal gate.

He snapped off the radio, planning on getting
out and opening the car door for her, but before
he could even undo his seat belt, she was already
there. Popping into the passenger seat with her
sunbeam smile.

"Hey!" she said in that gleeful voice of hers.
"Good morning."

Danny Garza, you're a damn fool.

"Morning." Roan grinned back, his chest growing tight with so many feels he couldn't name them
all. "Ready?"

She buckled her seat belt. "Ready."

The cab of his truck filled with her fragrance,
sweet as cotton candy and as clean as strawberry-
scented shampoo. The impulse to kiss her and see
if she tasted as good as she smelled gripped him
and it was all he could do to keep his hands on the
steering wheel and off Jazzy Walker.

"All set," she said, settling back in the seat and resting her hands in her lap. "Let's do this."

Five minutes later, they arrived at the Twilight Bakery. Honestly Roan wasn't even sure how they got there. Jazzy so dazed his mind. This time, he hopped out of the truck and ran around to the passenger side before she could get out.

Unfortunately, he forgot to put on the parking brake and the truck started slowly slipping down the incline. Oh crap. He raced back to the driver's side, but Jazzy had already leaned over to yank on the parking brake, and when he opened his door to find her stretched out across the seat, she peeked up at him through a sheaf of blond hair and grinned.

"Got it!" She giggled.

"Jazzy to the rescue," he said, sounding insanely out of breath. He got in and repositioned the truck.

"Don't think you have to help me out of the truck. It's nice that you're chivalrous, but I can take care of myself."

"It's an ingrained habit," he said, "but I won't do it if you don't want me to."

"No need. It's not like we're dating or anything," she said. "We're just friends, right?"

"My mom trained me to open doors for women, but now I see that's a throwback to the days when men believed women couldn't take care of themselves. Old customs are falling by the wayside." He glanced over at her. "You'll have to teach me the ways of your generation."

"Oh yes," she said with a grin. He loved how she smiled so often. "You're practically Methuselah."

"Maybe you should open doors for me?" he joked. "Where did my cane get off to?"

"You're not too old for me," she blurted, sitting right there in his truck parked in front of the Twilight Bakery.

"Wh-what?"

"I know you think you're too old for me, but you're not."

He didn't know what to say.

"You like me," she said. "I can tell, and I like you. So, if it's my age that's holding you back from kissing me, don't let that be an obstacle. I'm single, you're single. Why can't we have a bit of holiday fun together?"

With that, she hopped from the truck and made a beeline for the bakery, leaving Roan sitting with his mouth agape.

Inside the bakery, Jazzy stepped aside to let others pass, waiting for Roan to join her. "Let It Snow" was on the sound system and to distract herself, Jazzy imagined what the song would be like to sing on karaoke night. As the seconds ticked by and Roan stayed in the truck, her anxiety grew.

Why had she told him she liked him? Why had she practically begged him to kiss her?

Why? Because she'd spent the last two evenings sitting around a campfire with the man. Baking cookies, smelling his manly scent, listening to ranch noises, and wishing, oh so powerfully, for something more.

Greedy girl! She should have kept her big mouth shut. Instead, she'd impulsively told him what was on her mind. Had she scared him off? Would he tell her he could no longer give her baking lessons, considering that she wanted to jump his bones?

Aww, damn, Jazzy. You blew it.

She heard a vehicle door slam and darted a glance out the window. Roan had finally gotten out of the truck and was sauntering toward the bakery, adjusting his Stetson lower on his forehead. She couldn't see his eyes or get a read on his body language.

Her heart thumped harder with each step he took toward her. When he reached the door of the crowded bakery, she leaned over to open it for him.

His eyes met hers, murky and impassive.

Yikes! She had blown it.

"Roan?" she said, her voice coming out shaky.

He raised his eyebrows. "Yes?"

"Are you . . . is everything . . ." She pulled her bottom lip up between her teeth, worried it. "Are you cross with me?"

"Why would I be cross?"

"Because I said something you didn't want to hear."

"Who says I didn't want to hear it?"

She stared at him, hope pulling her mouth into an O shape.

"Roan!" A voice from behind the counter called to him.

They glanced over simultaneously to see the owner of the bakery, Christine Noble, limp around the counter to greet them. Once, Christine had been an avid skier whose Olympic dreams ended when a car hit her while she was out on a training run. Christine had won the Twilight Christmas Cookie

Contest so many times, she'd been the first inductee into the Twilight Christmas Cookie Hall of Fame. Christine was in her early forties, married to a cutting horse trainer with four children. They lived in Jubilee, not far from where Roan lived.

Christine hugged them both, first Roan, then Jazzy and said with a bright smile, "Two of my most favorite people. Y'all come on into the back." She waved for them to follow her.

"You've got a long line of customers," Roan said. "We can wait."

"Amy's got it covered. She's a dynamo." Christine flapped a hand at the assistant behind the counter. "You two are special. Let's go check out the cookie vault."

"Cookie vault?" Jazzy giggled.

"Where I keep my top-secret recipes."

"And you're willing to share them with me?" Jazzy asked, stunned by Christine's generosity.

"I'm willing to share them with Roan," Christine said. "He and Claire gave me invaluable advice when I opened the bakery and I've just been waiting for the chance to repay his kindness."

Claire.

To Jazzy, the biggest sticking point in exploring a relationship with Roan wasn't their age gap, but rather, the ghost of his dead wife. Claire cropped up everywhere. Worse, after watching every single campfire cooking video Roan had uploaded to YouTube, Jazzy adored Claire too. She was clever and quick-witted and beautiful. She had a high beguiling laugh as sweet as an oboe and a sly way of looking at the camera that seduced the viewer.

No way could Jazzy ever compete with Claire's innate sensuality. Her hopes rode a downdraft and two words lit up her brain bright as neon signs.

Tread lightly.

Okay, she would pretend she hadn't said a word to Roan in the truck and if he didn't make a move, she'd just let things die out. They'd just go through Christine's cookie vault and pick out the most unique or difficult cookie to use for the contest. Roan had said that strategy would help her stand out in the crowd. She was scared that she couldn't pull off a complicated recipe, but Roan paraphrased Ellen Johnson Sirleaf. "If your dreams don't scare you, they're not big enough."

Christine led them down a small hallway. Her bustling kitchen buzzed with activity and delicious smells as they passed by it on the way to Christine's office that doubled as a tasting room.

"Have a seat." Christine waved them down into two chairs in front of her desk crowded with open notebooks which were filled with photographs of cakes, cookies, and pastries for weddings, graduations, family reunions, and other large celebrations.

She plopped down behind the desk, reached into the bottom drawer, and pulled out a large metal file box. The box sported numerous Christmas stickers. The top was labeled with masking tape in Christine's handwriting.

Top-Secret Cookie Recipes.

"You may go through and take as much time as you want, but you can't take the recipe with you," she said.

"Can we snap a photo?" Roan asked.

"For you, yes. I trust that you won't tell anyone I shared my secret recipes with you." Christine shifted her gaze to Jazzy. "You're also sworn to secrecy."

Jazzy pantomimed zipping her lip and throwing the imaginary key over her shoulder.

With great reverence, Christine passed the box to Roan, who clutched it as if he'd been given the queen's gold.

"May you find the perfect recipe for you." Pressing her palms together, Christine bowed and left the room.

"Wow," Jazzy said, impressed. "The way Christine values those recipes you must have done something pretty special to get access to her vault."

"Eli and I are good friends," he said, referring to Christine's husband.

Still, it reflected on Roan's good character that someone as private as Christine trusted him with her secret recipes.

"We won't use whichever recipes we choose exactly as it's written, and Christine knows that," he explained. "You'll need to put your special spin on them, but we'll find a good recipe that jazzes up easily."

"Pun intended?" she asked, slanting him a provocative glance through lowered lashes.

A teasing smile lit his face as his gaze rambled over her body and back to her eyes. "Pun intended."

Jazzy felt herself blush and she ducked her head. While she enjoyed his frank approval, it embarrassed her a little. Did this mean they were moving forward? Could a holiday romance be blooming?

Her heart shimmied like a dog shaking off water. *Please*, she thought, *please*.

He opened the box in his lap and glanced at her. "Get closer so you can see too."

Before she could scooch over, he had a big strong hand on the arm of her chair and easily dragged it six inches nearer to him. She was so close that their chairs touched. She caught a whiff of his cologne, woodsy, warm, spicy. Nice scent. Guys her age rarely wore cologne. She'd bought Giorgio for Danny at Christmas one year, but he'd never worn it.

Jazzy's nose twitched. "Is that Giorgio?"

"What?" Roan blinked at her, a yellowed index card in his hand, his brow furrowed in confusion.

"Your cologne."

"Oh yeah," he said. "Claire claimed it's my signature scent. I don't know about that. I just like the smell. I'm sure there are other colognes out there I could try if you don't enjoy it. I don't mind switching."

The man was willing to switch his signature cologne for her? That was something, huh? It almost made up for the Claire and Danny associations to Giorgio.

"Wh-why would you switch your cologne for me?" she asked.

His gaze locked on hers. "Did I hear you wrong in the truck?"

"Um . . ." She licked her lips absentmindedly, realized how it might look and stopped herself mid-lick, swiftly sucking her tongue back into her mouth.

"Didn't you say not to let age be an obstacle if I was interested in you?"

"I did," she squeaked, hardly able to catch her breath.

Now that they were actually talking about dating each other, she felt weird and excited and a little terrified where this might lead.

"We'll take it slowly," he said. "We've got a lot of issues to address before we take things to the next level."

"Issues?"

"My dead wife and your ex-boyfriend."

"Uh, I'm not interested in getting that deep."

"What do you mean?"

"I'm leaving town as soon as the holidays are over. I'll accept the job from Traveling Nurses when they offer it. I thought this . . . we . . . hmm . . . could just hook up maybe?"

He studied her for a long moment, his dark eyes giving no clues to his emotions. The butterflies in her stomach fluttered hard. "I see."

"Is that a problem?" She winced and braced herself for rejection.

"I don't do casual sex anymore, Jazzy. That was fine in my twenties, but after I got married and we had Trinity . . ." He shook his head. "My wife and daughter became my everything. I'm not jumping into anything that could put Trinity in harm's way. Trust is important to me."

"Trust is important to me too and I adore Trinity."

"My daughter adores you too, which is my worry. She attaches easily and like you said, you'll be off to see the world after New Year's. I don't think a holiday hookup is in either of our best interests."

"You're absolutely right. Forget I ever said anything. The last thing I'd ever want is to hurt Trinity," Jazzy said. *Or you. Or me.* "The very last thing."

"That said," he continued, "I recognize it's time I moved on from Claire. It's been over two years since I've . . ." He gulped. "Been with anyone."

So, he was rusty. She was too. "Same page."

"Maybe a rebound relationship, especially with someone kind and trustworthy, is what we both need."

"Maybe," she whispered, her heart thumping hard in her throat. Could he see the vein in her neck pounding? Did he have any idea how much she wanted him? Rebound man. Uh-huh. She could see it. But would that be enough for her?

The sultry light glistening in his eyes said he wanted her too.

Whew. Heady stuff.

"There's a lot to consider," he said.

God, his maturity was such a turn-on. Danny would have had her half-naked by now. Not to knock Danny. He was a decent guy, but like most men in their twenties, he wanted lots of quick sex. She was enjoying Roan's much slower pace. His deliberateness made her feel like she meant something. Even if they couldn't be more than a hot Christmas hookup.

"So, we'll see about proceeding with caution?"

"Uh-huh." She felt so breathless she could hardly speak. She kept imagining what he looked like bare chested and sprawled out on her bed.

"Yellow light. Feel this thing out. See if it's a path we both want to go down."

"I agree."

"Okay, then." Roan nodded. "Now that we have that ironed out, let's find a cookie recipe."

CHAPTER 10

They settled on a rugelach after Roan convinced Jazzy that he had a plan for elevating Christine's basic recipe into an award-winning cookie. The only thing left was to hone Jazzy's culinary and campfire skills. Unfortunately, they had less than two weeks to accomplish that goal. That meant they'd have to spend every spare moment together.

Not that Roan was complaining.

Being around Jazzy was like strolling through a magical forest. With her, the world shone brighter, and Roan felt himself fully living in the moment. Colors were more vivid. Music more melodious. Flavors more scrumptious. The cinnamon in the rugelach samples Christine gave them lingered on his tongue long after he'd swallowed the last mouthwatering bite.

"You seriously think I can make something as delicious as Christine's rugelach?" Jazzy asked as they left the bakery and joined the throng of shoppers in the town square.

"We can make it even better."

Jazzy stopped walking and gnawed her bottom lip. "My only worry is that rugelach is technically a pastry and not a cookie."

Roan halted beside her. "We'll slice the dough into cookie-sized circles before we bake them. They'll look just like a cookie. I'll bet you that no one else will make rugelach in a Dutch oven. I've won enough of these things to know what the judges are looking for. Trust me. The rugelach is a winner."

She angled her head to study him, a lock of golden hair falling prettily against her cheek. Good heavens but she was beautiful. It was all he could do not to reach out and brush the curl from her face. To use the errant strand as an excuse to touch her as he had with the chocolate on her chin the first night they'd baked together. It seemed forever ago.

His heart clutched. What was he doing? Did he seriously think he could have casual sex with her and not suffer repercussions? Bad idea.

"Well, well, well." Andi Browning's voice yanked Roan's attention to the showy blonde in front of them. She had hold of Danny Garza's wrist and appeared to be dragging him toward the Twilight Bakery. "Fancy meeting you here."

Roan shot a glance over at Jazzy. Her serene smile warmed his soul. She wasn't letting her nemesis get the better of her.

"Where else would I be but gathering material to win the bake-off?" Jazzy asked.

"You *do* know the recipes must be original." Andi was speaking to Jazzy, but eyeing Roan. He could almost feel the heated intensity of her stare.

Overhead, the breeze ruffled the tinsel garland

mounted to the awning of the pet supply store next to the bakery. The door to Fruit of the Vine, the storefront from a local winery, on the north side of the square stood open and the sound of Billie Holiday's "I'll Be Seeing You" mingled with the Christmas song "All I Want for Christmas Is You" piped from the courthouse speaker system, creating an oddly euphonous combination.

"I do know that." Jazzy deepened her smile and earned Roan's admiration for her calm serenity under pressure. "But all recipes are built on a basic foundation and there's no better baker in town than Christine. Isn't that why *you're* here as well?"

"No," Andi said with a toss of her hair. "Danny and I are going in to taste cakes for our wedding." She put a hard inflection on the word *wedding*.

Roan shot a look at Danny. The younger man flashed a sheepish grin. He shifted his weight, glanced at the ground, and when he raised his head, his attention locked on Jazzy.

That expression on Danny's face—one of a man who'd figured out he'd made a grave mistake—bothered Roan. Jazzy didn't need this fickle dude messing with her head.

Jazzy didn't seem to notice Danny watching her. Her gaze latched on to Andi.

Roan's shirt collar felt itchy.

"Whatcha gonna bake?" Andi batted her lashes at Roan.

What game was that woman playing?

"Rugelach," Jazzy said before Roan could send her a warning glance.

Did Jazzy always do this with Andi? Hand her nemesis the ammo to use against her? The downside of being open, honest, and trusting, projecting her own good qualities onto others and assuming they would think and act the same way.

"It's just one of several recipes we're considering," Roan said.

"Rugelach?" Andi lifted an eyebrow. "Is that a cookie?"

"Christine sells them as cookies. Why? Do you think rugelach violates the contest rules?"

Please hush. Gently, he squeezed her elbow, hoping Jazzy would get the hint.

"Nah." Andi shook her head. "I'm sure rugelach is fine. The rules just say no brownies or bars."

Jazzy looked uncertain and shifted her gaze to Roan. He draped his arm around her shoulder and pulled her close, letting her know he had her back.

"Have fun at your cake tasting," Jazzy said with a fixed smile and a wriggle of her fingers. Then she linked her arm through Roan's.

Roan had just enough time to see Danny scowl before Andi hauled him into the bakery.

Well now, had Roan just become some kind of bargaining chip in Jazzy's rivalry with Andi? He sure didn't mind her arm hooked around his elbow, but he didn't like being a pawn in a Jazzy-Danny-Andi mind game. He deserved better than that. Especially after what Jazzy had said to him in Christine's office.

"Would you like to cut through Sweetheart Park?" he asked, trying to figure out the best way to approach the subject.

"Sure! I love Sweetheart Park this time of year. Oh, who am I kidding. I love it all year round. The park is sentimentality at its best." She leaned into him, her head level with his shoulder and his nose filled with her honeyed scent.

Arm in arm, they walked under the candy cane archway that led into a winter wonderland. Twinkle lights adorned every tree. Garlands, ribbons, and bows decorated the park benches and wooden footbridges spanning the small tributary of the Brazos River as it fed into Lake Twilight. There were wooden cutouts and blow molds, inflatables, and animatronics—Santa and his reindeer, a North Pole village complete with Mrs. Claus and an army of elves, Frosty the Snowman, the Grinch, and a lavish nativity scene.

Amid the holiday designs were the permanent starry-eyed fixtures in Sweetheart Park. They strolled past the Sweetheart Fountain, a statue of Jon Grant and Rebekka Nash, two of the town's founders, locked in the enrapt embrace of reunited lovers. An engraving on a plaque beside the statue told the story of their legendary romance and ended with this promise: throw a coin in the fountain, make a wish to reunite with your first love, and it would come true.

Roan and Claire had been high school sweethearts and they'd broken up when they'd gone off to separate colleges, but distance couldn't keep them apart. Later, Claire had told Roan she'd thrown twenty dollars' worth of coins into the fountain and made wish after wish that they would find their way back to each other. It was a silly myth, of course, he and Claire had been destined all along.

But then he'd lost her. There was no town legend that told you how to move on after a loss like that.

Jazzy tightened her grip on his arm and he looked down at her.

"Thinking of Claire?" she murmured.

He nodded.

"It must have been so hard to lose the love of your life."

Again he nodded, struck by the kindness in Jazzy's eyes. It took him a second to find his words. "She'd want me to move on. Claire was whimsical and she had a big imagination, but she was practical too. She liked to say it took all kinds of love to make the world go round. I think she was right."

"Twilight just chooses to focus on teenage romance because it lures more tourists' dollars," Jazzy said. "But teenage love is quite often not much more than rampant hormones. It's infatuation, not true love. That's the message of Jon and Rebekka that gets lost. They had to spend fifteen years apart for infatuation to grow into mature love."

Roan wondered if she was thinking about her high school romance with Danny Garza, but he didn't really want to know. Claire wasn't a threat to his budding feelings for Jazzy. His wife was gone and couldn't come back. But Danny Garza had been staring at Jazzy with regret in his eyes.

C'mon, Sullivan. Is that true or is it just your insecurities talking?

Fair question.

He steered Jazzy around the fountain, happy to leave the kissing sweethearts behind. They passed by more Christmas decorations. Tiny Tim, Scrooge, and the three ghosts that visited the miserly man in *A Christmas Carol*. A gingerbread town populated with gingerbread people and an array of Peanuts characters outfitted in Christmas clothing.

Toward the end of the park exit loomed the Sweetheart Tree, which during the holidays doubled as Twilight's Angel Tree. The names of needy children, written on white plastic snowflakes, hung from the lower branches of the two-hundred-year-old pecan tree.

Assembled around the base of the pecan was a white picket fence along with a weathered sign asking people not to deface the tree. Countless names scratched into the bark of the old tree defied the edict. Squarely in the center of the tree, outlined with a heart, were the names of Jon Grant and Rebekka Nash. The original tree-defacers.

A few years back, the chamber of commerce had the bright idea of encouraging tourists to buy engraved metal charms and attach them to a wire frame around the tree to stop the tree whittling. Not only did it cut down on the name carving, but the charms brought in extra revenue for the town's coffers.

Roan had grown up in the tree-carving era, and Claire had scratched their names into the bark with a paring knife in big lettering. He'd protested, but Claire's joy prevented him from stopping her. He'd secretly felt guilty about the inscription ever since. He knew without looking exactly where their names were, underneath a knothole on the back side of the pecan.

"Oh look," Jazzy said, bending down. "One of the angel snowflakes fell from the tree."

Her fanny was in the air and Roan couldn't help looking. What a view! But he didn't want to ogle, she wasn't an object. Quickly, he turned his head and saw Danny Garza standing alone at the Sweetheart Fountain some yards away.

Where was Andi? Had the couple finished cake tasting already? Curious, he studied the younger man.

Then Danny reached into his jeans' pocket, pulled out a coin, and threw it into the wishing fountain.

Jazzy hung the fallen snowflake back on the tree and straightened to find Roan standing with his head down and his hands jammed into his pockets as if he was chilled, but he wore a jacket, and the weather was mild. His body language said he was shutting himself off.

Was he thinking of his late wife?

"Is your name on the tree?" she asked.

He nodded but said nothing and kept his hands in his pockets.

"Can I see?"

He let out a deep breath, it wasn't quite a sigh, and he led her to the back of the tree out of view from the other park visitors. Overhead, plastic snowflakes dangled, creating a concealing canopy.

Roan pointed to the bark beneath a prominent knothole.

Jazzy tracked his finger to the carving, discerned it from all the other names hewed there. *Claire loves Roan 4 Life.*

Ahh, darn it. Jazzy's heart stumbled over itself. "Claire carved this?"

"She was impulsive sometimes," he said. "Where are your and Danny's names?"

"I wouldn't let him deface the tree." Jazzy chuckled. "He wanted to, but I'm such a rule follower and I couldn't help feeling sorry for the poor old pecan that has to bear the burden of so much ripe, young love."

"Kind," Roan murmured. "Even to a tree."

"What?" Jazzy blinked up at him, hearing something odd in his voice.

"You're a truly kind person, Jazzy Walker."

She felt her cheeks heat. "Oh, I have my moments."

"Do you?"

"Yes." She tilted her chin upward.

He had one forearm resting on the tree, his body half turned toward her. She was facing him and feeling a little unsteady on her feet. There was a look in his eyes that sent a thrilling army of goose bumps spreading over her skin.

Roan cleared his throat.

Jazzy leaned in.

He lowered his head.

From the outdoor speakers mounted in the trees, Michael Bublé sang "It's Beginning to Look a Lot Like Christmas." Jazzy stood stock-still, barely breathing. Every hope in her body aching for a kiss.

Briefly, Roan touched the tip of his tongue to his upper lip.

She gulped. What would she do if he kissed her? Better question, what would she do if he didn't?

"I can't stop thinking about you," Roan murmured.

Fresh sweet shivers. "Probably because you're baking again because of me, and it's fired up your passion."

"I'm fired up all right, but it's not about baking." His tone came out deeper than normal.

"No?" she said, sounding so breathless that she wasn't sure if he heard her or not.

"For you to win this contest, we need to work closely together for hours, every single day until the competition."

"That's not a problem for me." She met his gaze dead-on.

Roan didn't flinch. "If we do this, I'm serious about it."

"Me too. I intend on taking that trophy away from Andi Browning."

"I'm not talking about baking."

"Oh." She pursed her lips. "You mean . . . *us.*"

"I do."

Suddenly the chills of excitement vanished, and stifling heat swamped her body. She wanted to shed her jacket, fling her arms around Roan's neck, and tell him she was all in for a rebound romance.

"So . . ." she said.

"So?" He arched one eyebrow and peered at her with a comically quizzical grin.

"Are you going to kiss me or not?"

His grin widened and he cocked his Stetson back on his head. Roan's arms went around her, and his masculine scent filled her senses. She could hear traffic passing on the road paralleling the park, but drivers couldn't see them because of the stone wall barrier. Not that she would have cared if they could.

Jazzy went up on tiptoes, and closed her eyes, wanting to savor this moment without distraction. His pressure was firm, but his lips were soft. Tender. She sank against him, wrapped her arms as tightly around him as he held her.

Roan gently parted her lips with the tip of his tongue, and it was as electrifying as she'd hoped. Honestly, more so.

She softened her jaw and got fully into it as he kissed her thoroughly. Scale of one to ten? So far this one was shooting for top billing of her all-time best kisses. That thought made her feel a tad disloyal to Danny, since he'd been her first, but she couldn't lie to herself.

Roan was a far better kisser than any man she'd ever kissed.

Especially when he pulled her closer and just kept going. His tongue caressed the roof of her mouth and she started thinking of other ways he might use that wicked tongue.

Wow! Wow! Wow! She better check her socks after this and make sure he hadn't knocked them straight off.

Finally, he pulled back to take a breath and her eyes flew open to gauge his reaction, but Roan kept going.

He held her so tight her breasts pressed flat against the hard expanse of his muscular chest.

Her fingers reached up to stroke his face, the stubble of his beard rough against her skin. He cupped her face between his palms and softly kissed her forehead, eyelids, the tip of her nose, and each cheek before he found his way back to her mouth.

Sexy sensations rolled over her body in waves. His palms were warm as he moved his hands to her jaw and held her in place while he explored her mouth deeper and deeper, triggering every erogenous zone in her body.

She gave a quiet whimper and fisted his shirt in both hands.

He moved his lips to her throat, and she threw back her head, allowing him access to the vein that throbbed there. She loved having her skin sucked at that pulse point and he seemed to go straight to the spot with unerring accuracy. It was as if he knew exactly where she wanted his mouth to be.

When he nibbled the spot, Jazzy came undone.

Ooh, ooh, this was moving way too fast. She hadn't expected this kind of chemical reaction and frankly, it scared her. She was so hot and wet and if they hadn't been in the park, standing beside the tree carved with the name of him and his late wife, she could very well have had sex with him on the spot.

The out-of-control element scared her. Jazzy liked her life happy and even-keeled. Nothing even-keeled about the desires rushing through her. Her desire for him freaked her out. Wound up so tight that one more tick would break her.

She pulled away from him, backed up quickly, readjusted her clothes. "Well."

"Well?"

He looked earnest . . . and hungry. As hungry for sex as she felt. Somewhere along the way, his Stetson fell from his head and lay on the ground behind him.

All that kissing had chapped her lips. She cleared her throat and dropped her gaze. Looking him in the eyes overwhelmed her.

"You lost your hat." She bent to pick it up and as she straightened, found herself eye level with *Claire loves Roan 4 Life.*

CHAPTER 11

After that world-rocking kiss, they went to lunch at Pasta Pappa's. They both ordered the caprese chicken salads and had a surprisingly easy conversation, discussing baking contests.

At one point, Jazzy reached across the table to touch his hand and smiled at Roan like he was her North Star. He felt wildly happy.

But now, on the way back to the ranch where they would start baking soon, doubts crept back about the wisdom of a short affair.

He cast a glance at Jazzy's profile. Her skin was pristine. No wrinkles or lines. He wanted to kiss her again so badly it scared him.

What in the hell are you doing, Roan Sullivan? You're gonna get hurt.

Why had he kissed her? At Sweetheart Park for heaven's sake. It didn't get any cheesier than that. He pulled his Stetson down lower and kept his eyes on the road.

She sat in the passenger seat, chatting gaily about

nothing in particular, but she didn't fool him. She was trying hard for light and breezy.

Did she like it or hate it? He thought she'd liked it. She'd been very responsive, her body molding to his as she'd kissed him right back.

"Is that the first time you've kissed anyone since Claire?" she murmured as if reading his mind.

Roan ran a palm over his mouth. "It is."

She nodded and said nothing else.

Roan guided the truck toward Jubilee, trying to figure out what was going on in her head . . . and in his own.

"It was a terrific first kiss," she said.

He gulped. "But?"

"No buts." She shook her head and offered a small smile. "Just . . . it felt . . . *wow*."

There was something she wasn't saying. "You can tell me the truth. It won't hurt my feelings."

"That is the truth. Your kiss was knee-wobbling. My knees actually wobbled."

He shot a glance over at her. Jazzy's lips were puffy, hair mussed, cheeks pink and windblown.

My kiss? He'd thought it was *their* kiss. "And that's bad because . . . ?"

"It's not bad at all. In fact, it's very, very good."

Ahh, he got it now.

"You're afraid because the kiss was *too* good. You worried that I was thinking of Claire when I kissed you."

"Were you?"

"No."

"You sure?"

"I won't lie to you, Jazzy," he said. "*Ever.* Know that for certain. While Claire and I had a solid marriage and a great sex life—"

Her wince cut him off.

"I'm here with *you*, Jazzy. For as long as this lasts. I want to get to know *you* better. That kiss was between you and me. No ghosts allowed. Got it?"

Her smile returned along with the light in her blue eyes. "Got it."

"I'm talking about the ghost of your relationship with Danny as well," he said, recalling seeing the younger man throwing a coin into the Sweetheart Fountain.

"You're a much better kisser than Danny." She giggled.

The gleeful sound lifted Roan's heart. Danny might pine for Jazzy, but maybe Jazzy didn't pine for her ex.

"I shouldn't have said that. It was unkind to Danny. We had our good times."

"Ain't gonna lie, Jazz," he admitted. "It stokes my ego a bit that you think I'm a better kisser than Danny, but in his defense, I am older, wiser, and more experienced."

"Hmm." Her grin widened. "Maybe that's what I've been missing all along. An old pro."

"Are you calling me old?"

"I'm calling you seasoned. It's a good thing."

"I'll take your word for it." Roan chuckled and saw the tension ebb from her shoulders. She was relaxing again. "So, we've got a game plan?"

"Game plan?"

"We don't compare each other to our former partners," he said.

"We've got a game plan." She bobbed her head.

He reached for her hand and when she took it, his nerve endings fired up like his new John Deere tractor.

Oh boy, he was in serious trouble.

By four o'clock that same afternoon they were on Roan's patio. Jazzy crouched to feed the flames in the firepit. She couldn't stop thinking about that phenomenal kiss. Or stop turning her head to sneak peeks at Roan's firm, rounded backside when he bent over to gather more wood from the stack by the barbecue grill.

Yummy.

But even as she admired him, she felt panicky at the thought of starting a fling with her baking tutor. Why had she suggested they explore their attraction? It was completely insane. Roan was still mourning his wife. For heaven's sake, he'd kissed her in front of a tree carved with his and his wife's names.

Red flag.

Roan's sister, Rio, had taken Trinity to story hour at Ye Old Book Nook, and they were all alone. Jazzy had instantly liked the lively woman and they both remembered they'd met once at a civic event several years earlier.

After Rio and Trinity left, Roan taught her how to make Christine's rugelach recipe for a test run. The dough sat nearby on a covered cookie sheet, waiting for the fire to create enough embers for

Dutch oven cooking. Jazzy still had trouble regulating the temperature enough to bake the cookies without burning the bottoms.

Being alone with Roan made Jazzy a wee bit uncomfortable. Not because she was scared of him in any way. Rather, she was afraid of her own escalating desires for this tall, lanky cowboy. She'd spent hours with him over the course of the past several days and she learned the ins and outs of campfire cooking and she couldn't deny they were growing closer.

But where would it lead? What would happen when the competition was over? What would she do when Traveling Nurses offered her a job?

Roan had cued up an oldies playlist, Billy Joel sang "Leave a Tender Moment Alone" from the outdoor speakers. Jazzy jolted at the timing of the tune. Or maybe the song had come on unnoticed before and triggered her train of thought. Confused, she rocked back on her heels, gaze still hooked on Roan's sexy butt showcased in tight Wranglers.

He straightened, looked over, and caught her gaze. "Would you like to pick the music?"

"Wh-what?"

"You were frowning at the speakers."

"Was I?"

He smiled. "What do you like to listen to?"

"Billy Joel is fine. I like all kinds of music."

"That didn't answer my question."

"How about some holiday music to set the Christmas cookie baking mood?"

"On it." He carried the armful of wood over to where she was and stacked it next to the firepit, then headed to his phone to change the music. Soon, George Strait's "Christmas Cookies" livened up the scene. It was her favorite Christmas song.

He reached out a hand to her.

Jazzy peered up at him.

Roan's chocolate eyes and warm smile melted her heart. She took his hand and he pulled her to her feet. They stood there a moment, staring into each other's eyes. This would be the perfect time to pull away, offer an excuse of tending the fire.

But there was another pull tugging her toward him.

Desire.

Roan slipped his arm around her waist and waltzed her to the beat of "Christmas Cookies." Charmed, Jazzy gazed into his eyes.

The song ended as did the dancing, but Roan didn't immediately let her go. He was looking down at her and her heart was thumping like mad.

"Maybe I kiss you again?" he murmured.

"Please." She closed her eyes.

His lips came down on hers and their kiss was just as good as before, maybe even better. Jazzy went up on tiptoes, pushed onward by hungry need, wrapped her arms around his neck, and cradled his head in her palms. The feel of his silky hair in her fingers stoked the fire building inside her.

"Jazzy," he whispered against her mouth. "You are incredible, but I have no idea how we got here."

"Shh," she said. "Stop talking and kiss me, cowboy."

Caution. Wind. Thrown.

Roan's self-control unwound. If only Rio hadn't

taken Trinity to story hour, this wouldn't have happened.

Yeah, blame it on your sister for wanting to spend time with her niece.

He should stop kissing Jazzy. Take a break before this turned into something neither one of them were really ready for.

But his body wasn't taking the hint. Jazzy parted his lip with her tongue and he just let it happen. Part of him calculating if they had enough time to take this to the bedroom before Rio and Trinity returned. The nobler part shaking his head in disappointment. If and when he and Jazzy had sex, he wanted it to be perfect. She deserved that. Hell, *he* deserved that. While it would be easy as pie to have a quickie with her, he wasn't going to do that. Roan wanted to take his time.

But her sweet lips flew him straight to the moon. She pressed her soft, slender body against his and whispered, "You smell so darn good I want to gobble you up." Then she kissed him, slowly, sensually, passionately.

Feeling caught in rising floodwaters, Roan groaned. The music played "Winter Wonderland" and he could hear the fire crackling as it consumed the mesquite wood and warmed the air around them. Or maybe it was just the heat the two of them generated.

He tightened his grip on her, one hand moving up to stroke her nape. She shivered and pressed closer until there wasn't a millimeter of space between them. The kiss ignited into a blistering melding of teeth and tongues. It was one of those primal, desperate kisses so intense that Roan couldn't even think. Words dropped from his head and fell like sparks into the void of sensation.

Hot. Wet. Tasty.

He was gone. She had stolen every last bit of sense he possessed. His mind had found two words and wasn't letting go of them. Issued an edict.

Bed! Now!

Roan clinched his hands into fists to keep himself from scooping her into his arms and throwing her over his shoulder like a caveman.

Jazzy pulled back, looking as dazed as he felt. He heard a buzzing noise that seemed very far away. Oh crap, he'd gone too far. Lost himself. He couldn't even feel his feet on the deck.

"Roan," she whispered.

"Yes?" He stared at her through glazed eyes, breathing heavily, still hearing the faint buzzing.

"Your phone is ringing."

"What? Huh?" Roan swiveled his head to where he'd left the phone resting on the outdoor kitchen counter beside the covered rugelach dough. His phone moved with the vibration. "Oh."

He wanted to ignore it and start kissing Jazzy again, but he was a parent and didn't have the luxury of ignoring phone calls when his daughter wasn't with him. Reluctantly, he left Jazzy's side and moved to pick up the cell just as it stopped ringing.

Rio's number was on his screen.

Paternal panic took hold of him and his mind leaped to worst-case scenarios. Something bad had happened, he just knew it. That's what he got for indulging himself. He was a dad. He didn't get to act like some randy teenager.

Damn him.

Jazzy came over and put a hand on his forearm. "What's wrong?"

"Rio," he said. "I've got to call her back. Can you excuse me?"

"Sure, sure. I'll go check on the fire." She wandered to the firepit, giving him privacy.

He couldn't help watching her walk away, wistfully, both disappointed and relieved that the phone had interrupted them. No time for regrets. Just as he was about to hit Redial, his phone started buzzing again.

Rio.

He pressed Accept.

"What is it?" he barked at the same time his sister spoke.

"Trinity."

"What's wrong? What's happened?" His body went both hot and cold simultaneously.

"Don't panic."

He paced, jamming his hand through his hair. From the corner of his eye, he saw Jazzy looking over with concern. "Tell me!"

"We're at the hospital—"

"What did you do to my daughter?" he asked, knowing as he said it that he was being too harsh.

"Roan, calm down," Rio said. "It's not that bad."

"You're at the hospital, it's not good. It's never good when someone is at the hospital."

"I know you don't mean to snap at me. I know

you're having flashbacks to Claire. I understand that, but if you don't stop and take a deep breath, I'm ending this conversation."

Jazzy was at his side again, apparently his agitation was worse than he realized. She held out her palm. "May I speak to Rio?"

Silently, he gave her the phone. His blood was pumping so hard he could barely inhale. How was he supposed to take a deep breath? His baby girl was at the hospital. Something had gone horribly wrong. Trinity had been suffering while he'd been kissing Jazzy.

"Hello, Rio," Jazzy said into the phone. "I'm here with Roan. Yes, he is pretty upset. Can you tell me what's happened?"

She was so calm, so controlled. He was jealous of her composure. But of course, it was easy for her. She was a nurse, and she wasn't a parent.

Jazzy was nodding to something his sister was saying. Roan pressed both palms against his forehead and paced faster. He was working himself up and he knew it.

Settle down.

"We'll be right there," Jazzy said. "Thank you so much, Rio."

"What is it?" Roan said as she ended the call. "Tell me the truth."

"Truly, Roan, it's minor. Trinity will be okay. Please sit down and try to take some deep breaths."

Jazzy's hand was around his arm and she was easing him down into a lawn chair, the same way she had when he'd almost passed out at the hospital.

"Rio and Trinity were leaving Ye Old Book Nook and you know how uneven the sidewalk is on that side of the square. Well, Trinity tripped and fell face-first and cut her chin deeply enough to require stitches."

"What! Why doesn't someone fix those old bricks? Why wasn't Rio holding Trinity's hand?"

"Trinity wanted to carry her new book purchases. Rio's not at fault. It was an accident. Accidents happen."

"She's not fine! Her chin busted wide-open on town square bricks. My daughter could get an infection."

"Roan," Jazzy said sternly. "Listen to me. Your anxiety has gotten the better of you. That's understandable. But you need to pull it together for your child."

She was totally right. He felt like a dope for losing his cool. He was the dad. He was supposed to be the one everyone depended on.

"Trinity is fine," Jazzy soothed. "My stepmom, Sarah, was doing a reading for story hour. She gave Rio and Trinity a ride to the hospital. She'll be right as rain. They'll probably give her a shot of antibiotics and a tetanus vaccine if she hasn't had one."

"She's going to be okay?" he asked, his body feeling as if he'd just drank an entire pot of coffee—shaky and wired.

"Give me your truck keys and I'll drive us to the ER. Everything is going to be just fine."

He looked her in the eyes, grabbed his cowboy

hat from the hook where he'd hung it when they started baking. "You promise?"

"I swear it. Now, come on." She held out her hand like she was offering him a lifeline.

Without hesitating, Roan took it. "Thank God you were here."

CHAPTER 12

By the time they got to the hospital it was after six. Charlie was passing by with a suture kit in his hands when they walked up to the Emergency Department desk.

Jazzy's best friend stopped in his tracks and did a double take. "Lambchop, what are you doing down here? Did they call you in from your vacation? Nightshift is short three nurses. They're out with the flu."

"No, no. I'm still on vacation."

"Better hide, then. If Lonnie sees you, she'll try to rope you in."

"We're here for Trinity Sullivan," Jazzy said, reaching over to touch Roan's shoulder.

"Oh." Charlie eyed Roan as if seeing him for the first time. "Y'all come this way. I'll take you to her."

"Are you the one treating my daughter?" Roan asked.

"Yep. Just about to sew up that little chin."

Charlie motioned with the suture kit for them to follow him.

Roan reached for Jazzy's hand.

Jazzy interlaced their fingers and gave his hand a reassuring squeeze. She was honored to be here in his time of need.

They reached the door of the exam room. Roan caught sight of Trinity sitting on the edge of a gurney, a bloodied compression bandage on her chin. He dropped Jazzy's hand and raced to his daughter's side.

"Daddy!" Trinity flew into his arms.

At the sight of the loving father cradling his vulnerable child, Jazzy transported back seventeen years to this very same examination room, and her dad, Travis, sat at her side during an asthma attack. Tears welled in her eyes, and she blinked them away. This was about Trinity, not her.

Rio stood in the corner looking glum. Sarah was also there, sitting in a chair on the other side of the gurney. Her stepmother gave Jazzy a loving smile and silently mouthed, *I love you.* She knew where Jazzy's thoughts had been.

Grateful for her stepmother's support, Jazzy smiled back. Strengthened by Sarah's unconditional love, Jazzy went to Rio. Hoping to reassure her that she'd done nothing wrong.

Roan sat on the gurney with Trinity in his arms. Vividly, the girl told her dad what had happened. "And then I tripped and dropped my books." Tears came to Trinity's eyes. "Daddy, my new books got dirty and one ripped."

"The one that got torn was a copy of my latest book," Sarah murmured. "I'll replace it for her."

"See there. It's going to be okay. Sarah will get you a new book."

"And Charlie will sew up your chin," Jazzy said. "We'll fix you right up."

"Okay." Trinity hiccuped and wiped a tear from the tip of her nose with the back of her hand.

"Now that the cavalry is here, I think I'll scoot." Sarah picked up her purse.

"Thank you for the ride," Rio said. "I was much too nervous to drive."

"Anytime," Sarah said. "My pleasure."

"I'll walk you out." Jazzy linked her arm through her stepmother's. To Roan, she said, "I'll be right back."

He nodded, but barely seemed to notice. All his attention stayed focused on his child. He was such a great dad.

Once they were outside in the hallway, Jazzy said to Sarah, "That must have gotten your blood pumping."

"It always hurts my soul to see a child get hurt. I don't know how you work pediatrics." Sarah shook her head.

"Someone has to help the children. Why not someone who was a sickly kid herself?"

"Trinity's poor aunt was beside herself. She was too upset to drive. Of course, I brought them. They'd been at my event."

"I know Roan appreciates it."

They went through the pneumatic doors and into

'hat happened?" Andi asked, her eyes round-
 she entered the room.
 thought it was your day off. Weren't you and
 y going cake tasting?" Charlie asked.
 e were, but I got called in since so many nurses
 t with a flu. Had to rain check the cake."
 at explained why Danny had been throwing a
 nto the fountain when he was supposed to be
 ng cake tasting with his fiancée.
 , you're down here why?" Charlie's words
 out muffled from behind his medical mask.
 y latest pediatric admit left a teddy bear
 here. Have you seen it?" Andi sidled closer
 an and Trinity.
 id you check the front desk?"
 rst thing I did," Andi said a little tartly.
 aven't seen it," Charlie grunted.
 nity wriggled. "I—"
 arlie, who'd started in on the final stitch,
 d, the needle halfway in his daughter's chin.
 h, try and sit still, honey," Roan coached
 Charlie's almost finished. You're doing great.
 little bit longer."
 nity pointed to the far corner of the room.
 ne turned to see where Trinity was pointing.
 on the floor, was a much-loved blue teddy
 ith a missing eye.
 h, there it is. Thank you for your sharp eye,
 " Andi picked up the teddy bear and tucked
 her arm. She paused at the door, watching
 lie completed the last stitch and clipped off
 gling thread with suture scissors. "Could I
 you a moment, Roan?"

the parking lot, Jazzy's arm still linked through
Sarah's.

"Speaking of Roan," Sarah said with an encouraging smile. "Is something going on between you
two besides baking lessons?"

"What makes you ask that?" Jazzy felt her
cheeks heat.

"Ahh, answering a question with a question.
You're cagey, Miss Jazz. I take that as a yes?"

"We've kissed," Jazzy confessed, a thrill running through her at the memory. "And we've
kicked around the idea of dating."

"But . . . ?"

"How do you know there's a *but*?" Jazzy asked
as they reached Sarah's SUV.

"The look on your face when you talked about
dating. You like him and apparently, he's quite the
kisser, but you have doubts."

"I do have doubts. I don't want anything serious. I'm leaving Twilight and I don't want to hurt
him. He's so kind."

Sarah cupped Jazzy's cheek. "I had my doubts
about your dad."

"Because he was a single father?"

"That was a consideration. I couldn't decide if I
loved Travis for who he was as a person or if it was
just because he was such a great father and so good
with you. I worried I was romanticizing him."

"Roan and I are light-years away from that.
We're kicking around being each other's rebound
person."

"I see. And that's all you both want?"

"Yeah."

"Well, then, as long as you both are clear on what you want, you should be okay. No one should get hurt. Where the problem comes in is if you're not being honest with yourself about what you truly want."

"Did that happen with you and Dad? He wasn't your high school sweetheart like so many people in town."

"No, but your father and I did have a history." Sarah sighed dreamily. "We were next-door neighbors, and I had a childhood crush on him. That was something else I had to sort out. Fact versus fantasy."

"You dreamed of him when you were fifteen and put a kismet cookie under your pillow," Jazzy said, supplying the story she'd heard so many times growing up.

"Exactly. At least you don't have that to wade through."

"I want to get to know him better, if you know what I mean, but now I'm gun-shy about sex. It's been so long."

"Danny," Sarah said with a click of her tongue. "He sure did a number on your self-esteem."

"I can't put all the blame on Danny. I was the one who didn't recognize that he was unhappy."

"Darling, it's not up to us to make other people happy. They have to sort it out for themselves."

"I know that, but I could have been more sensitive to Danny's needs."

"Jazzy, you are the most kind, empathetic, optimistic person I know and from what you've told

me, meeting Danny's needs meant th[at] dim your own light so he could shine[...]

"You want to know something iron[...]

"Absolutely," Sarah said.

"Now Danny dims his light so An[...] Funny how that worked."

"That's his problem. You deserve a[...] relationship. Try not to let the past weigh[...] too much, sweetheart."

Rebound sex with Roan sounded bett[...]ter. "I'm working on it."

"Good girl." Sarah gave Jazzy a h[...] into her car. "If you ever want to talk,[...] where to find me."

Roan sat on the gurney holding Trinit[y] while Charlie Cheek sewed up her c[...] had cried a little when Charlie num[...] with lidocaine, but she was a trooper.

Anxious of Jazzy's return, he kep[...] the door. He missed her. It was just[...] them in the room—Charlie, Roan, [...] Rio had gone to the cafeteria to get t[...] fee. He knew it was an excuse. His s[...] get weak-kneed at the sight of blood[...] to ask Charlie personal questions a[...] it seemed out of line.

"Hey, Charlie," a woman's voic[...] doorway.

Charlie was in the middle of a[...] look up. "What do you want, Ar[...]

Roan glanced over to see the m[...] ing him like he was Wagyu beef[...]

Not Mr. Sullivan. *Roan*. As if they were on familiar terms. "Now?"

"It won't take a sec."

"I'm in the middle of something important, Andi." Roan did not want to talk to the woman. What was taking Jazzy so long?

"Charlie just finished." Andi waved at Charlie, who'd gotten up off his stool to put the suture needle into the red sharps disposal container mounted on the wall.

"What's this about?" What was the woman up to?

"The cowboy cookie challenge."

"No need for a private huddle. Just tell me what's on your mind."

"I . . ." She shot a glance at Charlie. "Don't want to say in front of him."

Charlie rolled his eyes. "Fine. I'll go check on another patient." To Roan, he added, "I'll be right back in a sec to arrange Trinity's discharge."

"Or, you could just stay with Trinity and finish her discharge paperwork right now, while I have a word with Roan in the hallway." Andi seemed determined to get him alone.

"Can you hang out with Trinity for a short minute?" he asked Charlie.

Charlie nodded, snapping off both latex gloves in one smooth, practiced motion. Roan noticed Jazzy had the same skill. Must be a medical personnel thing. "If you make it really quick."

"Will do." Roan lifted Trinity and set her down on the gurney. "Stay here with Charlie, I'll be back in two shakes of a lamb's tail." Then he gave her

a soft, playful bop on the end of her nose and followed Andi into the hallway.

Jamming his hands into his pockets, Roan
hunched his shoulders and ducked his head. His
default defensive posture. Realizing what his body
was saying, he took his hands from his pockets,
straightened, and met Andi's gaze head-on.

"What is it?"

Andi smiled but it wasn't an authentic smile
like Jazzy's, and she fluttered her eyelashes the
way she had at the bakery that morning. "I . . .
want something."

"From me?" The hairs on his nape stood up.

Andi walked two fingers up his arm to his shoulder, getting way too close and in a sultry voice said,
"You're the only one here."

He stared at her point-blank. "Are you trying to
seduce me?"

"Oh!" Andi glanced down. "No. Me?"

"Yes, you." He narrowed his eyes.

She pressed a dramatic palm to her chest.
"Whatever gave you that idea?"

"Your hand on my arm, uninvited."

"You flatter yourself, Mr. Sullivan. And while
I do appreciate the compliment, I am an engaged
woman." She stuck her left hand under his nose.

"So, what *do* you want?" he asked, understanding she had no qualms flirting with him if it would
secure what she wanted, even if she was engaged.

"I want to hire you."

"For what?" Did Andi need another horse tamed?
If so, she'd have to wait. He had no openings in his
schedule.

"Why, for you to teach me how to cook over a campfire. I heard you were taking on students."

"You heard wrong."

"You're telling me you're not teaching Jazzy Walker how to bake in a Dutch oven?"

"I'm telling you that's none of your business."

Andi looked taken aback, but she recovered quickly, posting up a sly expression. "Ahh, so you two *are* dating. I told Danny you were, but he said Jazzy didn't date grandpas."

"I've got to get back to my daughter." Roan turned. He had no idea if Danny had really said that, or if Andi was lying for her own purposes.

"Wait!" She grabbed his arm.

He turned back, shook off her hand. "What is it?"

"I need help. I don't know how to bake over a campfire. I keep burning the cookies. How much is Jazzy paying you? I'll double it."

Ahh, so Andi was struggling just as much as Jazzy with campfire cooking. Nice to know.

"I'm not for sale, Ms. Browning." He pulled his Stetson down lower over his brow and headed for the exam room door.

"Mr. Sullivan?"

He stopped, suppressed a sigh. "What?"

"What's so special about her?" There was a wistful note to Andi's voice that surprised him.

"Who?"

"Jazzy Walker. Why does everyone love her so much? She's not a winner. She loses every time she goes up against me and still everyone loves her. The more I stomp her ass, the more everyone loves her."

"I guess we have a different definition of *winner*, Andi."

"What does that mean?"

"Look," he said. "You got Jazzy's high school sweetheart, what else do you want?"

"You." Andi locked eyes with him.

Roan's pulse jumped and he backed up.

"To teach me campfire cooking," Andi quickly amended.

"Never gonna happen, Ms. Browning. Not in your wildest dreams."

CHAPTER 13

"You should have seen how pissed she was," Charlie said, relating the interaction between Andi and
Roan earlier that evening. "Seriously, I took the
fire extinguisher off the wall. That's how sure I
was that Andi would burst into flames after Roan
told her no."

"You did not." Affectionately, Jazzy bumped
against her best friend as they sat side by side on
barstools at the Recovery Room for their usual
Friday night rendezvous.

"Well, I should have done it," he said. "If she'd
been a cartoon character, she'd have steam rolling
out of her ears."

Because of Trinity's mishap, Roan canceled their
baking lessons for the weekend, saying he needed
to spend more time with his daughter.

Jazzy got that, she truly did, but she couldn't help
feeling like he was also taking a break from *her*.

Totally fine. Everyone needed breathing room.

Feeling aimless in the first free time since she'd

had since baking with Roan, she'd called Charlie and he met her at the bar when his shift was over.

"I was dying to go to Roan's house to check on Trinity, but I thought I might be moving too fast for him. Thanks for agreeing to hang out with me and talk me down."

"No prob, Lambchop, but you're buying." Charlie caught the bartender's eye, held up two fingers. "Tequila shots. Don Julio."

"Whoa!" Jazzy said. "The good stuff." She shook her head to the bartender and said, "Make mine well."

"God, please no cheap-ass tequila. I'm paying. I'm a sipper, not a shooter." Charlie shook his head, then pointed his finger at Jazzy as they simultaneously said, "Title of your sex tape," and burst out laughing.

"Which one do you want," asked the bartender, holding the two different tequilas in question.

"One shot of Don Julio, one well shot, and we'll split the check."

"Got it." The bartender poured up a shot glass for Jazzy and tequila snifter for Charlie and brought them sliced limes and kosher salt.

"What are we celebrating?" Jazzy asked, raising her glass.

"Your first infatuation since Danny. So fun. I'm thrilled you're moving on. To Roan." Charlie clinked glasses with her.

"To Roan," Jazzy echoed.

"With his help you stand a real chance of beating Andi in this bake-off. Andi sucks at building a campfire as much as you do."

"Oh, what faint praise."

"I calls it as I sees it." He laughed.

"Such a sage."

"Honestly, I hope you know what you're doing."

"I'm becoming a better baker."

"I'm not talking about the cookie challenge."

"Oh?" She studied his face. "What *are* you talking about?"

"This thing with Roan."

"What thing with Roan?" Jazz made a what's-this-crazy-talk face. "There's no thing with Roan."

Charlie sighed and shook his head. "Who are you lying to? Me or yourself?"

"Both, I guess," she whispered.

"Ahh, now we're getting somewhere." He took a sip of his tequila and motioned at her shot glass. "You gonna shoot that?"

"Are you going to give me some advice I don't want to hear?"

"I just might."

Jazzy picked up a lime slice. "I forgot which order it goes in. Haven't done tequila slammers in ages."

"Lick, shoot, suck."

Their gazes met and they said in unison, "Title of your sex tape."

"Although . . ." Jazzy teased. "Wouldn't a better sex tape title be *Lick, Suck, Shoot*?"

"Jazzy!" Charlie let out a cackle and swatted her arm. "Does Roan know about the dirty mind behind your sweet face?"

"He does not."

"Therein lies the problem."

"Problem?"

"You should have seen him taking up for you with Andi." Charlie got a dreamy look in his eyes.

"What?"

"It was so romantic. Roan is investing in you, Lambchop. Are you ready for that?"

"You're wrong." She sprinkled salt on the web of skin between her thumb and index finger. Licked it off, downed the tequila, and sucked on the lime wedge. Made a face and sputtered, "N-neither one of us wants a long-term relationship."

"Aww." Charlie nodded. "I'm seeing a picture emerge. Are we talking booty calls?"

"Maybe." Jazzy nodded. "We haven't gotten there yet, but if something happens it'll be strictly casual."

"You sure?"

"Why?"

"Because the Roan Sullivan I saw in my ER this evening is head over heels for you, even if he doesn't realize it yet."

On Saturday evening, December 10, Jazzy and Sabrina curled on the couch watching Christmas movies on the Hallmark Channel.

Jazzy had spent the day alone, cleaning house and then browsing the internet for ways to elevate the basic rugelach recipe Christine had given her. During a commercial, she picked up her phone to check social media and saw Roan had texted.

The second she saw his name on the screen, she grinned helplessly and her pulse did a happy dance.

ROAN: Hey.
JAZZY: Hi!
ROAN: Sorry to bail on our lessons again.
JAZZY: No worries. How's Trinity?
ROAN: That kid is indomitable. She thinks having a chin cut is cool.
JAZZY: How R U?
ROAN: Honestly? Still rattled. It kills me to see Trinity hurt.

Jazzy sent a hug emoji, then immediately worried she was being too familiar.

ROAN: Want 2 bake 2morrow?
JAZZY: I thought you needed a break.
ROAN: I miss U.

Jazzy stared at the text. Roan missed her? A hot thrill ran through her body. Taking a deep breath, she texted back. Miss U 2.

ROAN: Come by the ranch after church?
JAZZY: See U around 1.
ROAN: Looking forward to it. Nite.
JAZZY: Nite.

Later, Jazzy went to bed, and fell promptly asleep with dreams of Roan dancing in her head.

An hour after Sunday church services with her family, Jazzy found herself in Roan's kitchen casting him a sidelong glance as he got out the ingredients for rugelach dough.

Trinity sat at the kitchen table molding kitty cats from the brand-new Play-Doh that Roan bought her for being brave about the stitches. The red-and-white-checkered oilcloth tablecloth delivered a pleasant crinkling sound as the girl rolled a ball of the modeling compound for the next kitty's head. She already had three cats lined up. The child was quite good at molding. Perhaps she had a future as an artist like her auntie Rio.

"I'll let you make the rugelach while I start the fire to speed things up. You've gotten pretty good at fire building this past week."

"Meaning that I need more work on my baking skills?" she asked.

"Gotta have both skills to win this competition," he said. "Once you master the basic rugelach recipe, the next step will be making it your own. We also need to find a second cookie recipe for when you move on to the finals."

When. Not *if*. She smiled at him, grateful for his confidence in her.

"And then the final step will be learning how to control the temperature of the fire?" she asked.

"Yep. That's the trickiest stage of all."

"Would it be okay if we did all the steps together?" Jazzy asked, realizing she enjoyed him hanging out in the kitchen, giving her tips and techniques. "You calm my nerves."

"Really?"

"Uh-huh . . ." She paused. "Significantly."

"You calm me too, Jazzy." He searched her face and said in a whisper so low she barely heard, "While at the same time, you electrify me."

They peered at each other and a sweet shiver went down Jazzy's spine at the heated look in Roan's eyes. She gulped past the lump in her throat.

Hard.

A brief knock sounded at the back door just before it opened. "Yoo-hoo, it's Mom."

"Grammy!" Trinity hollered, tossed her Play-Doh on the table, and ran for her grandmother coming through the mudroom.

Seconds later, Mrs. Sullivan, dressed in an elegant satin cocktail dress, came into the kitchen holding Trinity in her arms. "You're going to have one cool scar, Doodlebug."

Gingerly, Trinity touched her chin. "I fell down."

"So, I heard. Don't touch your chin, sweetheart. You don't want germs getting into your cut." Roan's mom planted a kiss on her granddaughter's forehead. "Oh," she said, spying Jazzy. "I didn't know you had company. Hello, Jazzy. How are you?"

"Once I perfect rugelach, I'll be doing great, Mrs. Sullivan," Jazzy said.

"Please call me Ava. After spending time with you in the hospital over this little toot's tonsillectomy, I feel like we're old friends."

"I agree, Ava," Jazzy said, even though Trinity had only been in the hospital for a day and a half. Roan's mother had visited much of that time and the woman was keen on conversation. "I enjoyed our talks."

"Not to sound rude or anything, but what are you doing here, Mom?" Roan asked.

"Don't tell me you forgot." Ava Sullivan shook her head.

"Forgot about what?" Roan frowned.

"You *did* forget." Ava shot Jazzy an exasperated glance over the top of Trinity's head. "The grandmother-granddaughter tea party is from four to six at the Bolger Mansion."

"That's today?"

Ava made a tsk-tsk noise. "You've had a lot on your plate. It's my fault. I should have reminded you."

"I'm sorry, Mom. Trinity's not dressed for a formal tea party. Rain check?"

"Aww. It's the annual grandmother-granddaughter tea and this is the first year Trinity's been old enough to sit still for the event."

"I've just got too much going on."

"Why don't you leave it all to me? I'll get Trinity dressed and then I'll take her home for the night. Would you like a sleepover with Grammy, kiddo? Grampa is making tacos for dinner."

"Yay! Tea party! Sleepover! Tacos! Canna go, Daddy, canna?"

"You sure you want to?" he asked.

"Yes!" Trinity declared.

"You won't see me again until tomorrow morning," he said.

"Tea party! Sleepover! Tacos!"

"I've been replaced by tacos," Roan said with faked forlornness. "Do you want to commit to this, Mom?"

"Absolutely, I can't wait to see her eyes light up when we walk into the Paradise Court at the mansion. I've been looking forward to this since Trinity was born."

"If you say so." Roan chuckled.

"The Bolger mansion tea party is pretty impressive," Jazzy said. "I never got to attend the grandmother-granddaughter Christmas tea, but my dad did take me there for the daddy-daughter dance after my mom left town when I was six. It meant the world to me. Trinity is going to love it."

"I guess it's a done deal, then," Roan said. "Let's find her a dress to wear."

"I'll take care of it. No worries." His mom hitched Trinity higher up on her hip. "You go on with your baking."

"You sure?" Roan asked.

"Positive. We'll be out of your hair in no time," Ava called over her shoulder and carried Trinity off to her bedroom.

"I can't believe I forgot the tea party." Roan gave a rueful shake of his head. "What kind of dad am I?"

"A very busy one," Jazzy soothed. "And Trinity having to get stitches on Friday threw you off your game."

"I've got to get better organized."

"You'll figure it out. I have complete confidence in you."

"Thanks," he said. Was he staring at her mouth? Maybe it was her imagination. Her gaze hooked on his lips and she remembered what they tasted like. "I appreciate the pep talk."

"I'm a former cheerleader. It's what we do."

"You must have been a fantastic cheerleader. I can just see you on the sidelines, cheering your team on to victory."

"Walking cliché," she said. "I was the head cheerleader, and my boyfriend was the quarterback."

"Let me guess," he said. "You and Danny were homecoming king and queen as well."

Her face flushed. "I had a terrific senior year."

"I'm glad for you."

"How about you?" she asked, watching him shift the flour into a bowl. "What were you like in high school?"

"I was working the ranch with Dad and didn't have much time for a social life," he said. "Until Claire and I started going out. She got me out of my shell."

"I'm sorry you lost her," Jazzy murmured, feeling a strange pang in the middle of her heart.

"It is what it is," he said gruffly. "Is the butter soft enough yet?"

Change the subject. Right. She got it. Jazzy poked the stick of butter with her finger and the foil packaging dented easily. "Ready to go, Iron Chef Roan."

He snorted playfully and rolled his eyes.

They'd just finished mixing the rugelach dough when Ava reappeared holding Trinity's hand and carrying an overnight bag. The little girl looked adorable in a burgundy velvet dress, matching tights, and black patent leather shoes. The only thing out of place were the stitches on Trinity's chin.

"You three stand together," Jazzy said, waving Roan toward his mother and daughter. "And I'll snap a pic."

Trinity mugged for the camera as Roan put his arm around his mother's shoulder. What a lovely family. The ache in her heart widened. Claire should be here with them. Not her. Life just wasn't fair.

Carrying the overnight bag, Roan walked his mother and Trinity to the car, and when he returned, Roan and Jazzy headed to the patio to get the fire going. The air was chillier than it had been on Friday and Jazzy wished she'd worn a coat instead of a heavy sweater. They stood huddled in front of the firepit, waiting for the flames to grow.

"You're cold. Go on in the house," Roan said. "I'll tend the fire."

"No way. This is my project."

"Okay." He extended his left arm toward her, holding open his coat. "Do you want to share body heat until the fire builds up?"

"Yes, please." She moved closer.

It wasn't until he'd pulled her against him, wrapped half his coat and his arm around her, that Jazzy realized maybe this wasn't such a hot idea. Not when she was already aching for him and his body against hers only stoked that blaze.

CHAPTER 14

When Jazzy slipped her arm around his waist and burrowed against his side, Roan just about came undone. He was the stoic type. A guy who kept his messy emotions tightly under wraps, but right now, his feelings were a huge, complicated muddle.

The minutes ticked by and they stood there, staring into the fire, not speaking. His body was doing things he did *not* want it to do. Growing harder the closer Jazzy pressed into him. Briefly, Roan closed his eyes, scrambling for some semblance of self-control.

"Ready?" she asked.

"Huh?" He opened his eyes, feeling the weight of her head against his shoulder. Hell yes, he was ready. He glanced down at her.

She peered up at him with the most innocent smile. Okay, it seems she had not noticed the hard-on. Why would she? They were side by side, facing forward, his coat camouflaging his anatomy. Thank God.

"The fire. It looks like there's enough embers for the Dutch oven," she said.

"Yes, right." He swallowed hard, wished away his erection.

She eased from his sheltering arm and moved toward the fire, sinking down on her knees in front of the pit. Her blond hair shone golden in the late afternoon sun.

That did not help things. His body grew even harder. To help hide what was going on, Roan jammed his hands into his pockets.

She reached for the insulated gloves he'd set out and dug hot coals from underneath the burning mesquite logs the way he'd taught her for Dutch oven baking.

"Good job," he complimented.

She turned to look up at him from her crouching position, a big smile on her face. "Thanks."

Terrified she was going to see his arousal, Roan dropped to his knees beside her, noticing with surprise that the pulse at her throat throbbed when his leg brushed against hers. He heard her draw in a deep, shaky breath and his own lungs squeezed.

"You okay?" he asked.

"Sure, fine, why wouldn't I be?"

"Because you just put the Dutch oven on the coals without putting any cookie dough in it."

"Oh well." Her laugh was as shaky as her breathing. "So, I did."

She leaped up and raced over to where they'd left the rugelach sitting on the outdoor counter. She looked so beautiful in the slant of the dying sun through the oak trees. The orange light accentuated her high cheekbones and shimmering blue eyes. She looked like an oasis. Life-giving and welcomed.

Roan blinked, almost convinced she was a mirage, but nope, she was still there, still smiling. He rose to his feet. "Do you want me to put the dough in the Dutch oven for you?"

"No, no, I need to learn to do everything on my own. I've got to win this thing."

"Do know this, I'm on your team one hundred percent." He thought about telling her how Andi had tried to hire him, but he didn't want to stir the pot. Barring unforeseen circumstances, Jazzy was going to win this competition, Roan would make certain of that.

"Thanks."

He took the lid-lifter tool and raised the top on the Dutch oven. Jazzy came over and knelt down in front of the fire, gingerly easing the pastry rounds onto the bottom of the cookware with her insulated gloves. The cookies got a little misshapen in the process, but it didn't matter. For now, they were just trying to get the basic rugelach recipe baked over the campfire.

When she'd finished, Jazzy rocked back on her heels to give him room to replace the lid. Then, she used the fireplace shovel to disperse coals from the fire onto the lid and the baking had begun. Roan set a timer and they settled into the side-by-side Adirondack chairs to wait.

Roan got a text from his mom. A picture of Trinity eating chocolate cake at a table with other girls and their grandmothers. His daughter looked supremely pleased with a smear of chocolate on her cheek. He chuckled.

"What's funny?" Jazzy asked, leaning in. "Or am I being too nosy? It's perfectly okay to tell me to mind my own beeswax."

"Beeswax?" Amused, he caught her gaze. She smelled so darn good, just like Christmas morning.

"Oops, sorry about the beeswax thing." She laughed. "I work with children all day."

Smiling, he turned his phone screen around so she could see the picture.

Jazzy brought her knees to her chest, looking completely relaxed and at home. "Oh my goodness, what a happy face! She's having a blast."

"I should let her hang out with Mom more often," Roan said. "She needs a motherly influence. I never think of things like tea parties."

"You're a dad. You're not supposed to. It really does take a village to raise a child," Jazzy said.

"I often feel like I'm coming up short."

"You're doing a fantastic job in my book," Jazzy went on. "Trinity is a happy, healthy little girl."

"You can't tell that from her busted chin."

"All kids fall down. Stitches and casts are bound to happen as children explore their world. It's no reflection on your parenting."

Roan winced. "It sure feels like it is."

Jazzy reached over to pat his arm. It was a small gesture, easy and quick, but it undid him in a way Roan hadn't expected. She was such a bright ray of sunshine and he wanted more of her light, but he couldn't help worrying his darkness would sully her.

Then she interlaced her fingers through his and whispered, "I'm so glad you're on my side."

"Why?" he asked point-blank.

"Why what?"

"Why do you like me?"

She looked at him as if he'd sprouted a second head. "Why *wouldn't* I like you? You're smart and hardworking and you've got buckets of love to give. You should see the way your eyes light up every time you look at your daughter. Warning, Roan, I'm a sucker for tough guys with tender hearts."

"Is that what attracted you to Danny?" The second the words tumbled out of his mouth Roan wished he'd bitten his tongue off.

Her cheery expression wobbled, but only for a second. "Danny is yesterday's news. Let's not talk about him."

"You sure there's nothing still simmering between you?"

"Absolutely." Jazzy bobbed her head. "I'm not going to lie, Danny did mean a lot to me at one time, but we just weren't a good fit."

"Why is that?"

"I'm too Pollyanna for him. Danny's got a dark side he enjoys wallowing in and I don't need that negative energy in my life."

"And yet, you were attracted to him."

"In retrospect, I thought I could save him." Jazzy rolled her eyes. "I know, I know. I'm hopeless."

Roan leaned in closer to her, until only the arms of their Adirondack chairs were in the way. Their fingers still interlaced. "Are you trying to save me, Jazzy Walker?"

"No," she whispered.

"You sure about that?"

"Positive."

"Would you be upset if I told you I saw Danny throwing a coin into the Sweetheart Fountain the day we kissed by the Sweetheart Tree?"

She locked eyes with him and didn't miss a beat. "I don't care what Danny does. His life is his own."

"Even if he's wishing to get you back?"

She let go of his hand, reached up, and cupped his face in her palms. "Silly man," she murmured. "I don't want Danny Garza, I want *you*." She said it with such conviction his heart skipped a beat.

"Jazzy?"

"Yes?"

Roan sucked in a deep breath and he would have kissed her if the timer hadn't gone off and the moment vanished.

"Rugelach time!" She slipped out of her chair, away from him, pulled on her insulated gloves, and went for the lid lifter.

While she wasn't quite skillful, she did a good job of removing the coal-laden lid and setting it aside. She hooked the lifter tool around the Dutch oven handle and moved it to the bricks. Anticipating her need, Roan handed her the long-handled spatula, and she flipped the rugelach from the oven back onto the baking sheet.

"Oh yay! They didn't burn on the bottom," she

said, looking so excited by that small victory a swell of pride nearly strangled him.

After the cookies cooled, Jazzy scooped one up and bit into it. "Ooh sooo good. These are better than kismet cookies!"

"Shh," Roan teased, putting a finger to his lips. "Don't let anyone from Twilight hear you say that."

"Seriously, try one."

He nibbled a cookie. "You knocked it out of the park."

"Now all that's left is making this recipe my own and finding a second cookie recipe."

They were alone. Trinity was with her grandmother. Roan's ranch hands lived in a bunkhouse at the back of his four hundred-acre spread. There was no one else here. The fire crackled merrily in the pit, the breeze had a bracing nip in the air, bringing with it the smell of cedar. Horses nickered in the field. This was home. The place he felt most secure.

She leaned against the brick wall surrounding the firepit, her lithe body silhouetted in the gathering dusk, the dancing flames at her back. The look in her eyes was hypnotic. No doubt about it, she'd woven a spell over him.

Reaching out, he took her hand and pulled her close.

"Oh," she said, sounding breathless again.

He was breathless too.

She peered into his eyes for a long moment, both of them holding their breaths. The evening was thick with possibilities. Trinity was gone for the night. For the next twelve hours or so, he had zero responsibilities.

"You think we can have a holiday fling without getting hurt?" she murmured.

"I can if you can."

"I don't want to get hurt and I certainly don't want to hurt you." She gnawed her bottom lip and looked adorable.

"Ditto." He searched her face.

She offered a faint smile. "So, no reservations?"

"You're out of my league."

She snorted. "Seriously, you think *I'm* out of your league? Man, they named a freaking Dutch oven after you. Who gets an honor like that?"

"You could have any guy you wanted, Jazzy. You're young and beautiful and optimistic and you've got your whole life ahead of you."

"You talk as if you're a hundred years old. You're only ten years older than I am, Roan."

"A decade is a long time."

She mumbled something under her breath that he couldn't quite make out, but the word *stubborn* seemed to be in there.

He pressed his palm to the nape of his neck.

"Am I making you uncomfortable?" she asked and arched an eyebrow.

"Yeah," he said. "Kind of."

"Is it my positive outlook that has you worried?"

"What? No? I love your upbeat personality."

"Really? I'm not too much sunshine and rainbows?"

"That's some crap Danny fed you, isn't it?"

She shrugged but looked embarrassed.

"Jazzy Walker, you are a damn magical unicorn and I adore that about you and anyone who can't appreciate you for who you are isn't worthy of your time or worry." He took both of her hands into his and peered deeply into her. "Got it?"

"Got it."

He saw a glimmer of tears in her eyes, but her big smile told him they were happy tears. He moved his hands up her arms to her shoulders, then he cradled her face between his hands, holding her still so she couldn't look away.

"You hear me?"

"I hear you loud and clear, but how about we stop talking now."

Roan opened his mouth to say something, but she put a finger to his lips and shook her head. "Shh."

"I—"

"Shh."

He pressed his lips together tightly and stilled, wondering what she would do next.

Jazzy went up on tiptoes to wrap her arms around his neck. "You may kiss me now."

"Oh, I can, can I?"

Nodding, she slowly licked her lips with her sweet pink tongue and Roan was a goner. He didn't even try to argue with himself. She wanted him. Lord knew he wanted her. He captured her mouth with his and that was all she wrote.

He meant to keep the kiss soft, exploring, but Jazzy dragged him into fresh territory in sixty seconds flat. Increasing the pressure. Hungrily shoving her fingers through his hair, moaning low in her throat. Inviting him to let go.

And then she whispered, "Take me, now."

He heard the urgency in her voice, felt it in his own hard body. She was singing his song. They were both gasping and wide-eyed.

"Please," she said.

"Not here. It's too cold and there's no soft place to land."

"So, take me to that soft place."

"You got it," he croaked. He scooped her into his arms and carried her into the house toward the bedroom he'd once shared with Claire.

CHAPTER 15

Once they were outside his bedroom, Roan hesitated.

"Change of mind?" Jazzy asked, her heart in her throat.

"Change of venue." He pivoted on his heel and carried her down the hallway.

Boom, boom, boom went her pulse. If she wanted to back out, now was the time. Jazzy did not want to back out, but she was scared. Not of Roan, but of her own tangled emotions. She tended to fall hard and fast. Or at least that's how it had been with Danny. He'd been her only serious relationship to date, so she didn't have much to go on. Sex with Roan would cement her budding feelings for him.

Was she really ready for that step?

"Second thoughts?" he asked, eerily reading her mind.

She tightened her arms around his neck and peered into his eyes. "Are *you* having second thoughts?"

"I am not, but there's no harm in waiting. I want this to be special, Jazzy. I want it to be right."

"Which is why you're taking me to the spare bedroom?"

"I thought it'd be better than the bed I shared with Claire."

"Spot-on." Now things were starting to get weird, and they'd lost the sexual momentum they'd built up on the patio.

He set her down in front of the guest room door. "Still sure?"

In answer, she took hold of his shirt in both fists and stared him straight in the eyes. "Kiss me!"

"Jazz—"

"Don't blow this, Sullivan."

"Pun?" He chuckled.

A noise of frustration burst from her throat and she pushed him against the door, pressing her soft body into his hard one. The man was pure muscle. His eyes widened and his smile faded. "Jazzy—"

"Shh, shh." She undid the buttons on his shirt and separated the material, her mind going wild at her boldness.

Was she truly doing this? Taking charge? Showing him exactly what she wanted from him? Her brazenness surprised her. She was more of a follower than a leader, but there was something about Roan that brought out her secret wild woman. She'd been dreaming of this for days.

"There's no need to rush," he said. "Mom won't bring Trinity back until midmorning tomorrow. We have all the time in the world."

Did the idea of time scare her? Was that why she was rushing things? Was she afraid Roan would change his mind, and this would slip through her hands? What did she really want from him? Hot sex? Or something more? But how could she hope for something more when they were both on the rebound and she'd leave town in January?

"I'm afraid," she said and then hiccuped.

"Afraid of what?" His tone was so gentle, so understanding that it scared her even more.

"I'm afraid . . ."

"Yes?" He waited.

"I'm not experienced enough for you. Danny is the only guy I've ever been with."

He sucked in an audible breath. "Ahh," he said. "Now *I'm* scared. How can I live up to the love of your life?"

"Danny wasn't the love of my life. He was just my first boyfriend."

"There's nothing like your first love, Jazzy."

"Well, I have to stand in Claire's shadow. I've seen her on the YouTube recordings. She was extraordinary."

"She had her flaws like anyone else, Jazz. Don't canonize her."

"How do we leave our past partners at the bedroom door?" she asked.

Roan gulped. "I don't know."

"We need a clearing ritual."

"Huh?"

"I know it sounds woo-woo, but it's just symbolic. A visual to help release whatever needs clearing from your life. My friend Charlie and I do smudging. We learned it in group therapy when we were kids. It's the placebo effect, obviously, but it's surprising how well it works."

"Smudging?" Roan shook his head. "I have no idea what you're talking about. Told you, you're way out of my league."

"Don't start with that again." She swatted his arm lightly. "You burn a stick of sage and write down or recite aloud an intention that expresses your desire to let go of whatever it is that's keeping you from moving forward."

"You got a stick of sage on you?"

She pulled a rueful face. "No."

"I've got ground sage in the spice cabinet. Would that work?"

"Since the whole thing is symbolic and there's nothing magical about a sage stick . . ." Jazzy shrugged. "Sure, why not?"

They went to the kitchen and Roan got out the sage.

"What can we put it in that we could burn and wouldn't damage the container?"

"I have a marble mortar and pestle."

"Perfect. We just need the bowl part. Is that the mortar or the pestle?" she asked.

"Mortar." He got it from the top of the cabinet and passed it to her.

She shook in a healthy dollop of sage. "Do you have a lighter?"

He retrieved a long-handled grill lighter.

She took the lighter and the sage-filled mortar down the hall to the guest bedroom, Roan following at her heels. Pausing at the door, she said, "Let's have a moment of reverence for who we were and where we've been."

"Um, okay." Roan closed his eyes and bowed his head.

The sight of him looking pious ripped her resolve to shreds. Who was she to insist he perform a ritual to let go of his late wife? She wished she'd never started this in the first place, but they seemed to need some kind of permission to have sex.

Question was, why?

Roan opened one eye and peered at her. "Are we done with this part?"

"Yes." She paused, anxious to give him a way out if he was having second thoughts. "Open the door and walk through the threshold. Crossing the threshold signifies a new beginning. If you don't wish to go forward, don't cross it."

Without missing a beat, Roan opened the door and stepped inside, no hesitation. She was the one lingering at the threshold, lighter and sage-filled mortar in hand.

Roan looked at her, hand outstretched. The room was bare-bones. A bed and dresser. A TV on a stand. Some serene artworks on the walls. Not much trace of Claire in here. Safe enough. Jazzy took his hand, took a chance, went to him. His accepting smile strengthened her.

"What now?" he asked.

"Think about what you want to release, and I'll do the same," she said. Danny popped into her mind, and she saw him growing smaller and dimmer until he faded. Then she flicked the lighter and put the flame to the dried sage.

It flared immediately, threw smoke and the stench of burnt sage into the air. She walked around the room, chanting, "The past is released, the future is now."

The flame grew higher, and the mortar got too hot to handle. She juggled it between her palms. "Ow, ow."

"Put it down, put it down," Roan said.

"I don't want to burn your furniture."

"I don't want you to burn *you*." Roan took the mortar from her hand, kicked opened the door to the en suite bathroom, dumped the bowl of burning sage into the sink and turned on the faucet. He came back to her, took her hands in his. Her palms were pink and warm.

"Are you okay?"

She nodded.

"You sure?"

"You took it from me before I got burned."

"Well, the sage ritual worked. I certainly forgot all about the past in that moment," Roan said.

They looked at each other and burst out laughing. The flaming sage was the icebreaker they needed.

He brought her palms to his lips and softly kissed her skin. The pulse at her wrists beat wildly and when he kissed her lips again, Jazzy knew having rebound sex with Roan was the right thing to do.

Jazzy's little ritual had scared the crap out of him, but oddly enough, it did bring a sense of release. He felt alive again in a way he hadn't since he'd lost Claire. This was it. They were moving on from their pasts . . . together.

Fresh slate. Fresh start. He was ready for the next chapter.

He kissed her with every ounce of passion he had in him, hoping to show her just how excited he was about this.

About her.

They kissed endlessly. On and on and on. The air around them stinking of sage and their desperate hunger for each other. He loved getting to know her. Memorizing the noises that she made when he kissed or touched her in different places. She wriggled like a puppy when he licked the underside of her throat and moaned softly when he nibbled her earlobe.

Finally, air-hunger pushed them apart and they came up gasping. His hand slipped under her sweater and his palm rested just underneath her bra. His other hand threaded through her hair. His gaze beaded on her lips, full and glistening from their shared moisture.

"Wow," she whispered. "Just wow."

"Right back atcha."

He claimed her mouth again, his eager hands slipping down past the waistband of her loose-fitting jeans to cup her lush little fanny in both palms. She was wearing thong undies, he was pleased to note, and his hands filled with the soft padding of her butt. Another glorious moan slipped from her sweet throat as she worked the remaining buttons of his shirt and shoved it from his shoulders.

"Double wow," she said, raking her gaze over his torso. "You look even better than in my fantasies."

"You've been fantasizing about me?"

"Hell yes!" She peeked at his face. "Have you been fantasizing about me?"

"What do you think?" he asked, directing his attention to his rock-hard boner.

"Oh. My." She licked her lips and reached for the fly of his jeans.

Before he could haul in a deep breath, she undid the button and slipped down the zipper.

"Whoa," he said. "Slow down, Speed Racer. All good things are worth waiting for."

She made a sound of irritation. "Spoilsport."

"I'm not spoiling anything, honey. Here's one thing to know about older men. We like to take our time."

"Is that so?"

"We've learned much of the pleasure comes from anticipation." He ran a knuckle over her cheek and she gave a full body shiver.

"No kidding?"

He pressed his mouth to the hollow of her throat and sucked lightly.

She threw back her head and ground her pelvis against him. He talked a good game about self-control, but honestly, he was losing it. Especially now that she tugged her sweater over her head and tossed it on the table across the room.

Her breath came in quick, shallow pants, her breasts rising and falling in a tight, hot rhythm.

Her mussed hair sticking out from her head, and chin reddened with his stubble burn. He wished he'd shaved this morning.

His gaze roved her gorgeous body. Those full breasts, slender waist, and rounded hips. Her nipples beaded hard, thrusting upward through the thin fabric of her bra. Sexy as hell. Could he possibly keep up with her?

Teasing her, he kicked off his jeans and backed up, draping himself across the queen-sized bed and crooking a finger for her to join him, giving a come-hither stare.

She whisked off her own jeans, revealing the color of her thong panties matched her bra—crimson. Then with a sexy toss of her head, she moved over the foot of the bed toward him, but the comforter was satin, and she started to slide.

Roan grabbed for her.

Missed.

Went sliding himself.

Laughing, they ended up on the floor with Jazzy in his lap. Roan wrapped his arms tightly around her.

Their gazes met and he felt lost in a sea of conflicting emotions.

This step felt far too soon in their budding relationship and at the same time, not nearly soon enough.

"Do you . . ." Jazzy gulped visibly. ". . . still want to do this?"

"More than ever." He tightened his grip on her, letting her know any second thoughts were fleeting. "You?"

"This is just for fun, right?" An uncertain look settled over her features.

Was that what she wanted? Would he scare her off if he said no? He certainly scared himself.

"I want what you want," he said, which was true, but it sounded like a cop-out in this nondescript spare bedroom.

"I just . . ." She reached out to trace his cheek with her finger. "Don't want either of us to get hurt."

"Ditto." He smiled to let her see he was chill.

She moved her legs, straddling him. Then she leaned down and dipped her head to kiss him, the curtain of her beautiful blond hair falling against his face.

His body responded, hardening all over again as her lips captured his and she pushed him onto his back.

Her hands moved to his wrists, and she pinned his arms above his head. He let her, enjoying the shift as she deepened the kiss. If being in control helped her feel more comfortable, he was all for it.

Jazzy might seem sweet, but that wicked little tongue of hers took him prisoner and held him captive. He couldn't get enough of kissing her.

Her scent filled his nose, also sweet, like strawberry cotton candy, but there was an earthiness to her as well. A rich umami flavor that tickled his senses. She stroked the roof of his mouth with her tongue, exploring.

Roan couldn't stay passive. His body urged him to touch her, taste her, penetrate her. The yearning was powerful, overwhelming.

Their tandem breathing was ragged and shallow,

filled with urgency and need. She pressed her thighs into his sides, her small knees nestled against his ribs. She took her lips away and he instantly felt cheated.

Giggling, she sat back, until her butt was on his lower abdomen. His erection straining through his boxer briefs, eager to have at her. Her hair swung across her shoulders. A hypnotic sight that held him spellbound.

She looked glorious, her breasts raised and hard nipples clearly visible through her bra. He wanted at them. Reaching up, he went for the hook of her bra, one goal in mind. *Free those tits!*

But his fingers were shaking so hard, he couldn't get them to do what he wanted. He fumbled like he was seventeen again and behind the bleachers with Claire after their winning football game.

Poof.

The ghost of his late wife was between them again and he dropped his hand to Jazzy's waist.

This wasn't right. Thinking of Claire wasn't fair to Jazzy. Roan needed to rein himself in, get his focus where it belonged. On the warm and willing woman in front of him.

"You were thinking of her, weren't you?" Jazzy whispered.

Roan nodded. "I'm sorry."

"It's okay." Her tone was gentle and filled with empathy. "She was so important to you. How could you not think of her? You're having sex for the first time since you lost her. There's bound to be comparison."

He thought to ask if her mind was on Danny, but he really didn't want to know.

"This is a big step," she said, sliding off his belly and rearranging herself, stretching against his side. She rested her head on his shoulder and her lovely perfume filled his nose. "We don't have to do it all at once." She paused. "Or at all."

"No," he said. "I want this. I want *you*."

"I want you too."

"I do have something to confess," he whispered.

"I'm listening." She traced her index finger around his nipple.

Roan shivered. "Please don't do that."

"It doesn't feel good?"

"No, it feels too damn good. Keep that up and I can't promise to control myself."

"Oh ho." She tilted her head to flick her tongue over his nipple.

Groaning, Roan put his hand over his nipple. "Please. Wait. I'm trying to tell you something."

She stopped, sat up, and looked down at him. "What is it?"

"You told me you'd only been with Danny. Well, I'm in the same boat. I've only been with Claire." He braced himself. Waiting for her reaction. Believing she would tell him there was simply too much baggage to keep this up. "You're the second woman I've been with. I don't have a lot of experience."

"Oh, Roan," she whispered. "That's *such* a turn-on."

"It is?"

"Yes."

"Why?"

"You're trustworthy and I don't have to worry about catching something from you."

"Don't you want someone more experienced? Isn't that why you're attracted to older men?"

"Roan Sullivan," she scolded. "Let's get something straight."

"What's that."

"I'm not attracted to older men. I'm attracted to *you*."

"You sure?"

"Are you trying to sabotage this?"

"No." He lifted up on his elbows, his gaze fixed on those lovely breasts. "Maybe."

"You know what? I think we should stick a pin in this until you're really ready." She hopped up and reached for her jeans.

He jumped up too. "Is that what you want?"

She paused with her jeans held out in front of her. "No, but I think it's the sane option."

"You're right." He shook his head.

She looked disappointed in him, as if he'd failed a test. "You're not even going to try and fight for me?"

"Whoa there, missy," he said. "You're trying to ride two horses at once and I'm not sure you realize the mixed messages you're sending."

CHAPTER 16

Was she? Jazzy blinked.

"I'm too old to play games." Roan pressed a palm against his nape and looked resigned. "Either you want this, or you don't. I want to be with you, but if you aren't comfortable, I don't want to pressure you in any way. I don't want to talk you into something you're not one hundred percent on board with."

She had a dozen reasons to dress and get the hell out of there and only one reason to stay. She wanted this.

Wanted Roan.

"The sage burning didn't work, did it?" She offered him a smile.

"Maybe because sage wasn't in a stick?" Bemusement sparked his eyes.

"What if we just accept that there will be remnants of our past relationships with us and let that be okay."

"That sounds mature."

"Pros and cons," she said.

"Oh, we're doing that? All right." He nodded and she couldn't help noticing how amazing his muscled chest looked. "Pros. We both are insightful and self-aware. We're not walking into this blind."

"We're both loyal." She ticked off two fingers.

"Which can also be a con," he said, "because it keeps us loyal to our past relationships."

"Pro, we really like each other."

"Con, potential for screwing up our friendship."

"Pro, our chemistry is off the charts. The sex could be pretty damn good."

"Con," he said, his gaze latching on to hers. "I don't have any condoms."

"Pro," she said, licking her lips. "I do. My friend Charlie insists I carry them just in case."

"I like the way Charlie thinks." Roan chuckled. "I like *you*."

"C'mere," he said and crooked a finger at her.

She went. It might not be smart, but she really couldn't help herself. She wanted this man. Wanted his touch, his kisses. Wanted to feel his body inside hers.

Goose bumps fled up her arms and it wasn't because she was in her underwear. The room might be a little chilly, but she was blazing hot.

For Roan.

He wrapped her in his arms and hugged her for a long time and she let him, soaking up his warmth and strength.

Then his hand went to the clasp of her bra, but he hesitated. "Do you want this?"

"Yes."

"You sure?"

"I'm still here."

"That's definitely a pro." His fingers were at her back and she felt the bra give and fall away. He sucked in his breath and with reverence in his voice said, "God, you are so beautiful."

Her cheeks flushed and she ducked her head.

He hooked a finger under her chin and raised her face to meet his gaze. "You are special to me, Jazzy Walker. I want you to know that."

Tears pressed against her eyes, surprising her. "Thank you."

"I feel like you're a dream I never even dared dream."

"Oh, Roan, I feel the same."

Gently, he kissed her forehead, then the spot between her eyebrows before moving to the tip of her nose and her lips.

When his mouth fully closed over hers, they both groaned. She slipped her arms around his neck and pulled his head down, drinking him in.

With his hot hands all over her body and her lips tingling from his kisses, Jazzy could scarcely breathe. She tried to suck in air, but her lungs felt tight, and her pulse galloped. She struggled to inhale and made a small strangling sound.

Roan pulled back, peered at her intently. "You okay?"

"Uh-huh, just . . ." She fanned her throat. "Choked up."

"Aww." He pulled her to him for another hug and held her until her heart stopped racing. "It's okay. It's going to be all right."

"You promise?"

"Yes." He started kissing her again, slowly, sweetly.

She drifted, savoring everything, the taste of his mouth, the smell of his skin, the silk of his hair slipping through her fingers.

"Better?" he asked.

Grateful, she smiled. "Better."

Giving her a devastatingly wicked grin, he cupped her breasts and dipped his head to kiss first one nipple and then the other.

She clutched his shoulders, trembling at his touch. When he took a nipple into his mouth, she groaned and pressed against him, sliding her hands down his back, skimming her palms over his honed muscles until she reached his butt.

What a fantastic butt!

Grunting, she pushed at the waistband of his boxer briefs, tugging at the elastic. He was so busy blazing kisses up her neck, he didn't stop to help. She tried to shove them down low enough so he could step out of them, but they hung on his erection.

He laughed. The sound vibrated against her throat sending tingles up her jaw. "Greedy little thing, aren't you?"

"Some help here?"

"You shuck yours and I'll shuck mine."

"Deal."

They broke apart long enough to shimmy out of their underwear, and then flew immediately back into each other's arms.

After a long moment of red-hot kissing, Jazzy peeked at him. As if sensing a change, his own eyes flew open. They stared at each other, so close they were cross-eyed.

"Hey," he said softly.

"Hey yourself."

His eyes filled with an emotion she couldn't quite name. Lust for sure, but there was something more. A lot more. Reverence, hope, enjoyment.

Her heart clutched.

She closed her eyes and started kissing him again. His rock-hard penis throbbing against her belly. Oh dear, oh dear, oh dear, he was magnificent.

Grinding her pelvis against him, she gently bit down on one of his nipples and heard a ragged groan tear from his throat.

"Too much too soon, sweetheart," he murmured and stepped back.

Sweetheart. How she loved the sound of that word falling off his lips!

"Are we done?" she whispered. "Do you want to stop?"

"Just for a moment," he said. "Let me collect myself. It's been a long time and I don't want to end prematurely."

She slipped her hand down to touch him, but he grabbed her wrist and shook his head. "No," Roan said. "You're first."

"Um, what does that mean?"

"Let's take care of you and give me time to get myself under control."

"Oh," she said, still unsure what he meant. Was he talking about oral sex?

A fresh wave of goose bumps rippled over her at that delicious idea. Danny had never much cared for giving her oral pleasure and had only done so a few times. Of course, he'd sure liked it when she'd done that for him.

Stop comparing. You're with Roan. Be here now.

He didn't give her much time to think. The next thing she knew, he was peeling back the satiny comforter and guiding her to the bed.

The sheets were cool against her bare rump, a sharp contrast to his hot hands skimming down her belly. Erotic shivers shook her, and she arched her back as he traced his fingertips lower, igniting her nerve endings. His mouth started at her breasts, while his fingers kept walking lower and lower. He licked his way down, pausing to lavish attention in places where she giggled or squirmed. He seemed to know exactly where to touch, his instincts unerring.

Pro, she thought in a daze. *He's been around the block and it shows!*

When he got to that sweet spot between her hips, he went to his knees and looked up at her.

Jazzy met his sultry gaze. His brown eyes half-lidded and a soft smile lit up his face. Her body tensed with anticipation and longing as she waited . . .

And then he lowered his head and touched his tongue to her in a way that unfurled every inhibition she'd ever had about oral sex. She couldn't wait to see what he had in store for her next.

He strummed a spot she'd never had strummed before and in a matter of minutes her body rocked hard. She didn't know if she could handle it. What on earth was that man doing? She was a nurse. She understood anatomy but it was as if he'd found some new part of her she'd never known existed.

"Ooh," she cried and pushed herself against his mouth. "Oh, oh, oh."

He grabbed her hips and helped her arch closer. He moved his tongue, and she let out a joyful squeal so loud it embarrassed her.

Roan stopped what he was doing. "Are you all right?"

She felt herself blush and covered her face with a palm.

"Hey, hey. You okay?"

She nodded. He smelled so good.

He stroked her hair, cooed her name, drew out her name. "*Jazzy.*"

She shifted and peeked up at him. "That was interesting."

"Not bad for an old guy, huh." He wriggled his eyebrows and stretched out beside her.

Playfully, she swatted his shoulder. "You are not old. You're in your prime. Like fine wine."

"That's what they say to old guys," he teased. "Now, where were we." He slid back down the sheets to press his mouth at her sensitive spot again.

She squirmed. "I'd rather have sex with you."

"You don't like this?" His tongue stroked her.

"Oh, I like it very much," she said. "I just want to merge with you."

He gave her a wry grin and looked down at his penis. "Little Roan is just aching to be with you too."

"There is nothing *little* about Roanie," she said with a growl and pounced, tackling him to the mattress and pinning his wrists.

"Roanie?" He laughed. "Kind of on the nose, but I'm not complaining."

She almost asked him what Claire had called his member but bit her tongue before it came out.

Con, she thought, *dead wife land mines*.

Jazzy leaned down to give Roanie a kiss and he instantly sprang to attention. "Your turn, fella."

"Are you having a private conversation with my penis."

"I am." She giggled. "Is that a problem?"

"Not in the slightest."

She kissed the head of his penis.

Roan hissed like he'd sat on hot coals.

"Oh, too intense? I can back off." She shifted again, went to nibble his chest, and traced her fingers over his skin the way he'd done to her.

A guttural groan poured from his throat. His approving noises made her feel powerful, and her heart was pumping so hard she could feel it thumping against her throat. She paid close attention to every part of him that she plied with her tongue. Noticing everything he liked or didn't. His jawline. Steely and strong. His scar at his collarbone. He wriggled when she touched her tongue there.

"That bothers you?" she asked.

"Freaks me out a bit."

"What happened?"

"Thrown from a wild mustang when I was fifteen. Compound fracture."

"Ouch. Collarbone PTSD. Will steer clear."

"Maybe one day," he said, "I'll be able to get past the ghost of that fall."

"No worries, I'll just concentrate on your earlobe." She took his earlobe between her teeth and lightly bit down.

That brought a moan and he clutched at the sheet with a fist. Aha! Good to know. Roan liked his ears nibbled.

She took her time, torturing him shamelessly before she finally scooted back down his body.

Roan ran his hand through her hair as Jazzy lowered her head and brought her mouth down over his hard shaft.

She licked and swirled, stroking her tongue up and down. Tasting his salty flavor. He moved his hips in rhythm with her mouth. The tension built and built until he rolled away from her.

"No, no. Not like this. Not the first time. I want to be inside you, Jazzy."

Panting, she dropped to the floor. "I'll go get the condom! Stay right where you are!"

She ran naked through Roan's house, searching for where she'd left her purse when she heard a car door slam and the sound of Trinity and her grandmother walking up to the back door.

Con, Jazzy thought as she froze deer-in-the-headlights style. *He's got a kid who's about to see you naked.*

CHAPTER 17

Jazzy burst through the guest bedroom door.

"I haven't twitched a muscle," Roan said, lying supine, his stiff penis jutting proudly in the air. "Promise."

"Get up! Get up! Your mom and Trinity are back!"

"Oh, sheet cake!" Roan leaped from the bed.

The back door slammed closed.

"They're in the house!" Roan and Jazzy whispered simultaneously and stared at each other, wide-eyed and alarmed.

"Roan?" his mother called. "Jazzy?"

"Get dressed!"

They both grabbed for their jeans. Roan yanked his pants up, but they stopped at his knees.

"What the heck?" he muttered, looking perplexed.

At the same moment, Jazzy's baggy jeans pulled up almost to her breasts. "Wh-what?"

"Roan? Jazzy?" Footsteps.

"Daddy?" Trinity's little voice sent fresh panic shooting through Jazzy.

Roan looked down at the jeans stuck on his lower thighs, then darted his gaze back to Jazzy's.

"Wrong jeans," they said.

Shucking off their pants, they handed them to each other. Roan pulled on his jeans, grabbed his T-shirt, and raked a hand through his hair. He looked as deranged as Jazzy felt.

"Yew-hoo?" His mother's voice was moving away from the guest bedroom, thank heavens.

"Daddy?"

"Stay here," Roan hissed softly.

"And get trapped?" she whispered.

"We can't come out of the bedroom at the same time."

"Good point."

Roan headed for the door.

"How do I get out of here?"

"I'll find out what's going on and get rid of my mom."

"What about Trinity?"

"I'll put her to bed and then you can leave."

Jazzy didn't like that idea. She was starting to feel claustrophobic and more than a little foolish.

"Roan?" his mother called again.

"Gotta go," he said and slipped out the door.

Jazzy stared at his retreating back, heart squeezing with complex emotions—disappointment, relief, sadness, delight, optimism.

So much optimism that she wasn't sure it was healthy.

She traced her bottom lip, recalling the sensation of his mouth on hers, and shivered. Well, why not? Optimism was her default personality setting and it had served her well.

They might not have been able to complete their time together, but the chemistry was off the charts and she couldn't wait for another chance to explore it.

"Mom," Roan said, coming down the hallway, the tile cool against his bare feet. "What are you doing here?"

His mother and Trinity were at the opposite end of the corridor coming from his bedroom. His mother was carrying his daughter's overnight bag.

"There you are!" Trinity ran to him, arms wide.

He swung his daughter into his embrace and held her close. "I thought you were going to spend the night at Grammy's house."

Kissing his daughter's cheek, Roan met his mother's gaze over the top of Trinity's head.

"She got homesick," Grammy said.

"I wanna sleep in *my* bed," Trinity announced.

"Okay," he said, resisting the urge to glance over his shoulder at the guest room.

"I tried to talk her out of coming home," Mom said.

"No worries at all. You can always come home, Trinity. *Always*," he reassured his daughter.

"What were you doing in the guest bedroom?" his mother asked, an amused smile on her face as if she'd guessed what had gone on behind closed doors.

"Um, um." *Think of something quick!* "Wrapping packages."

"Christmas presents?" Trinity asked, wriggling in his arms. "I wanna see."

"We can't spoil the surprise," Roan said, then feeling guilty for his deception, he dropped his voice to an exaggerated whisper. "The presents are for Grammy and Gramps."

"Oh," Trinity said and immediately looked disinterested. "Nothing for me?"

"Santa is bringing your presents." Roan lightly tickled her.

Trinity giggled, rested her head against his shoulder, and looked at him with adoring eyes. Roan melted. "I've been nice. Not the least bit naughty."

"Not even when you flushed your Hot Wheels down the toilet?"

"I tol' you." Trinity folded her arms over her chest and looked exasperated. "That was an assident, Daddy."

God, how he loved her. Roan squeezed her so tight he could feel her little heart beating. Shame burned the nape of his neck. His child came first. Always. But it wasn't fair to Jazzy to keep her hiding out in the guest bedroom.

"How was the tea party?" he asked.

Trinity made a face. "I don't like hot tea . . ." She paused, then added, "So, they brought me hot chocolate with little pink heart marshmallows. I liked that."

"No kidding?" He ruffled her hair and kissed the top of her head again.

"The cookies had sprinkles on them, but they weren't as good as yours," Trinity declared. "And I got to meet Alice in Wonderland. She is bootiful."

"That's wonderful."

She crinkled her nose. "I didn't like the Mad Hatter, though. He talked too loud and smelled funny."

"Mad Hatters are like that." Chuckling, he shook his head. "I'm glad you're back safe and sound. Thanks for taking her, Mom. I hope she wasn't any trouble."

"No trouble at all. You heard her. She wasn't the least bit naughty."

"Was Santa at the tea party?" he asked Trinity.

"No, but there was hundreds and hundreds of Christmas trees."

His mom held up four fingers.

"We're really going to have to work on your numbers," Roan said.

"Where's Jazzy?" his mother asked. "Her car is still in your driveway."

"Jazzy's here?" Trinity's face lit up.

Gee thanks, Mom. Roan didn't want to lie, but neither did he want them knowing Jazzy was still here. Deflection seemed the best choice. "It's bath time, Doodlebug. C'mon, let's get you in the tub."

"Can Jazzy give me a bath?" Trinity asked.

"Nope. You're stuck with dear old Dad."

"Aww, man." Trinity paused. "Can Jazzy read me a story after my bath?"

"No," Roan said. Was his daughter already too attached to the pediatric nurse? *Trinity's not the only one.*

It was true. His feelings for Jazzy were growing. He wanted her. Not just in his bed, but in his life after this cookie contest was over.

That was a problem. Jazzy was leaving town. She wouldn't be around for long and he couldn't just bring someone willy-nilly into Trinity's life. He was a dad. He had responsibilities. He had to be extra careful.

For the sake of everyone involved.

Jazzy stood with her ear pressed against the guest room door, trying to eavesdrop on Roan's conversation with his mother and daughter.

When she heard her name, she dithered. Should she go out and say hi, revealing she'd been hiding in the bedroom? Or lie low and wait until Roan let her know the coast was clear?

She cast a glance over her shoulder and considered a third option. Sneak out the bedroom window. She'd brought her purse with her when she'd fled back to the guest room. It would be easy enough.

Sneak away in the night like a thief.

That didn't seem very dignified, but her anxiety latched on to the idea. *Do it. Go. Get out of here*.

Right now, she felt like an afterthought. Which was fine. Totally fine. She got it. His kid came first. That was one of the things she adored about him. He was a father, first and foremost, and the last thing she wanted was to get in the way of that bond.

Despite their passion for each other, Jazzy was super glad his mother and Trinity had interrupted them. They'd been moving too fast. Burning too hot.

Go home.

Roan and his family were still talking in the hallway. Trinity chattering away about the tea party.

It was now or never.

Jazzy slung her purse over her shoulder, went to the window and raised it. Cold night air rushed into the room. Carefully, she took off the outer screen and set it on the ground, dropped her purse out first, and then crawled from the window, one leg at a time.

She landed in a fallow flowerbed, grabbed her purse, now covered with dirt and leaves, and made a run for it. Heart pounding hard in her throat, she jumped into her car and backed out, just as she saw Roan come out of the house to watch her drive away.

When she got home, she saw that he'd texted her.

ROAN: Sorry about that. Trinity got homesick.
JAZZY: No worries.

He didn't respond immediately. Jazzy showered, washing away the scent of Roan that clung to her skin, put on her pj's, brushed her teeth, and got into bed, Sabrina beside her, by the time her cell dinged again.

ROAN: Rain check on the baking lessons tomorrow?

Disappointment sent her stomach plunging to her feet. Everything okay?

ROAN: Sure, sure, just really busy.
JAZZY: Day after tomorrow?
ROAN: Pretty busy that day too.
JAZZY: The day after that?
ROAN: Let's play it by ear.

Uh-oh. This wasn't a good sign. Had she blown things with him by moving too fast? Hauling in a deep breath, she texted K and added a smiley face emoji to show there were no hard feelings. Let me know when.

There. The ball was in his court. If he contacted her, fantastic. If not, well at least they hadn't gone all the way. She'd gotten out before she'd fallen in too deep. It was cool. Fine. Great. No sweat, Chet, as her dad would say.

Roan did not text back.

She tried not to take it personally, told herself she wasn't taking it personally, but as she drifted off to sleep, a voice in the back of her brain whispered, *Liar*.

"I'm so glad you called," Jazzy's stepmother said as the hostess ushered them through the antique store portion of the Painted Parrot Parlor three days later. "It's been ages since we've had lunch together, just you and me."

A hostess led them through a beaded curtain into the tearoom filled with vibrant colors and all things parrot—parrot dishes, parrot statues, parrot branded merchandise. This time of year, Christmas decorations adorned the parrots. The tree in the middle of the room, in front of a crackling fireplace, was a twelve-foot spruce tree, laden with parrot ornaments. Low parrot sounds piped in through a speaker system created a jungle atmosphere in a place it did not fit.

She and Sarah knew the women seated at the tables. The Painted Parrot Parlor was a hot spot for the ladies-who-lunch in Twilight, and it was a rare male who darkened the door. They waved across the room and exchanged many "hellos" and "how-are-yous."

The hostess passed them off to the server who held out two menus cut in the shape of parrots.

Sarah shook her head. "We know what we want."

"The croissant chicken sandwich," Jazzy said. "With cranberry sauce on the side."

When Jazzy was thirteen, and got her first period, Sarah brought her here to celebrate Jazzy becoming a woman and they'd ordered the same sandwiches. The food had been so delicious, they ordered the same thing every time.

"You got it. You want chips, fries, or the fruit cup with that."

"Fruit cup," she and Sarah said in unison and grinned at each other. The worry that had been gnawing at Jazzy since she'd climbed out of Roan's window that night abated in the face of their happy routine.

"Peach tea to drink," Sarah said. "With honey and lemon."

"Same for you, hon?" the server asked.

"Yes. Thanks."

The server smiled and went off to fill their order.

"Now," Sarah said, settling into the plush padded chair. She reached across the table to touch Jazzy's hand. "Tell me what's going on."

"Don't tell Dad. I'm not ready for him to know yet."

Sarah pantomimed zipping her lips, ticking

a lock, and throwing the pretend key over her shoulder.

"Roan Sullivan and I are dating . . ." Jazzy paused. "I think."

"You think?"

Quickly, Jazzy told her a G-rated version of what had happened the other night. "I crawled out the window like a dufus so I wouldn't have to face his mother and Trinity. I feel like an idiot."

"Why?"

Jazzy shrugged. "I don't know. I understand his daughter must come first. I really do. It's just that . . ."

Sarah waited expectantly, her gaze hooked on Jazzy's face, and her hand still on top of Jazzy's arm. "You know you can tell me anything."

Jazzy nodded. "I know."

"Please don't feel obligated to share something you're not ready to share," Sarah added. "But you did ask me to lunch out of the blue, so it seems you want to talk."

Pausing, Jazzy considered how to phrase her question. "What was it like dating my dad when I was little? I mean, when it came to finding private time with him."

"Ahh," Sarah said, leaning back and folding her arms in her lap. "Bringing out the tough questions."

"Is that too personal?"

"Not at all. I'm just afraid you won't like the answer."

The server appeared with their order. When the woman was out of earshot, Sarah unfurled her napkin, settled it in her lap and leaned across the table to whisper conspiratorially. "At least you *chose* to climb out the window."

"Pardon?"

"When you were little and at a sleepover with Andi Browning, you got homesick just like Trinity."

"Wh-what? Really?"

"Uh-huh." Sarah smiled, amused.

"I did?"

"I was in town for a book signing and staying at the Merry Cherub B&B. I'd gone out in a paddleboat and didn't realize a wind warning was in effect. A gust caught the boat and blew me to the middle of the lake. Then it started sinking. Your father came to my rescue."

"You and Dad told me that story before," Jazzy said. Many times. Usually when they told it, they shot each other knowing glances and grinned. Jazzy slapped a hand across her mouth. "OMG, was that the first time you and Dad—"

"Your father brought me back to his house because I was soaking wet. I took a shower, and he gave me his bathrobe to wear—"

"I don't need the deets, Sarah." Jazzy put both palms over her ears.

"Okay." Sarah chuckled. "Let's just say things were getting really heated between us, if you know what I mean."

"I get it." Jazzy held up a stop-sign palm.

"Andi's mom pulled in the driveway, just when your dad and I were about to—"

Jazzy could barely remember a time when she and Andi weren't rivals, but Sarah's words knocked loose a memory. It had been a sleepover with several other eight-year-old girls, and they'd ganged up on Jazzy, teasing her for needing an inhaler and she'd started crying, which only fueled the taunts. Even now, she felt hot shame heat her cheeks. Was that the moment things had shifted between her and Andi?

"It was the first time you'd ever had a sleepover with anyone besides your aunt Raylene," Sarah went on. "I think Andi's mom, Sandy, wanted to date your dad. Sandy had just gotten divorced and was inviting you and your dad to things, but then I came back to Twilight and your father forgot all about Sandy."

"I didn't know that."

"I don't think they ever went out, but I think they'd made plans to take you both to the pajama party at Ye Old Book Nook if memory serves."

"Instead, you and Dad hooked up."

"Not that night. That night, Sandy brought you home at the most inopportune time. Sandy pulled up in the drive and your father panicked. He grabbed my clothes, stuffed them into my arms and shoved me out the back door while I was still wearing his bathrobe. It was Christmastime, and it was cold."

"No!"

"Fact."

"I can't believe Dad did that to you."

"He panicked. I understood. Not at the time though." Sarah shook her head. "But after he groveled and offered a sincere apology."

"I'm gonna have to get on him for that." Jazzy wagged her head.

"Please don't say anything. I didn't tell you that story to embarrass your father. Just to let you know that when you date someone with kids, it can get complicated. That's all."

"I do appreciate you telling me, and I'll keep that in mind."

Sarah patted Jazzy's hand again. "Be patient with Roan. He's got a lot of stuff to work through."

"I know."

"And so do you, after Danny—"

"I'm over Danny."

"That may well be true, but he was your high school sweetheart and you do live in Twilight, the romance capital of Texas, and he did get engaged to your frenemy. There's emotion there. Don't let that interfere with Roan. You've got enough to navigate with him being a single father."

Jazzy considered telling Sarah about what had happened and ask her opinion about why Roan backed off, but that felt too personal. "I had no idea things were so dicey between you and Dad in the beginning."

"Not dicey . . ." Sarah paused. "There were just a lot of things to work through before we could be together."

"So, tell me this," Jazzy said, noticing her tightening chest. "Despite all the obstacles you and Dad had in your path to happily-ever-after, was it worth the work?"

Sarah beamed bright and in that moment Jazzy understood where part of her own optimistic attitude had come from. "Oh absolutely, sweetheart. Not only did I get the love of my life, but I also got the best daughter in the whole world." Tears in her eyes, Sarah reached across the table to envelop Jazzy in a loving hug.

This, Jazzy thought as she inhaled Sarah's lovely scent. *This is what I could one day have with Trinity.*

Immediate fear flooded her. *No, no. No thoughts like that.* She and Roan were temporary. A rebound relationship. Casual fun. But, oh boy, if she didn't stop these runaway feelings, she was going to get hurt.

Badly.

CHAPTER 18

Four days had passed since he'd last texted Jazzy on Sunday evening, and Roan couldn't stop thinking about her. He felt badly that things had fallen apart. He'd mishandled the situation. He should have called instead of texted or better yet, went to see her. He should have explained why he was so conflicted. But how could he explain to Jazzy what he didn't fully understand himself?

Honestly, he'd never expected to have these kinds of feelings ever again. And that scared the hell out of him. He'd loved before with all his heart and when he'd lost Claire it ripped his world apart. He didn't know if he could survive another loss like that. Much safer to protect his heart and his daughter. Trinity was getting close to Jazzy too.

But he felt like crud abandoning her baking lessons, especially when winning against Andi Browning meant so much to her.

He went to the barn to muck out horse stalls and mull over his options. Trinity was playing on the backyard swing set and he could watch her through the open barn door. Multitasking was a skill he'd cultivated as a single parent.

His cell phone rang. Roan slipped it from his pocket, saw Jazzy's number, and broke out in a cold sweat.

Should he let it go to voice mail? That's what a prudent man would do. Ghosting her wasn't easy. His hands turned sweaty, and he held his breath.

The phone rang a second time.

He inhaled, tried to corral his thoughts into something coherent. *I like you. I want to be with you, but I'm scared as hell I'll blow it.*

Third ring.

"Hello?"

"Roan?" a man's voice asked.

"Yes?" he answered, leery.

"This is Charlie Cheek. Jazzy Walker's best friend. I stitched up Trinity when she cut her chin."

"Yes, right. What can I do for you, Charlie?"

"Since Jazzy listed you as a contact, I thought you should know—"

"What's happened? What's wrong?"

"It's okay, she'll be all right."

Panic iced the blood in his veins. "What's happened to her?"

"She was trying to bake cookies on her outdoor grill, and she burned her arm enough to need emergency attention. She's in the ER right now, and while she's in some pain and needs treatment, they are second-degree burns, and she won't need hospitalization."

"Thank you for being there for her. I'm on my way to the hospital now."

"There's no need. I just thought you should know what happened. I'm hoping you'll continue her baking lessons. She can't do this without you."

"Yes, thank you, Charlie, for letting me know. I'll be right there."

"You don't have to come—"

But Roan had already hung up. He called his mom. "Can you watch Trinity for a bit?"

"Sure," his mom said. "Bring her over."

"On the way."

He propped the shovel against the stall door and zipped across the yard to the swings. "C'mon, kiddo," he said. "We're going to see Grammy."

"You did what!" Jazzy exclaimed as Charlie swathed her arm with burn cream and sterile gauze. She was sitting on the edge of the ER gurney while Charlie perched on a rolling stool. The burn stretched from her wrist to her elbow on the inside of her left arm.

"Don't squirm, Lambchop. I'm trying to work here."

"You had no right to call Roan, none at all."

"I beg to differ. Because you put him down as a contact, I do have a right. And if he hadn't stopped your campfire baking lessons you wouldn't have been out there messing around on your own and gotten burned."

"This burn has nothing to do with Roan. Nothing at all. I was clumsy and I'd let Sabrina outside to keep me company. She darted in front of me at just the wrong moment and I stumbled into the hot Dutch oven. Period. End of sentence."

"Don't blame Sabrina. You were clumsy because you were woolgathering over Roan."

"I wish like hell I'd never told you that."

"Ahh, but you did."

"Call him back. Tell him not to come up here."

"You call him."

"I will. Where's my phone?"

"Oops, it's in my lab coat pocket and I can't get to it." Charlie held up his gloved hands.

"Dammit, Charlie, why are you being a jerk?"

"Dammit, Jazzy, why can't you see the nose on your face?"

"What are you talking about?"

"You like Roan Sullivan and from the panic in his voice, I think he likes you too."

"You're wrong. He canceled our lessons."

"Did you ever think it was because he cares too much and that scares him?"

Jazzy paused. Really? Maybe? Did she dare hope?

"We've only known each other two weeks," she said. "How could that possibly be true?"

"It might be only two weeks, but you've been together for hours, working side by side. You've developed tender feelings for him, why couldn't he have developed them for you too?"

"He's hung up on his dead wife."

"How do you know?"

"He's got pictures of her all over the house."

"Maybe he's not had a reason to move on . . . until you."

"Whose side are you on? You're my friend, not his."

"I didn't realize there were sides."

Jazzy hadn't either.

"Are you searching for a reason not to move forward with this relationship?" Charlie asked, gingerly taping down the gauze covering her left arm.

"I don't know. Maybe."

"Do you want to be with him?"

"I do, but I'm not so sure he wants to be with me. Besides, if Traveling Nurses hires me, which I'm sure they will, I'm outta here."

"Why don't you ask him if he wants more than a casual thing?"

"Because I'm afraid he'll say no."

"Isn't it better to know the truth so you can move on rather than live in limbo?"

"Yes," she admitted.

"Jazzy." Roan's voice pulled her attention to the doorway. His troubled eyes and worried expression tugged at her.

"Hey, Roan," she said, surprised by how much relief flooded her body. He had come. He *did* care. While she was mad at Charlie for calling, she was so glad he had.

Roan walked into the room and with each step closer to her, Jazzy's pulse thumped harder.

"I've got another patient to check on," Charlie said, bouncing to his feet and scurrying out the back door that led to the employees' corridor.

Leaving her alone with Roan. *Boom, boom, boom.* The pounding in her ears was so loud she could scarcely hear.

Roan took the stool Charlie vacated. His gaze latching on to her bandaged arm. "Is it painful?"

"Not much right now. Charlie gave me a pain-killer."

"I hate that you got burned," Roan said. "I blame myself."

"Why? It's not your fault."

"I shouldn't have stopped your lessons."

"You can't hold my hand forever. I'll have to do it myself at the cook-off anyway."

"You weren't ready to go it alone. I didn't teach you enough fire safety."

"I'm not your responsibility, Roan."

"Jazzy." He met her gaze head-on. "I'm so sorry."

"For what?"

"Freaking out the other night when Mom brought Trinity home. Standing you up . . . acting like a jerk."

"Totally understandable. I get it." She wasn't about to let him know how hurt she'd been when he discontinued her lessons.

"When you hightailed it out the window before we even had a chance to talk, I . . . well . . . I got my feelings hurt and to protect myself, I shut down." He hesitated. "Shut you out."

"I shouldn't have climbed out the window. That was childish of me."

"Mom was confused when she came back outside to find your car gone."

Jazzy picked up the pillow off the gurney, covered her face to hide her shame and mumbled, "I'll never be able to look her in the eyes again."

"Don't feel embarrassed. Mom likes you."

Jazzy lowered the pillow, peeked at him. "She does?"

"Very much."

"Oh."

"So do I."

"Really?"

"Don't pretend you don't know. The last night we were together . . ." He shook his head. "That was big for me."

"Me too."

A nurse appeared at the door with forms in her hand. Jazzy knew her. They'd gone to nursing school together. "I've got your discharge paperwork here."

"Thanks, Teresa."

"Is he here to drive you home?" Teresa gave Roan an approving gaze.

"No," Jazzy said at the same moment Roan said, "Yes."

"You don't need to be driving. Not with Toradol on board."

"Huh?" Roan blinked.

"That's nurse-speak." Jazzy laughed. "Toradol can make you drowsy and they gave me some when I got here and it's kicking in." Jazzy yawned, proving Teresa's point.

"That's it. I'm driving you," Roan said.

"How will I get my car home?" she asked. "It's in the Emergency Room parking lot."

"You let me take care of that," Roan said. "Time to get you into bed."

"Yes," Teresa said. "Get some rest and start healing before the bake-off. I can't wait for you to beat the pants off Andi. We're all getting really tired of her bragging about what a wonderful baker she is."

"Thanks for the support," Jazzy said.

"Anytime." Teresa winked. "Just sign these forms and read over your home care instructions and we'll get you out the door."

"I'll go bring my truck around," Roan said and sauntered out.

Teresa watched him go and sighed. "I wouldn't mind if he were taking me home to bed. Are you two dating or is he just giving you baking lessons like Charlie says."

Jealousy knifed Jazzy's chest. "Dating," she said. "We're definitely dating."

Teresa looked disappointed. "Well, good for you. No more moping over Danny Garza?"

"Nope," Jazzy confirmed. "None."

"With good reason. Danny's still an overgrown kid." Teresa stared at the door where Roan had disappeared. "But there goes a *real* man."

"For sure."

"You're a lucky woman, Jazzy."

Yes, she was. She always tried to find the sunny side of life. But when it came to Roan, she felt unsettled and off-balance. Their courtship was a roller coaster, and she wasn't so sure she had the stamina to stick around, even for a short ride.

Time to change your ways, cowboy.

No more running from his feelings. No more hiding from his fears. He wanted a deeper connection with Jazzy and he ached to break from the cocoon of two years of emotional isolation. Roan wanted to love again.

Wanted to love Jazzy.

He could fall for her so damn easily. If he could lower his guard and open his heart to the possibility.

They had just stopped off at the pharmacy for the antibiotics and the pain pills the doctor had prescribed. Roan glanced over at her bandaged arm and winced. His fault. Her burn was all his fault.

The radio was on low, and he could hear the weatherman announcing the winter storm headed their way. He'd been a rancher long enough to see and smell bad weather coming. He'd already texted his ranch hands to get the livestock under shelter. Trinity was with his parents, so he didn't have to worry about her. The only thing on his plate right now was getting Jazzy home and tucked into bed.

"Wow," Jazzy said. "The sky is darkening fast. I think the storm will hit sooner than predicted."

"Hopefully, I can get you home and settled in before I head back to the ranch," he said, guiding his pickup through the town square.

Shoppers bent over against the wind, clutching their coats closer around themselves. Beside him, Jazzy shivered.

Roan turned up the heat. The temperature outside had dropped ten degrees while they'd been in the hospital.

"Home sweet home," she said as he pulled into her driveway. She unbuckled her seat belt and hopped out before he'd even killed the engine.

"Thanks for the ride home. You don't have to re-trieve my car. I'll get Charlie to pick me up on his way to work tomorrow."

"Whoa, whoa," Roan said. "I'm not going to leave you all alone with a storm coming. Not until I'm sure you're going to be okay. You've had a painkiller—"

"A mild one," she said, standing in the driveway looking at him.

"And because of that, you might not be thinking clearly. I'm coming in to get you settled."

She looked relieved but put up a mild protest. "I don't want to impose. You need to get home to look after your own stuff."

"Trinity is with Mom and Dad and the ranch hands are taking care of the ranch. I'm at your dis-posal, Jazzy."

"I don't want to cause problems."

"No problem at all."

"Really, I—"

"Jazzy," he chided. "I want to help. Let me help . . . *please*."

She shivered against a fresh blast of wind, and barely nodded.

"C'mon. Let's get inside." He got out of the pickup and went to her, sliding his arm around her shoulder as he guided her to the door, while at the same time hitting the lock button on his truck remote.

She sank against his body and he could feel her gratitude in how she slipped her arm around his waist.

He was glad he'd been pushy. Normally, he wasn't

so insistent, but he owed her. She'd done so much for him and Trinity, it was his turn.

They stepped over extension cords snaking across the lawn for the animated Christmas display and when they got to the front door, he took the house key from her and unlocked the door.

Even before they stepped over the threshold, he could smell Christmas in the air—pine, cinnamon, gingerbread. It smelled like home. Or at least the way his home used to smell when Claire lived there.

A pang of sorrow punched him in the gut, but he shoved it aside. The past was in the past. Now he was here with Jazzy.

First off, he met her tabby, Sabrina, who went to him like they were old friends, weaving around his legs like a lovesick eel.

"Wow," Jazzy said and picked up her cat. "Sabrina's doesn't usually take too well to strangers."

"I like cats," he said. "But Claire was allergic, and I thought I'd wait until Trinity was older before getting a house pet."

Jazzy stroked Sabrina's head and invited him farther into her home.

The place was tidy, but he'd expected no less from her. And decorated just as aggressively as the front lawn. Everywhere he looked he saw happiness and good cheer. A large Christmas tree done in red and white lights and ornaments. Gaily wrapped packages underneath the tree. A nativity scene laid out on a long sideboard and on the coffee table, a Christmas village. And at the fireplace mantel, red-and-white stockings.

A lot of stockings. At least a dozen. Names embroidered on the fluffy white cuffs. He stepped close to read the names—*Travis, Sarah, Crystal, Charlie, Sabrina.* Her family, friends, pet. Other names too. Many people he knew from Twilight.

Two stockings that didn't quite match the others, hung on the end. They looked bought later than the rest. When he saw the names on those two stockings, the breath left his body. *Roan. Trinity.*

She'd added stockings for Roan and his daughter to her mantel.

Bombarded with feelings, he turned to her.

Jazzy was smiling at him like he was life-giving sunshine, and she was a sunflower.

"You put stockings up for us?"

"You and Trinity have become a big part of my life this holiday season," she said. "I was hoping maybe you could come over for Christmas Eve or Christmas Day to celebrate with me."

"You . . ." he said but couldn't find additional words to express what he was feeling for her in that moment. Gratitude for sure. Joy. Tenderness. A dash of fear that this was actually happening and . . .

The beginnings of love.

Holy cow, he should run, but that was the last thing he wanted.

"When did you buy these?" he asked.

"Yesterday."

After he'd already snubbed her, she'd remained openhearted and optimistic.

"You're not upset are you?" She looked suddenly worried.

"God no," he said. "Why would I be upset?"

"That I assumed you and Trinity might want to drop by my house for Christmas." She nibbled her thumbnail as if she was scared he'd reject her. "I have stockings for all my friends. I didn't mean to overstep my bounds. If I did, please tell me and I'll take the stockings down. I didn't—"

"Jasmine Walker." He growled low in his throat.

"Yes?"

"There's nowhere Trinity and I would rather be on Christmas than spending time with you."

CHAPTER 19

"Really?" Jazzy peered into his eyes, hope pressing against her chest. So much hope.

"Really. Besides my parents and Rio, you are top on my list of people we want to spend the holidays with."

"No kidding?"

"I can't seem to stay away from you, no matter how hard I try." He sounded both wistful and eager. "When Charlie called me and told me you'd gotten burned, I couldn't get to the hospital fast enough. Honestly, if a cop had been in the vicinity, I would have gotten a ticket. I ran a red light."

"For me?"

"Damn straight."

"Roan," she whispered. "What's going on here?"

"I think I'm falling for you."

"I think I'm falling for you too, but I'm scared. This is supposed to be temporary." Sabrina wriggled in Jazzy's arms, wanting down.

"Ditto. I never intended for this to happen," he

said. "I tried to keep you at arm's length but being with you has brought me back to life."

She blew out her breath through pursed lips and set Sabrina on the floor. The cat bolted to the fireplace hearth and began grooming herself. Nervously, Jazzy straightened to find Roan's eyes on her.

"I feel guilty for the way I've handled things between us, and I want you to know I'm sorry. You deserve better. I—"

She stepped closer. Went up on tiptoes and put an index finger to his lips. "Shh, Roan. It's okay. Everything is just as it should be."

"You got burned. Because I wasn't there to help you with the fire."

"My own clumsiness. No fault of yours."

"I shouldn't have stopped our lessons."

"You needed space. You needed time to think. We were moving too fast. Both of us have had our share of pain. We're skittish."

"You're the most understanding woman I've ever met."

She wasn't. Not really. But she did want only the best for Roan and Trinity, and if that meant she had to butt out of their lives, she would do it. From outside the house, the wind gusted and sent the chimes on her back porch dancing, various vibrating tones rippling through the air.

"The last time we were together . . ." Roan paused and held her gaze. "Things got pretty intense."

"Very."

"I've never wanted a woman as much as I want you," he said.

"Ever?" she whispered, hating that she sounded so vulnerable.

"Never, ever," he confirmed, his brown-eyed gaze locked onto her.

"Not even with—"

"*Never.*"

Seriously? He and Claire had been high school sweethearts and Roan was telling her the chemistry with his wife hadn't been as intense as what she and Roan now shared?

A flash of crackle-bright lightning lit the room, followed immediately by a boom of thunder. They both jumped as sleet started pelting the windows. Sabrina let out a yowl and sprinted under the couch.

"You should go," she said. "Before the roads start icing up."

"I'm not leaving you alone in this mess."

"Trinity needs you."

"She's safe with my folks."

"So . . ." She hitched in a breath. "You're willing to risk getting iced in with me?"

"I told you, Jazzy, there's nowhere else I'd rather be right now."

"Roan . . . I don't know what to say to that."

Taking care with her arm, he gathered her to him and kissed her. The kiss was just as potent, just as compelling as what they'd shared before. Had it really only been four days since they'd been together? It felt like eons.

He pulled back and looked down at her. "Are you hungry?"

"Yes," she said, sighing happily. "For you."

"C'mere," he said, guiding her to the couch. "I'm going to get you set up and then go make lunch."

"I can help."

"I know you can, but I want to do something special for you. So, you rest right here." He eased her down on the couch and covered her with the plush throw blanket. Sabrina came out from under the couch to settle into her lap.

Finding the remote control, Roan switched it on and set the channel for the local noon news. "You can keep an eye on the weather."

"That's a good idea."

"I'll get a fire started in the fireplace."

There was wood stacked on the hearth and a fire-starter log on the grate. In no time, Roan had a fire going and she got to watch his magnificent backside as he worked. Getting pampered was nice. Really nice.

He straightened and winked at her. "I'll go raid your kitchen and see what I can find to make a meal."

"Don't go to a lot of trouble, Roan. I have TV dinners in the freezer."

"You need a solid meal for healing," he said.

"I'm not sure what ingredients I have on hand."

"You leave that to me." He came to the couch, leaned over to kiss her forehead, and then disappeared into the kitchen.

Jazzy listened to him rummaging around, enjoying the sounds of him cooking for her. Nice. She curled up on the couch with Sabrina, mindful of her burned arm and watched the weather.

"Expect sleet for the next twenty-four hours,"

the weatherman warned. "Bring in pets and plants. The temperature will slide down into the upper teens tonight."

Jazzy shivered, pulled the blanket more tightly around herself and closed her eyes as the weather report shifted into a sports update. She must have dozed off, because the next thing she knew, Roan was in the room carrying a serving tray laden with two bowls of tomato soup and two grilled cheese sandwiches and a side dish of bread-and-butter pickles. Sabrina hopped down from the couch to stretch long before trotting off.

"Yum!" she said and moved to push herself up with her left hand, forgetting all about the burn. Pressure woke up the nerve endings and set them tingling. Wincing, she sank back.

"Easy does it." Roan settled the tray on the coffee table next to the Christmas village she'd set up and moved over to reshuffle the couch pillows to prop her left arm.

"Thank you."

He put a lumbar pillow across her lap and balanced the serving tray on top of it, and then he eased down next to her. "I don't know what you like to drink, so I just brought water."

"That's wonderful, thank you. FYI, iced tea is my jam, but I'm not picky. I'll drink most anything."

The news had given way to a Christmas movie. Hugh Grant, Colin Firth, Emma Thompson.

"Ooh, ooh!" Jazzy exclaimed. "*Love Actually*!"

"Pardon?"

"*Love Actually* is my favorite Christmas movie ever. Don't tell me you've never seen it."

"I've never seen it."

"Here, snuggle up." She spread her half of the throw blanket over him. "You're in for a treat."

They ate tomato soup and grilled cheese sandwiches and watched the movie, and when Jazzy teared up at the end, Roan reached for the tissues from the box on the end table and passed her a handful.

"Th-thanks," she blubbered and dabbed her eyes. "Did you like the movie?"

"I did."

"I love how realistic it is. Modern love is complicated and the movie captures that perfectly in every couple."

"Hmm," he said. "I guess I'm old-fashioned. While I enjoyed it, I really prefer the classics."

"Do tell." She turned toward him on the couch, her hair brushing against his shoulder, sending a ripple of sensation throughout her entire body. "What's your favorite Christmas movie?"

"Will I look too predictable if I say *It's a Wonderful Life*?"

"I knew it!" she crowed.

"*Miracle on 34th Street* is Trinity's fave. Although she's only four so she hasn't seen too many movies yet."

"*Elf* is coming on next." Jazzy pointed at the TV. "It's my second favorite."

"Mine too."

Her eyes sparkled. "Wanna watch it?"

"I'd rather do something else," he murmured.

"Oh? Is there another movie you want to see?"

"Nope." He leaned in closer.

"What *do* you want?" She wriggled her eyebrows.

"I'd like to get to know you better, Jazzy. We rushed things the other night at my place. How about we just talk?"

"Sure. I'd love that . . ." She put her hand on his knee. "Among other things."

"We don't have to have sex tonight."

"But it's not off the table, right?"

He laughed. "Let's just see what happens."

The wind blustered against the house, shaking sleet against the windowpanes.

"We're officially iced in," she whispered.

"I keep chains in my truck during the winter," he said. "I'm never truly iced in."

"Darn it. I should have known you'd be prepared for anything."

"I called Mom while I was prepping the food. Trinity is happy as a clam. Rio's over there and keeping her entertained. She's in good hands. Trinity and Rio adore each other."

"So, you can fully relax."

"I can."

"And no one's going to show up unexpectedly on my doorstep." Jazzy paused. "You don't get that much time to yourself, do you?"

"Single fatherhood is a full-time job," he said. "But I wouldn't change anything. Trinity is my heart and soul."

"A little piece of Claire you'll always carry with you."

"Yes." He hesitated. "Does that bother you?"

"Not at all. *Love Actually* is my favorite Christmas movie, remember. I get how complex modern life is."

They were in the middle of the couch, their bodies turned to each other, their heads resting on the back of the couch as they gazed into each other's eyes. It felt so easy here with him. So peaceful.

They started talking, getting to know each other better. Roan told her how he'd gotten into campfire cooking. When he was growing up on Slope Ridge Ranch, his parents had turned the place into a wedding venue for cowboy weddings to earn extra income. His parents had bought a chuckwagon to use for weddings, parties, and other catered events. Cooking on the chuckwagon had been Roan's first job. From his dad, he'd learned to man a smoker like a professional and had quickly honed his skills. He started entering contests, mainly for the exposure to help grow the family business, but he'd gotten so good at campfire cooking, that the catering eclipsed the wedding venue.

When he and Claire married, they bought the ranch from his parents so the senior Sullivans could retire to a condo on Lake Twilight. Slope Ridge Ranch started making more money off the barbecue than the cutting horses. Claire was the one who brought desserts to the menu, adding Dutch oven cobblers, cookies, and dump cakes. Then Claire got pregnant with Trinity and Roan took over the campfire baking. For two wonderful years, life had been like a storybook—financial success, a thriving YouTube channel, critical acclaim, and a healthy loving family. And then Claire had a minor surgical procedure that went awry, and everything came crashing down. He stopped cooking. Sold the chuckwagon. Pulled the plug on the social media accounts and concentrated on raising his daughter. It was all he had stamina for.

"You knocked me out of my rut, Jazzy," he murmured. "I'm grateful for that."

"Same," she said. "After Danny dumped me, I threw myself into volunteer work. It helped ease my grief, but it kept me from focusing on my own wants and needs. You've given me the skills I need to pursue what's quickly becoming a passionate hobby. Baking."

"What kind of things were you interested in before you met Danny?"

"Goodness, that feels like a lifetime ago." She paused, remembering. "My dad's a game warden, so I grew up in the great outdoors—hunting, fishing, hiking, boating."

"What were your favorite activities out of those?"

"Oh, boating for sure, with catch-and-release fishing a close second. I love the water and it's the reason I bought a house a stone's throw from the marina. Walking around the lake is my main form of exercise. It's four miles, round-trip." She described her daily walks, how the activity got her out of her head and into her body.

Roan listened intently as she told him about her excursions on Lake Twilight and the Brazos River. She spoke of how, as a kid, she loved rising before dawn with her dad to hit the best fishing spots before other anglers showed up. She lit up as she detailed the joys of sitting in the johnboat with her dad, watching the red bobber floating atop the water for signs of a fish strike, and eating the PB&J sandwiches they'd packed. She heard her voice take on a dreamy quality as she accessed those memories and shared them with him.

While the sleet fell outside, they talked about the things that meant the most to them, letting down their guards, being open with each other in a way they hadn't been before. She talked about what it was like spending her life in and out of hospitals until she was eight years old. He spoke of watching Trinity's birth and how becoming a father had changed him forever.

The conversation kept going. He shared the things he loved about cutting horses. She discussed being a pediatric nurse and the sense of fulfillment her job brought to her life. They delved into TV shows they liked, books they enjoyed, and places they'd traveled. They avoided nothing except the finer details about Roan's relationship with Claire and Jazzy's with Danny. Neither one of them wanted to erect stumbling blocks in their escalating emotional intimacy. They could delve into that later if need be.

It delighted Jazzy to discover, that despite their ten-year age difference, they had a lot in common. Turned out they both loved Skittles and Starburst, particularly the strawberry and cherry. They agreed that the lost art of square dancing deserved a revival, and that Saturday morning was the happiest time of the week, and there was nothing more soothing than spending time in nature. They laughed to learn neither one of them could whistle, snap their fingers, nor roll their tongues. They both preferred beer to wine, cake to pies, and sweet potatoes to russets. Morning people by nature, they had trouble staying awake past ten thirty at night. They both spoke rudimentary Spanish and shared the same favorite color, blue. Although Roan preferred the darker tones while the lighter blue-green hues attracted Jazzy most. Their musical tastes dovetailed, both into country music, especially songs and artists with a bluegrass tinge.

When it came to their dislikes, they found their least favorite things complemented each other. He hated ironing. She loved it because it gave her a chance to zone out and she enjoyed the smell of spray starch. Jazzy didn't care for yardwork, but Roan loved the sense of accomplishment a well-manicured lawn gave him. He didn't like corner brownies, they were too crunchy, whereas she wanted only corner pieces, enjoying the crunch. She found balancing her checkbook tedious. He looked forward to Sunday afternoon when he did his finances. She hated doing dishes but didn't mind dusting. He was the opposite.

Finally, they fell silent, and just enjoyed sitting with each other in the quiet. The fire was dying down and required more wood to keep it roaring, but she was reluctant to break the magic of their getting-to-know-you gab session.

"How's the arm?" Roan asked after a bit.

It was only then Jazzy realized she'd been gingerly fingering the gauze bandage. "It aches a little, but not bad enough to take a painkiller."

"You sure?"

"You're all the medicine I need, Roan Sullivan." She leaned forward to plant a soft kiss on his lips.

"Jazzy." He breathed her name on a sigh.

"I'm so glad Danny asked Andi to marry him."

"What?" Roan pulled back, looking as dazed as if she'd yanked him from a deep sleep filled with sexy dreams.

"If Andi hadn't come into the Recovery Room that night flashing her engagement ring and bragging about how she was going to win the cookie challenge I would never have considered entering the contest."

"You wouldn't have gotten burned either," Roan pointed out.

"Totally worth it," she said, standing up. "It brought me here . . . to now . . ." She leveled a steady gaze at him and held out her hand. "To *you*."

CHAPTER 20

Roan stared at her extended palm. Every pulse point in his body ticked a desperate message. *Take her to bed, take her to bed, take her to bed.*

Biology was a ravenous bear, awakened from winter slumber, hungry to meet physical needs. But unlike a bear, he had a conscience. His mind warred with his body. His flesh wanted her, right here, right now, with a lust so strong it blunted the part of his brain screaming at him not to take advantage of the situation. Jazzy was vulnerable. If they made love now it would bind them in a way he wasn't sure either one of them was ready for. He was supposed to be the rebound guy. Not her forever lover.

But Lord, how he wanted her!

She loomed. Waiting.

He took her hand.

Jazzy tugged him to his feet.

He looked down at her.

They were both breathing heavily, a thin sheen of perspiration pearled on the little indention between her upper lip and her nose. Beer can tab, his father called that spot. Jazzy would know the medical name. He thought about asking her, anything to break the magnetic spell leading them to just one place.

The bedroom.

"Maybe I should go lie down," she said, her gaze hooked on his. "I feel a little dizzy."

Hell, so did he.

"Which way is your room?" he asked.

"This way." Interlacing their fingers, she turned and led him down the short hallway to a bedroom made for comfort. Everything in it was soft and plush and inviting from the frilly white bedspread to the low-wattage lightbulbs, to the queen-sized mattress loaded with pillows.

She led him to the bed.

He didn't resist. He wanted this too much to put up a fight and she seemed to want it just as badly as he did. Her knees were trembling. Hell. So were his.

"Let's get comfortable," she invited.

"Are you sure?" he asked, meeting her gaze, searching her eyes.

"I wouldn't have brought you in here if I wasn't. Are *you* sure, Roan?"

"Okay." He chuckled. "I can see how annoying that sounds."

Her smile engulfed him and warmed his heart. Throwing him a sultry look, she wriggled out of her jeans.

Roan sucked in his breath at the sight of her black lace panties. Not only because she was the sexiest thing he'd ever laid eyes on but also because he wanted so much more from her than sex.

She clicked her tongue and shook her head. "Hey, no fair. You're still dressed."

He unsnapped his jeans.

She watched his every move.

Slowly, he eased down the zipper.

She touched the tip of her tongue to her upper lip. Gulped.

He eased his pants down, casting suggestive glances her way as he went.

Jazzy made impatient noises.

Roan slowed down on purpose.

"Stop torturing me!"

He widened his grin and moved even slower.

"Need some help?" Her grin matched his own and she came toward him. Before he could answer, she dropped to her knees in front of him.

He took off his jeans, and kicked them across the room to join hers on the floor. They were both pantless but still in their underwear and shirts.

"Now, isn't that better?"

"Depends on your definition of *better*."

Her gaze drifted to his direction. Her smile turned wicked and then she looked up to meet his eyes. "Let's get this party started."

They finished undressing. Giggling, Jazzy scrambled onto the bed, bouncing like a teenager and patted the spot beside her. Roan joined her. They wrapped their arms around each other's waists and plunged deep into the mattress.

"Kiss me," she begged. "Kiss me like it's the end of the world."

She didn't need to ask twice, because Jazzy changed everything in his world. Roan covered her mouth with his and she clutched him in a frantic embrace.

Finally, Jazzy let out a soft hiss and wriggled away.

"What is it? What's wrong?"

"My arm."

"Oh, Jazz. I'm sorry. I forgot about your burn. This is silly. We shouldn't do this. You're hurt."

"I'm just fine. We just need to be a little careful. It's only my arm. The good stuff is just fine." She giggled again and the bubbly sound lifted his heart.

"Are you sure?"

"One hundred percent."

"I don't want to hurt you."

"You should know by now, Roan Sullivan, there's no escaping life's pains."

"I do know that," he said. "It's why I'm so scared."

She cupped his face in her hands and stared into his eyes. "I'm scared too."

"Do you still want to—"

In way of answer, she kissed him to shut him up.

He squeezed her tight, so grateful to have found her. She was a balm to his wounds. The pain of the man who'd lost his wife and become a single dad, the ache he hid from the rest of the world with a strong work ethic, slipped away and he wasn't afraid for her to see him bare naked and starving for her.

Jazzy.

She was as effervescent as her name. Lively and fun, but sensible and down-to-earth. The girl next door who grew up to be a raving beauty. *Jazzy, Jazzy, Jazzy.*

"Roan?" she murmured.

"Yes," he whispered against her lips.

"Could you go get the condoms in my bathroom vanity? I want you to make love to me now."

"If you're certain that's what you want." He didn't want to do anything she wasn't one hundred percent sure of, but it would kill him not to keep going. The day she'd abandoned him and crawled out the bedroom window had shaken his confidence and now he was gun-shy. He wanted her more than he wanted to breathe. But he wanted it to be right. He wanted this to be a wonderful experience for them both.

"I've never been surer of anything in my entire life, but I'm worried . . ."

"What about, sweetheart?" He pushed her hair from her forehead, peered down into her eyes.

"That I'll disappoint you."

"That can never happen."

"How do you know? I might be completely lousy in bed."

"Someone with your optimistic, can-do attitude could never be bad in bed. Don't give it a second thought."

"I don't know a lot of tricks or maneuvers."

"I don't need that. All I need is you. And if you want to learn tricks and techniques I would be happy to serve as your tutor."

"Really?"

"Hey, that's the benefit of sleeping with an older man, right?"

"Does it bother you?" she asked. "Our age difference?"

"Does it bother you?" It did worry him a bit. Their different phases of life. Roan in the settled and secure phase, Jazzy exploring and searching for what she wanted from life.

"Not in the least," she said.

"So, I won't worry about our age gap if you don't worry about disappointing me."

"Deal," she said. "Now that we have that squared away, I have an assignment for you."

"Oh?"

"After you get the condoms, hang out in the bathroom a few minutes."

"Why?"

"I want to get the room ready."

"Ready?"

"I want to make this special. I want to set the scene."

"It's not necessary."

"Still," she said. "I want to do this up right."

"Okay," he said. "This is your place, your show. I'll let you set it anyway you want."

The door opened a crack, and Roan poked his head in. "Ready?"

"Ready." She crooked a finger, inviting him to enter.

He came into the room naked, his bare chest a sight to behold. Jazzy lost her breath. This man was magnificent, and she was about to make love to him. She felt tremulous and a little dizzy. The moment had come.

His gaze was on her face and his eyes glistened in the light flickering candles. "You put on a robe."

"Just so you could take it off." Her voice came out high and light.

"Unwrap you like a Christmas present?"

"Exactly."

He came toward her, the wooden floor creaking beneath his weight. His eyes like lasers, burning her. Her heart rate sped up, kicking into a gallop. She couldn't recall ever being this excited.

"I thought you ran out on me," she confessed.

"I almost did," he admitted.

"Why?"

"Because I want you too damn much."

"And that's bad?"

"It makes me feel out of control."

"Me too. You're not alone. We're in this together."

His rough masculine fingers went to the tie holding her robe together and slowly, he undid the sash, exposing her bare breasts and belly.

He lowered his head then, fitting his mouth over hers. His kiss was insistent, intense, much different than the soft, gentle kisses he'd given her up until now. There was a power behind this kiss. Electricity. Danger. She thrilled to the sensation.

Roan's kiss took her to a place where she'd never been before. A place that drove all her attention to the physicality of him. Everything was him. The sight of his honed muscles, the taste of his masculinity, the smell of pure cowboy. Her body tingled in response and everywhere he touched, with his lips and his hands, she caught fire.

He was careful to avoid brushing against her

bandaged left arm and she admired how he was able to be both cautious and wild. A single father and yet at the same time a very sexy man.

She sank against him and closed her eyes. He kissed her forehead, his lips warm and firm. He moved down the bridge of her nose, to her eyelids, first one, and then the other. From there he moved to the tip of her nose and then to her mouth again. It felt as if he'd always belonged there and had finally come home.

"I can't take much more of this," she panted, pulling back and looking up into his eyes. "I want you. I need you. Take me, *please*."

He slipped her robe from her shoulders and let it drift to the floor, wrapped his arms around her, scooped her up, and carried her to the bed. She felt special in his embrace. Cherished. Treasured.

"Now, please."

"You got it." Roan took control. Not the least bit hesitant. Joining her on the bed and pulling her down on top of him. His hot mouth in charge.

His aggressiveness didn't frighten her. Not one little bit. She knew she was safe with him and met his forcefulness in kind. She trusted him completely. No more doubts or fears.

They went at each other like animals, clutching and clawing, nipping, and nibbling. She was straddling him, each leg over his washboard waist. He took hold of her hair and tugged lightly, pulling her head back as he looked up at her, his long dark lashes softening the angular geometry of his face. His eyes, the color of Swiss chocolate, searching her.

He looked so handsome, a man in his virile prime. She wriggled with delight that he was hers. He was her man. And she was his woman. They belonged together. It was too soon to say it out loud, but she knew it in the depth of her heart, from the bottom of her soul. It was unsettling this certainty and at the same time rapturous.

Roan lowered his eyelids, and in that moment, he looked a little confused and vulnerable. As if he had just realized she had the power to shatter him like fragile glass. His expression shook her to the core. She could hurt him, more than he could hurt her. He'd loved and lost before. He'd walked a hard road. He was trusting her. Jazzy would do her best to not cause him pain.

Her heart turned to mush. This was no small thing. No insignificant joining. They were embarking on an important journey together.

Gently, he raised up on his elbows and leaned forward to capture one of her breasts in his mouth. The sensation derailed her, stirred her, made her ache for more. He knew just what to do and how to do it. The promise of happily-ever-after dangled in front of her like a carrot.

He moved from her achy nipple to the other one, stroking his tongue over her skin until she whimpered, helpless and hungry. He was looking at her again, his eyes on her face, watching her emotions play over her features. She could see her reflection in his eyes and was shocked by what she saw. A young woman, open and ready and vulnerable.

Roan shifted, sitting up tall in the bed, his back against the headboard. Jazzy in his lap now, her bottom against his hard erection. He wrapped his legs around her, pulling her closer. It wouldn't take much for him to slip inside her.

How she wanted him inside her!

She heard the crinkle of foil wrapper and wondered vaguely where he'd hidden the condom. It didn't matter. He was rolling it on.

Locked her leg around his waist, stared deeply into his eyes, felt herself falling as if she'd dived off a cliff into a cool, still pool of deep water.

It seemed impossible to look away. Their gazes locked. Welded. She could see his emotions play across his face—desire, trepidation, excitement, worry. Reaching up, she pressed the pad of her thumb between his eyebrows, ironing out the frown wrinkling there.

"It's going to be all right," she whispered, "it's all going to be okay. You and me? We were meant to be."

As soon as she said it, Jazzy started fretting. Had she overstepped boundaries? Had she jumped to conclusions? Was she building castles in the air? Had she assumed too much, too soon?

But no. He smiled, such a gleeful smile, it triggered her own grin and she was out of her head and right back into the moment. Right back into her body and the sweet blissful sensations Roan stirred inside her.

His hands were all over her and hers were all over him and man, oh man, did it feel good. Their mouths explored. She tasted him, salty and at the same time sweet. Kettle corn, she thought and laughed out loud. He increased the pressure, as he navigated her lips, her chin, the underside of her throat, her breasts, her belly, the tender spot between her legs.

She moaned and whimpered, giggled, and sighed. So many sensations coming at her from all sides.

"You feeling all right?" he asked.

"Never better. Don't stop."

"Yes, ma'am."

He kissed swirly circles of heat over her skin. Her body incredibly sensitive, raw, and ready. So ready for him.

"Please, please, I have to have you now!"

He made a guttural sound, more like an animal than a man. Lifted her up, and then tugged her down on his rock-hard erection. She rode him fierce and fast. His hands clamped around her waist and he held her in place as she pumped against him.

They grunted and groaned together. Traveling as one. Racing to the summit of their joining. Desperate to get there. Desperate for each other.

She felt the pressure building, expanding, beckoning. She *had* to get there. Nothing could stop them now.

It hit her like an earthquake, shaking her to her core, rattling her in a way she'd never experienced. The shudder gripped her low in her belly and spread out through her body in rhythmic clenches.

She broke apart, shattered as sure as glass dropped on concrete. Gasping, she fell forward, her forehead bumping against his. Her entire body instantly limp and quivering. The same thing was happening to him, she could feel his own reaction inside of her. He let out a cry. Her name. Jazzy.

"Wh-what was that?" she stammered.

His laugh was hoarse and happy.

"I'm not kidding," she said. "What was *that* feeling?"

"You never felt that before?" He looked confused.

Jazzy shook her head. "Nothing like that. I mean I've come close. I've had some pleasant sensations. But never that kind of soul-wringing release. What was it?"

"That, my love, was an orgasm."

"*Nooo*." An orgasm? All this time she'd thought she'd been having them, but boy had she been wrong. She couldn't wait to do this again.

"Yes." He nodded and looked just the teeniest bit smug. "Are you telling me that's your first one?"

CHAPTER 21

Yawning blissfully, Jazzy curled into Roan's side and promptly fell asleep. Her sweet scent, combined with the musky smell of their sex, tickled his nose.

Nothing had prepared him for the tender feelings churning inside him. He wanted to tell her to hell with being her rebound man. Yell from the rooftops that he wanted more. A lot more. But he had no right to ask that of her. Even if she didn't realize it, her emotions lay tangled up with Danny and if Roan told her how he felt, it would only confuse her. If she chose him out of confusion, he'd always wonder if she'd picked him for himself or because he'd given Jazzy her first orgasm.

Ah damn, this was getting complicated.

A hollow ache dug into his chest, but he ignored it. He'd known what he was getting into when he'd started something up with her. Known it was temporary. He was going to milk this for every bit of enjoyment he could get and give her pleasure in return. After all, he was an old hand at letting go. This fling was a growth opportunity for them both and that's the only way he'd allow himself to see it.

Jazzy's optimism had rubbed off on him. Any time with her was a good time. He wouldn't get greedy and long for a commitment she was much too young to give. He should know. He'd gotten married at her age. Claire had been twenty-two. And while things had eventually worked out, they'd had some tumultuous early years. Honestly, they'd been too young for marriage and it could easily have gone in the opposite direction.

He glanced down to see the top of her blond head resting on his shoulder. He could feel her breathing, the long, steady intake of air, the rise and fall of her chest against his. Jealous of her easy sleep, Roan closed his eyes and tried to stop thinking.

But his eyes felt dry and itchy, the way they did when he unloaded hay from the tractor. He massaged both eyelids simultaneously with his thumb and middle finger. Breaking things off with her would be tough, but he didn't have to do it now.

Her eyelids flickered as if she were in REM sleep, dreaming, he hoped, of him. She made a soft noise and burrowed closer. He couldn't resist wrapping one arm around her, savoring the heat from her lush body warming him. He wanted to swaddle her in a cocoon of love and keep her safe from the dark side of the world.

It wasn't his place to protect her. They weren't in a committed relationship. But damn if the urge didn't swell and press against his heart until Roan found it difficult to catch his breath.

In too deep.

He was in too deep and he didn't know how to back out of this without hurting them both.

"Roan," she murmured.

"You awake?"

"Uh-huh," she said lazily and traced a finger in the whorl of hair between his nipples. "Sorry I dozed off on you."

"I enjoy watching you sleep," he said, toying with her hair. "It's good you're getting some rest. How's your arm?"

She held up her left arm for him to see. "Just fine."

"All our rolling around in the sheets didn't get the pain stirred up?"

"I was too busy enjoying the pleasure to notice any pain. You turned my world upside down, Mr. Sullivan. You're amazing."

Her compliment turned him inside out and left him with a desire to give her nothing but pleasure and all the joy he could muster. He kissed the top of her head and curled his arm around her shoulder, letting her know he was as amazed as she.

With his fingertips, he gently massaged her scalp and her soft moan rewarded him. Each caress stirred her scent, the delicious feminine aroma he'd come to associate with Jazzy. The fragrance embedded, evermore imprinting into his memory banks. He would never forget this moment.

Her silky hair was soft and fine. He loved how it felt slipping through his fingers. She shivered against him and whimpered, signaling his touch was arousing her all over again.

It had been so long since he'd had intimacy

like this, and he'd missed the physical connection something fierce. He'd forgotten just how much snuggling and cuddling could rejuvenate a man. Sex, too, of course, but he enjoyed the aftermath as much as the act. Claire had said he was a unicorn among men, but he thought maybe that wasn't so true. Guys liked tenderness too. Some of them just didn't know how to show it.

He feared he'd lost the ability to connect in his anger and grief over losing his wife, but Jazzy had gifted her mind, body, and sparkling personality, waking him up, bringing him back to himself. What a beautiful present. He'd become a shell of a man, kicked in the teeth by life, putting one foot in front of the other and moving forward because he had to for his daughter. Then here was Jazzy, innocent as the first blush of spring after a hard winter. Breathing life into him, coaxing him to believe in grace and goodness again. She'd refilled and refreshed him in a way he thought long out of his reach. Brought light and happiness with her.

Staggered by the depth of his feelings for her, Roan shifted Jazzy around so he could have access to her delectable mouth, and he kissed her with such a rush of gratitude and thanksgiving that it left him breathless. Every fiber in his body pulsed with the need to tell her he loved her, but he couldn't do it. She was in his life for only a short time. He was the rebound guy. Saying he loved her would make it much harder to break up with her.

So instead of talking, he used his tongue to rouse her again and soon, he was reaching for another condom.

Their second time was softer, longer, more intentional. He lingered on spots, fully getting to know her body. Aware of how little time they had together and wanting to maximize it. Roan had lived long enough to understand life was short and you had to grab the good times while you could.

Finally, when they'd worked each other into fevered urgency, she arched her hips against him, dropped open her legs, and let him in. Her body was warm and wet and welcoming and Roan slipped right on inside.

Gasping, she locked her legs around his waist and tugged him in deeper. He wriggled his hips and found a solid fit. The two of them, one now. She hissed in her breath.

"You okay?" he asked, worried he'd hurt her.

"Absolutely fine. Keep wiggling those hips, cowboy. Yeehaw." Her enthusiasm fed his as she egged him on.

They moved as one, chasing the peak. The candlelight threw their shadows onto the wall and it was erotic watching their silhouettes. They changed positions, several times, trying out different styles and being careful not to hurt Jazzy's arm. His favorites were when they were face-to-face and peering into each other. Looking into her eyes as he moved over her body or she moved over him nourished their intimacy. For a long, good time they sated themselves with a consistent tempo that carried them higher and higher toward the pinnacle of their joining.

When Roan couldn't stand the pressure any longer, he stared into her bewitching blue eyes to see his own reflection there. He saw a man on the verge of falling wildly in love. A man tottering on the brink of losing his heart.

A groan pushed from his throat, ragged and hoarse.

A corresponding moan slipped from Jazzy.

They clasped each other. Called each other's name. They clung like shipwreck survivors to a life raft.

Together, they came apart. Shuddered with the release. Safe in each other's arms.

Then Roan felt Jazzy's warm tears on his skin. "What is it?" he asked, alarmed. "I hurt you. It's your arm, isn't it? I knew we shouldn't have done this."

"No, no. Please believe me. I'm fine."

"What is it, then? What's wrong? Why are you crying?"

She nodded. "Don't worry. They're happy tears."

"Why are you so happy that you're crying?" He sat up and reached over to flick her tears away with his thumb.

"Because I felt it twice!"

"Your second orgasm?"

"Uh-huh." She smiled up into his face. "I can't believe what I've been missing all this time. Thank you, Roan, for such a precious gift."

They slept in each other's arms and woke not long after dawn. Jazzy opened her eyes to find she was face-to-face with her lover. She watched him sleep for a bit before he roused and grinned at her.

She couldn't believe he was here in her house, in her bed. How had she gotten so lucky to land such an amazing man? *No putting the cart before the horse*, she scolded herself. *It's still too soon for that*.

"Want to cook breakfast together?" he asked.

"You betcha." Remembering everything about their night together, she grinned. It had been outstanding. Far better than anything she could have dreamed. "After a long hot shower."

"Together?"

"I'm game if you are."

Roan wrapped Jazzy's bandaged arm in cling wrap, then they took a shower together and got frisky again. Jazzy had her third orgasm within twenty-four hours. She'd gotten hooked on him. They dressed and padded to the kitchen to prepare breakfast. Roan checked in with his folks. Trinity was still sleeping and since the roads remained icy and the temperature below freezing, his mom suggested they keep their granddaughter for another day.

"Call me if she wants to come home," Roan said. "I'll put the chains on the truck and come for her."

He pocketed his phone and smiled at Jazzy. "We have another whole day to ourselves, Rainbow."

"Rainbow?" She smiled. "Did you just give me a nickname?"

"I suppose I did. Do you hate it?" He blushed and looked so adorable she couldn't resist going up on her tiptoes to kiss him. "You're like a rainbow after a storm, radiating hope with your colorful light."

"Aww! I love it." She nibbled his bottom lip. "Now I have to think of a good nickname for you."

He started humming the old Rolling Stones' song "She's a Rainbow."

"You are entirely too happy, Mr. Sullivan." Playfully, she poked him in the ribs.

"Hey." He beamed. "You aren't the only one who had three orgasms in one night."

Feeling as if she were in some fairy-tale movie, Jazzy playfully pinched his butt and he pinched hers in return. Then she giggled and rested her head on his chest.

Roan looked down at her with adoring eyes. Eyes shiny and sharp and appreciative. He looked at her as if she were the missing piece to his puzzle. Danny had never looked at her like that. Not once the entire four years they'd gone together. Not that she'd seen.

"So, you know what we need to do?" she asked, intertwining their fingers, and swinging their arms. Light. Breezy. Happy. So damn happy.

Moonstruck. That was the word for her feelings and the way Roan was looking at her. *Moonstruck*.

"What's that?" He leaned backward to kiss her cheek.

"We have to come up with a twist on the rugelach. I've made prune and apricot and while those were good, they're not knock-it-out-of-the-park good. Plus, we need a second recipe for when I make it to the final round."

"That's where I come in." Teasingly, Roan flexed his biceps. "You need something Christmassy."

"Exactly."

"Breakfast first," he said. "I think better on a full stomach."

"Avocado whole wheat toast work?"

"Simple and heart healthy. I'll mash the avocado. You toast the bread."

"On it!"

While they made and ate their breakfast, Jazzy threw out filling possibilities for her soon-to-be award-winning rugelach. "Pecans and honey?"

"That would be tasty." Roan got up to rinse their dishes and stack them in the dishwasher.

Jazzy noticed. Danny hadn't helped with chores unless she nagged. *Stop comparing him to Danny.*

"But not highly original," Jazzy said, taking out the measuring cups and the digital scale she'd bought on Roan's advice. Precise weight made for precise baked goods.

"What flavors suggest Christmas?" Roan rounded up the ingredients from the fridge including the cream cheese and sour cream that made Christine Noble's rugelach dough so special.

"Trinity would be a big help with this," Jazzy said. "I miss that little munchkin."

"Me too," Roan said. "This is the longest I've been away from her since her mom passed."

"Should we call her and get her input?"

"Let's do it." Roan called his mom and asked her to put Trinity on the phone. He switched to speaker mode so Jazzy could get in on the conversation.

"Jazzy and I are making cookies," he told his daughter. "And we want Christmas flavors. What are your favorite Christmas treats?"

"You're with Jazzy?" Mrs. Sullivan asked in the background.

"I'm at her house. We got iced in," Roan explained.

"Hi, Jazzy!" Roan's mom exclaimed.

"Hi, Ava. Hi, Trinity." Jazzy took the bread from the popup toaster.

"I'm so pleased you and my son are able to ride out this winter storm together."

Hmm, what did that mean? Jazzy shot a glance at Roan, who was grinning as he set the ingredients in front of the food processer she'd also bought on his suggestion. She was turning into a real, live baker.

He silently mouthed, *Mom likes you,* and Jazzy felt her face heat. She liked his mom too, and his daughter, but she wasn't so sure she wanted his mother putting two and two together. This relationship was so new. Fragile. She wanted it on solid ground before everyone in Twilight knew they were a couple.

"I wanna visit Jazzy," Trinity said.

"Soon as the ice storm is over," Jazzy promised. "You can help me make cookies."

"Yay!" Her high little voice brought a big smile to Jazzy's face.

"So, Doodlebug, what's your favorite Christmas flavor?" Jazzy asked, steering the four-year-old back to the topic at hand.

"Candy canes!"

Jazzy met Roan's gaze over his phone and shot him a what-do-you-think expression.

He shrugged. "Got any candy canes on hand?"

"They're all over my Christmas tree," Jazzy said.

They thanked Trinity and Ava, and after a few more pleasantries, ended the call.

"I've never had candy cane rugelach before," he said. "Do you want to give it a go?"

"What's the worst that could happen, right?" Jazzy shrugged. "We throw it out and start over?"

"What if we added a little chocolate?" he suggested. "Maybe as a drizzle on the cookie after it's baked?"

"Spot-on."

"Maybe some cinnamon as well?"

"Unusual combo."

"All the more reason to try it."

"Sure." Jazzy opened the cabinet and grabbed for the cinnamon. "Could you snag a candy cane off the tree?"

"You got it." He popped into the living room and quickly returned with a candy cane. "Kitchen mallet?"

"Top drawer on your left." She waved.

Roan found the mallet and smashed up the candy cane. They weighed and measured and added the ingredients to the food processor in stages. As Jazzy dumped in the cinnamon she'd measured, Roan said, "Whoa, whoa."

"What is it?" She blinked at him.

"That doesn't look like cinnamon." He picked up the bottle she'd just used and turned it around for her to read.

Ginger.

"Oh no." Jazzy groaned and smacked her forehead with her palm. "I should have read the label. I'm such a dolt. In my job, we read labels three times before administering anything. Why is it so easy for me at work and so hard for me to do that when I'm baking?"

"First of all, you're not a dolt," Roan said. "Secondly, we're making this up as we go, so there's no rules. Thirdly . . ."

"Yes?" She captured his gaze.

"This," he said and leaned over to kiss her.

"Hmm." She rested herself against his chest. "I'm really liking thirdly."

He chuckled and kissed her again, a kiss so fantastic it had her toes curling inside her socks. If she didn't break this off, they'd be back in her bed in nothing flat.

"Should we throw this mess out and start over?" She eyed the dough, turned yellow-orange with ginger.

"We've gone this far, might as well bake it up and see what happens."

"I like your adventuresome attitude."

They finished the dough and put it in the oven to bake. Tomorrow, they could try a different rendition in the Dutch oven.

Jazzy paced while the dough baked. She desperately wanted these cookies to work out. Her motivation was no longer besting Andi. She'd let go of that objective from the moment she'd started falling for Roan. She had only one thought about this baking challenge. Do Roan proud. Show him how much his help and talent had improved her skills. Show him there was a reason for him to return to campfire baking. People needed him and his expertise. Now she wanted to win for him.

"It smells pretty darn good," Roan said.

"So did the salt cookies I made with Charlie."

"Where's that Jazzy optimism I know and love?" he asked.

Love.

He loved her optimism. Did that mean he could fall in love with her too? *Chill out. Don't rush things. Enjoy the ride.*

When the cookies were out of the oven, they looked as good as they smelled. Roan added the chocolate drizzle. The dough was perfectly flakey. Better than any of the dough she'd made before. Jazzy poked a cooling cookie with her finger.

"I'm not scared to try one," Roan said, scooping up the cookie she'd poked and putting it in his mouth.

"Well?" She knotted her hands into fists.

He chewed thoughtfully and then a big smile spread across his face. "These are amazing, Jazz. Try one."

She popped a cookie into her mouth and the first thing she tasted was the chocolate followed by the subtle hint of ginger. It wasn't too much. Not too strong. Followed by the soft crunch of the melted peppermint tucked inside the dough. It was a tongue-tingly taste sensation and she reached for another cookie just as Roan did. They munched, oohing and aahing over their creation.

"The best recipes often come from happy accidents. You bake cookies just like this on Thursday and I guarantee you'll make it to the finals. Well done, Jazzy, well done."

"Really?" His praise washed over her like sunshine.

"Straight up."

"You honestly think I have a real chance to win the bake-off?"

"With this recipe? I certainly do."

"So maybe I should save this recipe for the finals and find another to perfect for the elimination round."

"Good idea," he said and stole another cookie from the plate. "We can start work on that next."

"I have the perfect name for these cookies," she said.

"What's that?"

"Chocolate-Gingermint Roanies."

"Roanies?" He looked amused. "Why?"

"Because I couldn't have done this without you."

CHAPTER 22

Roan couldn't stop watching Jazzy. She pirouetted around the kitchen on a baker's high. He got it. He'd experienced the same pleasure whenever he nailed a recipe.

"Will you be all right if you don't win?" he asked, worried because winning seemed to mean so much to her. While he thought she stood a good chance of victory, anything could happen in a competition and things could go south for even the most experienced baker.

"I'm going to win," she said with certainty, eating her third Chocolate-Gingermint Roanie. He thought it was sweet of her to name the recipe for him. "These cookies are amazeballs."

"You're amazeballs."

She blushed prettily and did another spin. "Mmm, mmm."

"I'm serious though," Roan said. "How much of a letdown will it be if the contest goes sideways?"

"Have a little faith in me, big man." She tickled him under his chin.

Roan wanted nothing more than to pull her into his arms and kiss her silly, but he resisted. She was such a joy to be around, and he hated raining on her parade, but he needed an answer to his question.

"Is this where I confess my pettiness and say finally beating the pants off Andi at *something* would feed my ego."

"You aren't petty, Jazzy. Not in the least." His gaze searched her face, aching for her to be honest and admit to him that if she won, she hoped she'd get Danny back. "But why is besting Andi so important?"

"Andi took everything from me, but most of all she took my pride. I'm trying to get it back."

"And Danny?" he asked boldly, locking his eyes on hers.

She blinked but didn't glance away. "I am *not* trying to win Danny back."

"You sure of that?"

"You said you're just the rebound guy," she countered, sounding defensive. "Why do you want to know?"

"Maybe I'm not satisfied just being the rebound guy," he blurted before he even knew he was going to say it. "Maybe I want more."

She sucked in her breath and her eyes widened. "Really?"

"After last night, I can't get the idea out of my head, but if you're still hung up on Danny, it's a land mine where I don't want to tread."

She stepped closer to him, touching the tips of her socks patterned with snowflakes to his bare toes. "Roan Sullivan."

"Jazzy Walker," he said, matching her serious tone.

"I am with *you* for however long this relationship works for us. You're the one I want to be with and no one else." She paused and gave him a pointed stare. "Got it?"

He searched her face, trying to find clues that she was deluding herself, but she peered into his eyes, unflinching.

"Got it."

"Good," she said. "Now could you please help me write down this recipe, so we don't forget it?"

What was at stake if she didn't win the contest?

Jazzy mulled over Roan's question. Clearly, he was jealous of Danny and she couldn't blame him. Hoping to show Andi up in front of Danny had been her primary motivation for entering the contest in the beginning. It was also the reason she'd applied for a job as a traveling nurse. If she couldn't turn Danny's head back to her, she wanted out of Twilight. She didn't want to see her ex marry Andi.

But that futile—and in retrospect, immature—motivation ended the moment she started having feelings for Roan. She was a one-man kind of gal and she'd lost respect for Danny as she spent more and more time with Roan. She still cared about Danny, sure. He'd been her first love and he'd taught her what she didn't want in a relationship. She owed him a debt of gratitude for that.

Roan was busy writing out the recipe on an index card, sitting at the bar looking studious. She studied him, and her heart quickened. He looked so handsome, so solid and reliable. He was a man you could count on. A man who did not trifle with feelings or run hot and cold.

Good grief, but she was crazy about him and she wasn't sure how it had happened so quickly. She was afraid to bank on her feelings because of how fast this whole thing was happening. The romantics in Twilight would say they were meant to be, but she'd thought that once about Danny and look how that turned out.

She would take her time with Roan and not rush into anything.

Um, you already rushed into his bed.

Yes, well, and now she was paying the consequences. Falling hard for him when it was too soon to let down her guard. Damn her eternal optimism.

He glanced up and caught her looking at him. Grinned. "What?"

"I was just thinking about last night."

"Me too," he said eyeing her with fiery delight.

"Would you like to . . ." She motioned toward her bedroom with her thumb.

Roan shot out of his chair, jumped to his feet. "I was just waiting for you to ask."

After another luxurious orgasm they lay on their backs, panting and staring at the ceiling. Her body was raw and achy in the most fabulous way.

How on earth could Roan possibly believe she'd want Danny when he could make her feel like this? Her entire body tingled from her toenails to the ends of her hair. She liked orgasms and she wanted a lot more of them.

From him.

"Wow," Roan said. "And here I'd been thinking things couldn't get any better than they were last night."

"Wonder if it'll just keep getting better and better as we get to know each other."

"I hope so."

"This has been so special."

Roan propped himself up on his elbow and gently stroked his fingers over her bare belly. "What's your idea of a perfect day?"

"Me?" Jazzy pondered the question. "Maybe a day spent on the water? Swimming, water-skiing, fishing. Dad transferred his love of nature to me."

"You have a good relationship with your dad."

"My dad's the best," she said. "He took such good care of me after my mom split. Just like you take such good care of Trinity."

Roan studied her a long moment. "Is that why you're attracted to me? I remind you of your relationship with your dad?"

"It doesn't hurt that you share my dad's good qualities, but my admiration for you goes far beyond how close you are with your daughter."

"How far beyond?" His voice came out husky.

She looked up at him. His eyes were heavy-lidded, his mouth quirked up on one side. "Fishing for compliments?"

"Just curious."

"I love how resilient you are. You've come through so much. You're a survivor, Roan. I appreciate your patience, your honesty, and how amazing your butt looks in Wranglers."

"Ahh," he said. "We're down to the truth of it. You want me for my hot bod."

She tickled him lightly in the ribs and he smiled at her.

"Keep that up and we'll be headed for orgasm number five."

"Is that a dare?"

"An idle threat. Sexy as you are, Rainbow, I need a little recovery time. I'm not as young as I used to be."

"Oh, hush up on that. You know your way around a woman's body. Age is wisdom."

"Not always. Some people keep making the same mistakes over and over."

"But not you."

"I try to learn from my flubs, but I'm not always successful."

"See, another thing I admire about you. You strive to be a better person."

"I admire how much you admire people. You've got a gift of always looking on the bright side."

"I take slams for that sometimes," she said. "I've been accused of toxic positivity a time or two."

"I'm guessing by killjoys."

"Mostly." She laughed.

"Forget those naysayers," he said. "There's nothing toxic about you, Rainbow."

"You didn't tell me what your perfect day was," she said.

"I'm doing it."

"No, really. What does a perfect day look like for you?"

"Being with someone I lo—er, care about."

Had he almost said "love"? Jazzy's heart pounded, and her mouth went dry. It was far too soon in their relationship to be throwing around words like *love*, but darn if her feelings for Roan weren't rapidly expanding. She looked at him.

He'd closed his eyes and his lips pressed tightly together.

She cupped his cheek in her palm and softly kissed him. "I agree," she whispered. "This has been a perfect day. We invented Chocolate-Gingermint Roanies."

"Yeah," he said, sounding husky. "We created something special together."

The way he was looking at her told Jazzy he wasn't talking about the cookies. They'd created much more than a twist on a traditional pastry. They'd carved out a new relationship. It felt heady and scary. She wanted to be with him. Yearned for this feeling to go on and on and on, but she was too nervous to hope for much. This was still so new, so fresh.

And it was moving pretty fast.

Maybe too fast?

Jazzy gulped. Okay, she was infatuated with Roan. Very. But could it grow into something more? Or should she just be satisfied with living in the moment?

Roan got out of bed, exposing her to a wonderful view of his sculpted body and extended his hand to her.

She grasped it and he gently tugged her from the bed. They stood naked in front of each other, grinning. This was getting addictive. She wouldn't mind having this view every day for the rest of her life.

Gloriously naked and unabashed, Roan guided her into the bathroom and helped her change the bandage. The wound was blistered and red, but it didn't look infected.

"I hate that you got burned," he said.

"It's all my fault."

"If I hadn't gotten scared and cut off our lessons, this wouldn't have happened."

"You don't know that. The accident was all mine."

"Still, I can't help feeling like I could have stopped it from happening if I'd been there."

"You're not a superman, fella, and no one expects you to be."

"Holding myself to too high of a standard?" he asked with a wry smile.

"Exactly. You're human. It's okay to be less than perfect."

"I'll try to keep that in mind." He kissed her forehead and the sweet brush of his lips lit her up inside all over again. "But I'm not going to apologize for wanting to keep you safe."

Oh heavens, he'd hooked her.

She splayed her palm over his heart and peered deeply into his eyes. "You have enough responsibilities without taking on my safety. I can take care of myself, Roan."

"And I adore that about you. How independent you are while at the same time being so communal and caring. It's a rare combo."

"Roan," she said, gathering the courage to

broach the topic that had been on her mind all day. "I want more than just a casual fling. I know I told you I was good with it, but inside . . ." She placed both palms over her own heart now. "My feelings for you are growing. I know that scares you. It scares me too, but some things are worth taking a risk over. You're worth the risk and I hope you feel the same way."

He looked at her with such gentleness she was certain he was going to say, yes, he agreed, and her heart clutched.

Instead, he smiled wistfully and said, "Let's just enjoy the moment, okay? We don't need labels."

She struggled to keep up a happy smile, but he'd struck a blow to her fantasies. Maybe there was a reason he'd wanted to be nothing more than a rebound man. Maybe he wasn't as all-in as she was.

"Right?" He arched his eyebrows.

"Absolutely. Living in the moment is what we should all strive to do."

He kissed her again, but it held less promise than his earlier kisses and she couldn't help feeling he was pulling away.

"The sun's out and the ice is melting. It's time I picked up Trinity and headed home."

"Yes, yes." She bobbed her head. "Go get your girl."

"Thanks for being so understanding." He strolled back to the bedroom.

She followed him, wrapping her bathrobe around her, and watched him dress. "Will you come to the semifinals?"

"Of course," he said, buttoning up his shirt.

"But we've only got six more days to find you another recipe and hone your campfire skills. I'll see if Rio can keep an eye on Trinity. That way we can spend the entire day tomorrow at my house, baking over the firepit."

"You mean it?"

"I wouldn't abandon you now, Rainbow." He chucked her under the chin. "See you tomorrow. Say nine A.M.?"

"Perfect." She folded her arms across her chest, unable to stop watching him. Mesmerized by the way he moved. A man fully in control of his fate.

He put on his boots and she followed him to the front door where he retrieved his Stetson from the hat rack and settled it on his head. She felt pulled like warm taffy. On the one hand, he kept telling her they should keep their relationship light, but on the other hand, he acted like they were a real couple. It messed with her emotions. She didn't know what to believe. His words or his actions.

Just freaking live in the moment, Jazzy. Just be.

Wonderful advice. But how did she do that when all she wanted was a happily-ever-after with Roan?

CHAPTER 23

Jazzy prepared for the biggest competition of her life.

For the remaining days leading up to the challenge, she and Roan spent their time searching for a second cookie recipe to use for the semifinals. After testing out ten, they settled on Claire's recipe for Pecan Delights. Jazzy felt a little weird about competing with his late wife's recipe, but after they altered it and perfected the baked goods, she decided the end result was almost as good as the Chocolate-Gingermint Roanies.

In between the intense baking, they took a few breaks to have some Christmas fun and went ice skating on Sunday with Trinity and Roan's family and had the best time. Monday, they joined carolers on the Pediatric Ward. On Tuesday, they did some last-minute shopping while Rio babysat Trinity. Afterward, Roan and Jazzy grabbed a meal at Pasta Pappa's.

As they were leaving the restaurant, they ran into Danny and Andi.

"Ready to have your ass handed to you on a cookie plate, Walker?" Andi taunted.

Jazzy smiled sweetly. "Ready as I'll ever be."

"It's so adorable you think you can beat me." Andi fluttered her lashes.

"Andi," Danny said and took hold of Andi's elbow. "Let's go eat."

Jazzy's eyes met Danny's. He looked apologetic.

"Y'all have a nice evening." Roan tipped his Stetson.

"See you on Thursday," Andi called over her shoulder as Danny dragged her into the restaurant. "For your trouncing."

"You've got to beat her," Roan said as he guided Jazzy over the uneven sidewalk on the way to his truck. "That woman is begging for a comeuppance. I can't believe how she treats you. I want to read her the riot act. I have to remind myself this is your battle, not mine."

"I think she's really sad," Jazzy mused. All this time, she'd been focusing on how pitiful she felt whenever she lost out to Andi. Until now, she hadn't even considered what was behind Andi's antagonism. "I feel sorry for her."

"Even though she stole your boyfriend?" Roan asked.

"I feel sorry for Danny too. They seem miserable together." Jazzy paused underneath a streetlamp as Christmas music filled the air. "I hate that for them. I wish they could be happy." She looked into Roan's face, felt the same thrill she did whenever she was near him. "The way we are."

the mesquite wood chips stacked by
, along with the scent of breakfast tacos
m a Tex-Mex restaurant off the town

ecked in and received an assigned con-
ber to wear pinned to the green-and-red
gave her imprinted with the contest logo.
number thirteen," Roan said.

thing I'm not superstitious, huh?" she
as he tied the apron around her waist
d her attach the number.

st a number," he said. "It has no power
n what you give it. I have every confidence
bility to ace this challenge and take home
en cookie statue."

she appreciated him and his family's en-
c support, she *was* starting to worry about
veryone down.

we allowed to help the contestants unpack?"
mother asked the registration clerk.

e, but only contestants are allowed in the
g arena once the competition starts," the
replied.

take Little Bit to the stands." Rio reached
nity's hand. The little girl was waving at the
le bleachers erected for the event. "Good
Jazzy."

hanks."

anna have a hug first?" Trinity asked, reach-
ut to Jazzy.

er heart—already soft as butter—dissolved
pletely as she crouched to give Trinity a hug.
Are you gonna win a baking trophy like Daddy?"

"You're a good person, Jazzy Walker," Roan
said and kissed her.

They hadn't had sex since the ice storm, and she
could feel the longing in his lips. She wanted him
as much as he wanted her. She missed having sex
with him, but neither one of them thought it was
a good idea to have sex with Trinity in the house.
Not as long as they were keeping things casual.
They didn't want to confuse the child.

But tonight, Trinity was with Rio.

"My house is just a few blocks away," Jazzy said
breathlessly. "Do you want to—"

"God, yes," he said.

Laughing, they ran all the way to her house
and had a quickie before Roan had to pick up his
daughter.

"Baking tomorrow?" Jazzy asked as Roan
dressed.

Roan shook his head. "Not the day before the
competition. You need to rest and clear your mind.
I'll come by on Thursday morning and help you
pack everything up."

She cupped his cheek. "How did I get so lucky?"

"You took a chance on a sad-sack cowboy and
brought him back to life." Then Roan kissed her
again while Sabrina sat on the end of the bed,
watching.

"Your cat is a perv," he said.

"Hey, this is her house." Jazzy laughed.

Roan kissed her forehead, winked, and sauntered out the door. Sabrina jumped off the bed to
follow him.

"Traitor," Jazzy hollered after the cat. Grabbed a pillow, fell back on the bed, daydreaming of building a future with Roan.

It was only after she showered and got ready for bed did she check her voice mail. She had a call from Traveling Nurses.

On Thursday morning, December 22, Roan showed up at the appointed time with Trinity in tow. At six A.M., the sun wasn't even up.

The competition didn't start until eight, but Roan insisted they begin early to ensure they didn't forget anything. He double- and triple-checked everything she'd loaded up the night before. He coached her on managing her time and anxiety and cautioned her against common cook-off pitfalls, regaling her with stories of his own competition missteps while Trinity napped on her couch.

"Thanks," she said. "You made me feel better."

"Now you're thinking like a competitor," Roan said. "You can do this, Rainbow. I have faith in you."

The Lake Twilight marina pavilion had been set up with two dozen firepits for the twenty-four contestants. It surprised Jazzy how many people had entered the challenge and how far they'd come. Bakers from all across Texas as well as Oklahoma, New Mexico, and Arkansas.

"This is a big deal," she whispered to Roan as they unloaded her supplies from his pickup truck. Trinity sat on the tailgate humming "Rudolph the Red-Nosed Reindeer" and playing a game on her father's cell phone.

"The campfire cook[ing]," Roan said.

"I had no idea campfi[re]

A horn honked and [she watched] Roan's parents pull up be[hind them with Trinity in the] back seat.

Ava Sullivan rolled do[wn the window this] morning for a baking cont[est

"Grammy!" Trinity said[, handing the phone] back to Roan.

Roan's dad parked their [truck and lifted] Trinity down from the tailga[te. She went skip]ing to her grandparents and a[ll of them made] old chatter. She told them a[bout the kitty waiting] for her at Jazzy's house and [the

Sabrina. Which Trinity called [the best] kitty in the world."

The fifty-eight-degree mor[ning was] quite temperate after the weeke[nd cold snap] that was typical of December [in east] Texas. Balmy weather often follo[wed] below freezing temperatures.

Roan and Jazzy each grabbed [a] cooler packed with baking supp[lies and headed] for the check-in table. His paren[ts followed and so] did Trinity and Rio, who were hol[ding hands and] skipping across the parking lot. T[hey sang] "Skip to My Lou" at the top of [their lungs. Rio] was such a happy child, secure in t[he love of his] family.

It was a sweet moment that melted [her heart.]

She inhaled deeply, appreciating t[he smell of coffee] and the sunshine and buzz of activi[ty.]

"That's the idea," Jazzy said.

"Yay!" Trinity clapped. "I like trophies."

Bolstered by the child, Jazzy stood up and waved goodbye as Rio and Trinity skipped off to the bleachers.

"How you doing, Rainbow?" Roan asked, massaging her shoulders as if she was a contender about to go into the boxing ring against the reigning champ.

"I'm good."

"You've got this."

"I'll help Jazzy unload the cooler," Ava Sullivan said. "Could you see your dad to the bleachers? He's still favoring that ankle, but he's too proud to admit he could use an arm to hold on to. Don't tell him I sent you."

"I'll take care of Dad," Roan told his mother, and then gave Jazzy a thumbs-up before heading over to his father, who was leaning against a pavilion pylon for support.

Ava helped Jazzy carry the cooler over to the firepit marked with number thirteen and together they started unloading the supplies onto the folding table provided. Mixers and food processors, along with electrical hookups were also provided.

"I sent Roan off with his dad so we could have a chat." Ava set a canister of flour beside the fire-engine red KitchenAid. The mixer sported a label that identified it as being on loan from Christine Noble.

"Oh?" Jazzy said, feeling a little unsettled. Her mind was on the baking contest and Ava had thrown her a curveball.

"I haven't seen Roan this happy since before Claire died and it's all because of you."

Jazzy didn't know how to respond, so she just smiled.

"You've worked your Jazzy magic on him."

"He's worked his Roan magic on me," Jazzy said, feeling her stomach tense. What was Ava getting at?

"I know you two just started dating and the last thing I want to do is put any pressure on you . . ."

Then don't.

"But I hope you win today. It would do so much to restore Roan's love of campfire cooking. He completely shut that down after Claire died. He got it into his head it was his fault she died, and campfire cooking was the reason why."

Jazzy nodded and bit her bottom lip and concentrated on lining up the wet ingredients—sour cream, cream cheese, butter, eggs. "I'll try my best."

Ava finished pulling the last of the supplies from the cooler and added them to the rest of the things on the table. She reached to take Jazzy's hand and squeezed it. "We're so happy for you and Roan. It's so good to see him smile regularly again."

"Thank you, Mrs. Sullivan," she said, touched by the woman's kindness, but also worried because things just seemed to be moving way too fast. She and Roan were good together, but she feared discussing their budding relationship would jinx things.

"Win or lose," Ava said. "We're cheering for you all the way."

"I appreciate that."

Ava gave her a hug and went to join her family in the bleachers. Jazzy turned to make sure she had everything she'd need to get started.

Charlie came bouncing up. "Lucky thirteen!" her best friend exclaimed. "It's a sign you'll beat Andi."

"Thank you for your confidence."

"I saw the Sullivans. You brought your own cheering section. I feel unnecessary."

"Oh no, no. You being here means the world to me, Charlie."

"How's the burn, Lambchop?" He eyed her bandaged arm.

"It's healing just fine."

"Well, take care with it," he cautioned.

"I'll do my best. Happily, for me, the best physician's assistant in Texas is in the stands."

"Don't even start with that. You're going to be fine. This whole thing is going off without a hitch."

"Hey, look at you. Are you taking over my job as the optimistic one?"

"I believe in you." Charlie's smile widened. "And I love you."

"Love you too."

"I'm gonna scoot. That lady at the registration table is giving me the evil eye. She muttered something about some contestants having too many well-wishers. As if there's such a thing as too many people wishing you well." Charlie waved a hand. "Oh, I meant to ask, did you ever hear back from the Traveling Nurses?"

"Yes." She'd gotten a voice mail from Traveling

Nurses, and they'd wanted her to schedule a final interview.

"Don't keep me hanging in suspense."

"I'm not going."

"Why not? What happened to traveling the world? Getting the heck out of Twilight."

Jazzy searched for Roan in the stands. He was bouncing Trinity on his knee. They both waved and her heart swooned. "I love my hometown."

Charlie followed her gaze. "*Ahh*, I see."

"I'm not turning down the job for Roan. We're not at that stage where we would change our lives for each other."

"Then why aren't you going to interview again?"

"I applied for the job to get away from Danny and Andi, but I've realized how stupid that is. I'm not going to let them control my life."

"Good on you, Lambchop." Charlie kissed her cheek. "Break a leg. I'll be in the stands with your man, rooting for you."

Her folks showed up next. Dad and Sarah and her mother, Crystal, with her husband, Tim, before they jetted off to Aspen the following day. Everyone hugged her and wished her well.

Jazzy waved goodbye. Her family joined Charlie and the Sullivans in the bleachers. Heck, her people took up half the stands. It felt so good to have so much support.

Roan and Jazzy might have decided to take their relationship at a leisurely pace, but their families were already mingling and merging. If things didn't work out with them it would get uncomfortable.

Bolstering herself with a deep breath, Jazzy pushed aside thoughts of a future with Roan and turned her attention to the firepit. She checked her watch. The competition started in two minutes.

Contestants were rushing around with last-minute prep. She felt a tickling sensation on her nape and swiveled her head.

And saw Danny staring at her forlornly.

Her stomach catapulted into her throat. He was inside the arena, standing beside Andi, who was talking fast, frowning, and gesticulating. Apparently something had gone wrong at her firepit.

Jazzy smiled kindly at him and raised her hand. Danny raised his in return.

Once upon a time, she'd thought she'd marry this man. Now she just felt sorry for him.

Andi saw Danny wave, and she shot Jazzy a malevolent stare. Jazzy thought about going over to wish her well in the competition but decided Andi would take it the wrong way. Minding her own business, Jazzy went back to cataloging her items. Soon after, the contest representative, Linda Godwin, entered the pavilion and took her place on a small makeshift stage, followed by a camera crew.

Goodness, Jazzy had no clue the event was being filmed. Feeling flustered, she smoothed her hair and adjusted her apron. She was ready.

Linda Godwin picked up the microphone and explained the rules. "Welcome to our first cowboy campfire cookie challenge. As a reminder, this is a cookie competition, so no brownies or bars are allowed. Contestants will be judged on their campfire-making skills as well as their cookies. Ten points will be granted for fire making, ten points for taste, ten points for appearance, and ten points for creativity. Six of the twenty-four contestants will move on to the final round for tomorrow's competition on Friday, December 23."

Her pulse quickened and she double-checked her ingredients. Everything was ready.

"Contestants, you have two hours to complete your cookie recipe," Linda continued. "When you've finished, please bring your cookies to the judging table." Linda then invited the three judges onstage for an introduction, one of whom was Christine Noble.

Once the reading of the rules and introductions were over, the contest representative did a countdown, and when Linda said, "Go!" Jazzy sprang into action.

She worked with calm precision, executing everything Roan taught her. She'd made a fire so many times over the past three weeks, it felt like second nature. Within minutes her fire was flickering, and she turned to make the Pecan Delights.

Jazzy didn't mean to look at Andi to see how she was doing. She certainly shouldn't waste time, but her gaze caught Andi's and she mouthed *Good luck*.

Andi scowled and lifted a middle finger.

It stung. That insult.

"Mind yourself, Jazzy Walker," she muttered and went back to her cookie dough.

It didn't matter what Andi was doing. What mattered was creating the best campfire cookies she could make. She would do her very best to honor Roan's tutoring, and may the best baker win.

"Your chin looks good," Charlie said to Trinity as she tilted back her head to show him the scar he'd stitched. "It's healing nicely."

Trinity rubbed her chin. "It doesn't hurt anymore."

Roan had taken her to their regular doctor to have the stitches removed during the time he and Jazzy had taken a break from each other. "Thank you for taking such good care of her."

His folks and Rio had wandered off for breakfast burritos, so it was just him, Charlie, and Trinity at the top of the bleachers.

"Just doing my job."

"And thanks for showing up to support Jazzy," Roan said.

"Dude, she's my best friend. She'd do the same for me in a heartbeat. I hope that's not going to be an issue."

"Issue? Why would your friendship with Jazzy be an issue?"

"I don't know." Charlie shrugged. "Danny didn't like her spending time with me."

Roan snorted. "I'm not Danny."

Charlie eyed Roan. "No, you are not."

"Don't worry. I'm not going to steal her time away from you."

"Sure, you are. It's natural. It happens whenever one of us gets into a new love relationship. We shortchange each other and that's fine, but Jazzy and I go way back, and we'll always be in each other's lives."

"I think that's wonderful. Besides, there's nothing for you to worry about. Jazzy and I aren't serious. We're just having fun."

Charlie studied him for a long moment with narrowed eyes. "Does Jazzy know that?"

"We've discussed it."

Charlie shook his head. "I thought you were a smart man, Roan Sullivan."

"What do you mean?"

"I've never seen Jazzy like this. Not even in the early days with Danny."

"Like what?"

"Head over heels. Oh sure, Jazzy was besotted with Danny, but it was puppy love and that would have run its course years ago if Danny hadn't gotten spinal meningitis."

"When was this?"

"When Jazzy and Danny were both eighteen. Danny developed Guillain-Barré Syndrome from the meningitis. It took him over a year to rehab and Jazzy, being the kind, caring soul she is, wasn't about to break up with him during his recovery. In fact, she was instrumental in nursing him back to health."

"I had no idea."

"Why would you? They were on a break from their relationship when Danny slept with Andi. As painful as that was, it was the best thing that could have happened to Jazzy. It woke her up and she finally saw they weren't right for each other."

"I hate to hear he hurt her so badly." Roan grit his teeth.

"I don't mean to trash Danny. He's actually a good guy deep down and he has been through some shit in his personal life, but he's still pretty immature. Jazzy needs someone who recognizes how special she is. Danny was too self-absorbed to get it."

"Jazzy is something special," Roan said, watching her glide from the prep table to the firepit, getting the Dutch oven ready for the cookie dough.

"She's in love with you, you know," Charlie said.

Roan startled. "Naw. We've only known each other three weeks. No one can fall in love that fast."

"You don't know Jazzy if you believe that. She's got a heart the size of Texas and an endless capacity for love."

"Did she tell you she was in love with me?"

"She didn't have to. She told me she's turning down a fabulous job opportunity as a traveling pediatric nurse."

"And you think I'm the reason why?" Gobsmacked, Roan blinked at Charlie.

"Well, it's either because of you or Danny, and from the way she looks at you, my money's on Roan Sullivan."

CHAPTER 24

Two hours later, Jazzy carried the plate of Pecan Delights to the judges' table. Unfortunately, she arrived at the same time Andi did.

Side-by-side, they extended their plates of cookies to Linda Godwin. A memory took Jazzy back to fourth grade. She and Andi were standing just like this in front of the corkboard posted outside the classroom, listing the names of the kids who'd auditioned for the school play and scored a role.

Andi had let out a squeal, did a little jig, and said, "Suck it, Walker. I win!"

Jazzy stared at the list, dejected. She'd practiced so hard to land the role. She'd run lines with her dad. Did her best to inhabit the character of Rebekka Nash. Consulted with Charlie's stepmother, Emma, for tips and techniques. And she'd been losing out to Andi ever since.

But not this time. This time, she would win. She was that confident in the skills Roan taught her.

Simultaneously, she and Andi turned to go back to their stations and bumped into each other.

And instantly sprang apart.

"Sorry," Jazzy murmured.

"Out of my way, Walker." Andi tossed her head and marched to her firepit.

Jazzy watched her former friend retreat. Andi had a stiff set to her shoulders and Jazzy knew without seeing her face that Andi's jaw was clenched. The tension that simmered between them for fifteen years bubbled up all over again.

She didn't like this long-standing animosity and wanted it to end. If she could win this contest, she and Andi would finally be even and then maybe they could let bygones be bygones and move forward, if not friends, at least as respected competitors.

If Jazzy was going to stay in Twilight, she ached for this outcome. Working on the same floor with Andi had become intolerable after her engagement to Danny. Honestly, Jazzy didn't understand why Andi was so hostile to her. She'd won Danny's heart. She'd gotten what she wanted. Why couldn't Andi bury the hatchet?

Maybe it's you. The thought popped into her head. *Have you really forgiven her for stealing Danny?*

Blindsided by the thought, Jazzy stumbled back to her firepit, tripping over an extension cord on the way. Dazed, she watched the judges munch cookies—tasting, examining, mulling over their decisions.

From the stands came cheering. The spectators offering words of encouragement. The camera crew walked around, filming the contestants as they awaited their fates.

Jazzy crossed her fingers and closed her eyes after the camera crew swept past her. *Please, let me win this one. Please, just this once let me do something better than Andi Browning.*

The judges put their heads together. Gestured at various plates of cookies. Compared notes.

"Pins and needles," said a contestant next to Jazzy. "Pins and needles."

"Good luck," Jazzy whispered to the woman.

"You too."

After what seemed like a hundred hours, Christine Noble passed an index card to Linda Godwin. Christine looked out across the campfire arena, caught Jazzy's eye, and winked.

Oh heavens, did that mean she was a finalist? Heart thumping, she interlaced her fingers, knotted them into one big fist and pressed her thumb knuckles to her chest.

"The six contestants who will be moving on to tomorrow's final round are . . ." Linda paused for dramatic effect. "Contestant number twelve, Sue DeBusk, for her creation, Raspberry-Dream Cookies."

The woman beside Jazzy squealed and jumped up and down.

"Congratulations," Jazzy told her and sincerely meant it.

Sue DeBusk blushed. "Thank you, thank you."

Linda continued, listing three more contestants. More cheering from the friends and families of the semifinalists.

Only two names remained.

Would Jazzy be among them?

She sought Christine's eyes again for confirmation that she still had a chance, but the baker was leaning over, whispering to another judge.

Andi's name hadn't been called either.

Jazzy hazarded a glance down the row of firepits to where Andi stood, head held high, looking absolutely confident her name would be called.

What if Andi didn't win?

The feeling of schadenfreude that came over Jazzy brought a flush of heat to her cheeks and she heard her dad's voice in her head. *None of that, Little Missy.*

"Our fifth finalist is a frequent winner of our local baking contests, contestant number twenty-two, Andi Browning!" the contest representative called out.

Andi actually curtsied to the judges.

Do not roll your eyes, Jasmine Walker. Be a good sport.

Yeah. That's what she'd been her entire life, a good sport. Accepting readily when things didn't go her way with as much grace as she could muster. Playing nice. Being kind. It was her essential nature, but sometimes, man, she just wanted to gloat.

She wouldn't give in to her shadow side. She might have unflattering impulses, but she wouldn't give in to them.

"And our last finalist . . ."

Enough with dragging it out. Please, put her out of her misery. Her heart was in her throat and her palms were sweaty.

Christine's gaze locked on Jazzy, and her smile was as big as a half-moon.

"Contestant number thirteen, Jasmine Walker, for her Pecan Delights. Congratulations. This is Jazzy's first time entering any culinary competition. Finalist on her first try is a huge accomplishment!" Linda tucked the microphone under one arm and put her hands together. "Let's have a big round of applause for all our finalists."

The audience broke out in enthusiastic applause.

"To all those who didn't make the finals, chin up, there's always the Valentine's Day cake competition. You can enter now at the registration table."

The contestants who didn't make the cut offered congratulations to those who did. Good sports. Jazzy smiled and thanked her well-wishers. The fans came down from the stands, flooding the competition arena.

She caught sight of Roan's Stetson in the crowd and her heart tripped over itself. It would take him and their families a bit to get through the bottleneck.

"Finalists, be back here in the morning by eight thirty to get checked in and settled for our nine A.M. start," Linda reminded everyone.

Andi came over. Jazzy braced herself for something catty and reminded herself not to respond in kind, no matter how tempting it might be. Kill 'em with kindness was her dad's motto and he'd drummed it into her head from an early age. She busied herself, tucking her supplies and ingredients back into the cooler.

"Congratulations on making it to the finals," Andi said.

Jazzy looked up, felt her eyes widen in surprise.

Quickly, she pasted on a smile. Andi was being nice? Why? "Thank you. Congrats to you too."

"Clearly, Roan Sullivan passed his talent to you through osmosis."

Ah, there was the dig. "Roan is very talented."

"Are you sure you didn't just have some cookies Roan baked hidden away that you served to the judges?"

"That would be cheating. I don't cheat, Andi." *I'm not like you.* Gosh, she wanted to say that so badly, but she wouldn't stoop to her level.

"And you wonder why you're such a loser."

Andi's words were a knife through her heart. *Don't rise to the bait. She wants to bring you down.*

Still smiling sweetly, Jazzy said, "You're entitled to your opinion."

Andi looked flummoxed and before she could respond, Jazzy felt Roan come up behind her.

"Congratulations, Andi," Roan said smoothly.

Andi flushed, and stammered, "Th-thanks."

Roan slipped his arm around Jazzy's shoulder. "Ready to go, Rainbow? Our folks want to take us out to lunch." He pointed to their families waiting near the bleachers, who were waving wildly and grinning at her. Sarah was holding a sign that said GO JAZZY.

Aww, it felt so good to have such support.

"I'll wrangle the ice chest," Roan said.

"See you tomorrow," Jazzy told Andi.

"You better bring your A game," Andi said. "I'm gunning for you, Walker."

"Duly noted," Jazzy said mildly, not giving her nemesis any fuel.

"Have a good day," Roan told Andi, hefted the cooler, and led the way out of the contest arena and toward the people waiting for them.

On the way out, Jazzy glanced back over her shoulder. Andi stood all alone, looking angry and confused as most everyone else left the pavilion. No one was there for her.

Not even Danny.

For the first time since Andi had stolen Jazzy's man, she felt a deep unsettling pity for her former friend.

On Friday morning, everything that could go wrong did.

It started out with Jazzy forgetting to set her phone alarm. She was so exhausted from the excitement of the previous day that she didn't wake up until Roan came knocking on her door.

He helped her get everything into the truck and drove as fast as the speed limit allowed. They got to the arena just as Linda Godwin was cordoning off the pavilion. She put up a hand and shook her head as they ran up carrying the cooler between them.

"I'm sorry but you're too late."

"It's six minutes until nine," Roan argued, showing the woman his watch face. "The competition starts at nine."

"The contestants were to be here at eight thirty. There's not enough time for Jazzy to get prepared before the starting bell."

"Not if you don't let her in there's not." The tips of Roan's ears turned red. He was angry on her behalf.

"I'm truly sorry, Mr. Sullivan," Linda said. "But it wouldn't be fair to the other contestants."

"How do you figure? Jazzy's the one behind the eight ball. If anything, her being late will give the other contestants an advantage."

Jazzy put a hand on Roan's arm. It wasn't his place to fight her battles. "Linda's right, Roan. I blew it."

"You know Jazzy's a pediatric nurse, right?" Roan said to Linda. "She does so much for the children in our community."

Linda hesitated, but finally said, "Rules are rules."

Jazzy's disappointment was an aching throb. This win meant so much, not only to her, but to Roan. After all this work, she wouldn't get to compete.

"You're the gatekeeper, Linda," Jazzy said, tension rippling across her shoulders. "You're the one with all the power. It's five minutes to nine now. Still time. Is there *anything* I can do to change your mind?"

Linda considered it. Jazzy could feel the seconds ticking down.

"Please." Jazzy put her palms together.

Unmoved, Linda kept shaking her head.

Christine Noble trotted across the pavilion to join them. "Is there a problem, Linda?"

"Jazzy's late."

"We haven't started the countdown yet," Christine said. "Surely we can cut Jazzy some slack. She was nurse of the year at Twilight General. I think that honor deserves a little consideration."

"No one is above the rules." Linda folded her arms over her chest.

"There's nothing that disqualifies someone from competing if they arrive before the appointed time." Christine pulled the flyer with the rules from her pocket. "Just as long as she's in the arena before the countdown."

"Maybe not, but it's unfair to the rest of the contestants," Linda said. "They all arrived on time."

"What if we poll the other contestants to see if they'd mind?" Christine asked.

Terrific. No way would Andi agree to bend the rules for her.

Part of Jazzy just wanted to throw in the towel, admit defeat, and chastise herself for not setting her alarm. She'd messed up. Big-time. But the part of her that was tired of always putting the needs of others ahead of her own, balked. She and Roan had worked damn hard, and she knew the Chocolate-Gingermint Roanies could win the competition. She wanted to win, not just to best Andi, but to prove she had what it took to be a winner.

"Look," Jazzy said. "If we stop and asked everyone it would already be too late. It's 8:57. I've spent three weeks learning how to bake and start a campfire. Please, give me a shot."

"Free baked goods for a month from the Twilight Bakery donated to the homeless shelter in your name," Christine said to Linda. "If you let her in now."

Why had Christine stepped in to help her? Did she want something from Jazzy?

"You don't have to do that," Jazzy said, that old childhood feeling of life being out of control gripped her.

At the same time Linda took down the rope. She gave a quick nod to Christine, "Deal, get in there."

Roan started to carry the cooler in for her.

Linda put up her palm to stop him. "Not you."

"I'll help." Christine grabbed one handle of the cooler and Jazzy grabbed the other and they rushed over to station six, her new firepit for the final round.

"Why did you do that for me?" Jazzy asked as Christine started helping her unload supplies. "I can't let you pay for Linda's baked goods."

"Linda is a transactional person. She wasn't going to cede her position without a monetary incentive. Don't worry about it, Jazzy. Let me do something nice for you. You do so much for others."

Linda was up onstage counting down. "Ten seconds to start . . ."

"But why do you care about helping *me*?"

"Because someone needs to put Andi Browning in her place." Christine grinned. "And after tasting your cookies yesterday, I think you're just the one to do it."

Christine's intervention was a godsend, but things went downhill from there.

Jazzy couldn't find the butter. Even though Roan had helped her restock. She wasn't an experienced enough baker to figure out a decent substitute on her own and they'd had to leave their phones outside the arena as part of the rules. She couldn't look it up. If she baked without the butter, the Roanies would lose their flakey texture.

While it was against the rules for anyone to

bring extra supplies to the contestant once the contest had started, there were no rules against bor-
rowing ingredients from fellow contestants.

"Sptt," Jazzy called to contestant number five,
a middle-aged real estate agent named Harmony
Boss. "Do you have any butter you can spare?"

"Oh, Jazzy, I'm sorry, no," Harmony said. "I'd
happily give you some if I had it."

"I understand. Thanks anyway." She didn't have
time to ask every contestant if they could spare
enough butter. She was already behind and why
would the contestants help her anyway?

*You gotta do something. You can't let this stop
you. You have to show Roan that his time wasn't
wasted.*

She glanced toward the stands. Their families
would arrive later, in time for the announcement
of the winners. For now, it was just Roan. His
eyes were on her. He gave her a thumbs-up and
mouthed, *You can do this.*

If only she were that confident in herself.

It would cost her time, but she'd find a way to
compensate. She left her station and hurried over
to the fourth contestant.

The camera crew, sensing something was up,
started following her. Oh great, just what she
needed. An audience.

Contestant number four started shaking her
head before Jazzy got the request out of her mouth.
Contest number three was a vegan baker. No butter there.

By the time she got to the second contestant, the

camera crew was breathing down her neck. Thank heavens they weren't filming live. If she looked as panicked as she felt, maybe she could request that she be edited out before the Chamber of Commerce posted the video on the town's website.

"What do you want?" asked contestant number two, a handsome guy about Jazzy's own age. She remembered from the contest brochure that he was from Oklahoma and cooked for a ranch.

"Butter."

He eyed her. "Why should I give you any?"

"To help a fellow contestant?"

"Why would I help my competition?"

"To be nice?" she ventured.

"What's in it for me?"

"What are you suggesting?" she asked, taken aback.

"What are you offering?" He winked.

"Never mind." She spun away and almost plowed into the cameraman, he was so close. "Oops, sorry."

Ducking her head, she rounded firepit number two, going back to her station.

"You're not going to ask me?" Andi's voice rang out.

With an inward groan, Jazzy turned to face her nemesis.

The camera crew zoomed in for a close-up of Jazzy's face, and then panned to Andi.

Forcing a smile that she did not feel, Jazzy asked her rival if she could spare any butter.

"Sorry," Andi said. "I need all the butter I brought."

Dammit! Why had she fallen for it? She knew better than to trust the woman. She'd stolen Jazzy's boyfriend for crying out loud.

"Thanks." *For nothing, witch.*

"I do have some coconut oil to spare," Andi said. "If you want that."

What did Andi have up her sleeve? *Don't trust her, you know better than to trust her.*

"Why are you being nice?"

"I'm a nice person," Andi said.

"Not in this dimension."

"Take it or leave it. No skin off my nose."

While the recipe called for butter, Jazzy would certainly try it with another oil if she could get it. The exchange might affect the way the cookies tasted, and they might not be as good, but she would have gone down fighting.

"I appreciate anything you can spare." That was true enough. "Thank you for the offer."

Andi fished a small glass jar of coconut oil from an adorable, red-gingham picnic basket and passed it to Jazzy.

The camera zoomed in on the handoff. Jazzy quelled her annoyance. The crew was just doing their job.

She took hold of the jar.

Andi held on.

Jazzy tugged.

Andi clung.

Good grief they were having a tug-of-war in front of the camera. Just when Jazzy decided to stop grappling, Andi let go with a wicked-sounding laugh.

Jazzy stumbled backward, the jar of coconut oil clutched to her chest.

Oklahoma Cowboy put out a hand to keep her from falling into his firepit. Okay, so he was a bit creepy, but at least he kept her from getting burned.

Jazzy felt her face flame hot. Embarrassed, she mumbled, "Thanks," and raced back to her station. The camera crew following her all the way.

The buzzer sounded. The baking halted. Whatever was on the plate was on the plate. No adding or taking away allowed.

Jazzy's hair had escaped her bun and was falling in strings around her face. Sweat beaded on her brow and collected between her breasts. She'd just fished three cookies from the Dutch oven and she wasn't allowed to remove any more. Thankfully, there was enough for the three judges, but not an extra one for her to taste to see how the Chocolate-Gingermint Roanies had turned out with the coconut oil substitute.

"Contestants, please bring your cookies to the judging table," Linda Godwin instructed. "Let's start with station one and proceed in order from there.

One by one, the contestants filed to the judges' table to deposit their cookies and return to their firepits. Jazzy was the last to deliver hers and by the time she got to the judges, her heart was pounding, and it was hard drawing a full breath.

This was it. The moment she'd been striving for.

Would she, despite all the hurdles, win? Or would Andi take one last thing from Jazzy?

Back at her station, she shot a glance at the bleachers. Her family had arrived, as had Roan's parents with Trinity. But she didn't see Roan. Her gaze swept the area and she found him from his Stetson, waiting just outside the cordoned-off area of the pavilion. He'd come down to support her.

Danny, however, was nowhere to be seen. Was it petty of her to notice he wasn't there for Andi the way Roan was there for her?

Her gaze met Roan's.

He blew a kiss.

A warmth spread through her and her heart knocked against her ribs. No matter what happened, Roan was here for her and she owed him so much for his help. She wouldn't have gotten this far without him.

While the judges scribbled on note cards, Jazzy reached for a cookie. Now that the competition was over, she could finally taste what she'd made and see if she stood even a ghost of a chance with the butter substitute.

She took a bite. Chewed.

Holy Holstein!

Whereas with the butter, the cookies had been a delicious original recipe, the coconut oil took the cookies from magnificent to legendary. Andi would kick her own butt over this. There was absolutely no way Jazzy could lose with these cookies. They were perfection itself. Light, flakey, chocolatey, minty, gingery. They tasted like Christmas.

A helpless grin crossed her face, and she shot

another look at Roan. He was still watching her, giving Jazzy his full attention.

She gave him two thumbs-up.

He swept off his cowboy hat and did a little jig.

The camera crew homed in on the exchange and then shifted to Andi, who'd caught all of it. She was glowering, her arms folded over her chest.

Giddy glee squeezed her heart. This was it. For once in her life, she was going to beat Andi Browning at something.

Finally. Finally.

The judges finished their note-taking. Jazzy was on pins and needles, the taste of the cookies lingering on her tongue. They consulted each other. It was a quick confab. They nodded in unison. Pointed at a plate.

Her plate!

Christine Noble motioned for Linda Godwin and passed the contest representative the notecard.

Linda waved the notecard exaggeratedly for the camera crew filming her. "We have a consensus."

Jazzy leaned forward, her pulse thudding so loudly in her ears that it was all she could hear.

"The winner of the first annual Twilight Christmas Cookie Challenge for her truly phenomenal Chocolate-Gingermint Roanies is our hometown girl, Jasmine Walker."

Trembling, Jazzy cupped her hands over her mouth as tears of joy filled her eyes. She'd done it! All her hard work paid off.

She'd won!

Roan leaped over the cordon rope, headed straight

for Jazzy. She seemed stunned, unable to believe she'd won. He didn't know what had happened in the beginning as he'd watched her beg ingredients from the other contestants, but she'd overcome the stumbling block to pull off the win.

He was so proud of her, he could burst.

Not caring a fig about the camera crew clustering around Jazzy, he brushed past them, and swept her into his arms. Squeezing her tight, he kissed her cheek as tears streamed down her face and he spun her around.

"I'm so damn proud of you," he whispered in her ear. "So proud."

"I did it," she said, looking awestruck. "I really did it. Three weeks ago, I had no idea how to bake and because of you, I'm a winner."

"You've always been a winner, Jazzy Walker," he said, feeling his own eyes turn misty. "Now the world knows it too."

"I can't believe you gave up this feeling?" she said. "You must go back to competing, Roan."

"I have nothing to prove," Roan said. "This is your time to shine."

The other contestants came over to congratulate Jazzy and sample the winning cookies. Even Andi.

Roan could feel the tension as Andi eyed Jazzy. "You owe me," Andi said. "If I hadn't loaned you the coconut oil, you wouldn't have won."

"You're right," Jazzy said. "The coconut oil put it over the top. Thank you so much for loaning it to me."

Andi munched a cookie. "They are quite delicious." She nodded. "I see what you mean."

Nervously, Jazzy clasped her arms behind her back. Roan put a hand on her shoulder letting her know he was here beside her no matter what.

"Too bad you're about to be disqualified," Andi said.

"Wh-what?" Jazzy blinked.

"Disqualified?" Roan glowered. "How do you figure?"

"These aren't cookies," Andi said. "This is fancified rugelach. Rugelach is a pastry, not a cookie and the rules clearly state the winning recipe must be a cookie."

Then she turned and swished off to the judges' table.

Five minutes later, the three judges sat eyeing Andi and Jazzy as the camera crew recorded the conversation. Jazzy couldn't believe the win was about to be taken from her. Andi had set her up from the beginning. She'd been doomed to fail all along. No matter what she did.

"Technically, a rugelach is not a cookie," Andi argued. "Even though Jazzy has sliced them thin to resemble a cookie, rugelach is a pastry."

One judge pulled a hand down his ZZ Top–style beard and grunted. The other tapped her pen against the stack of index cards. Christine Noble sat in the middle. The judge most likely to be on her side.

She could point out that Andi was the one who'd told her rugelach counted as a cookie that day outside Christine's bakery, but she accepted responsibility. She should have double-checked with the contest community before committing to the recipe. If she'd done her due diligence she wouldn't be in this spot.

Jazzy pressed her palms together. "I'm asking you to allow it as a cookie."

Roan stepped forward, his cell phone in his hand. "I did a Google search. Look at all the websites calling rugelach a cookie."

"This is a gray area," said the ZZ Top lookalike. "Ms. Walker did slice them in cookie shapes, and they are so delicious. I'd like to eat another one."

"The rules state no brownies or bars. They don't specifically say no pastries," Christine pointed out.

"Well," Andi said. "I didn't want to bring it up, but you're not exactly impartial on the subject."

"What are you talking about?" Christine asked.

Andi exchanged glances with Linda Godwin, who nodded. "You bribed Linda to let Jazzy into the arena after she'd cordoned it off."

Okay, enough was enough. Jazzy didn't like conflict, but she wasn't going to sit idly by and let Andi suggest Christine had done something wrong.

"Christine did not bribe Linda."

"She offered to donate a month of baked goods to the homeless shelter in my name if I'd let Jazzy in," Linda said. "I don't mean to be a tattletale, but rules are rules."

"It wasn't even nine o'clock," Jazzy said. "You closed off the pavilion too early. You were trying to stop me from entering when I had every right to be here."

It dawned on Jazzy that Linda not letting her in had been intentional. Could Linda and Andi be in cahoots? Anger burned her nape. From her peripheral vision, she caught sight of Roan. She could tell from his scowl and body language that it was all he could do not to jump in to defend her. *Aww.* He was such a good guy, letting her fight her own battles. She hated that this was happening when he'd helped her so much.

"The contestants were to be in position at eight thirty. I had a right to close down the pavilion anytime between eight thirty and nine." Linda pulled herself up straight and lifted her chin.

"You penalized me for arriving late," Jazzy said.

"You should have been here on time." Linda wasn't budging.

"Did you offer Linda free baked goods in exchange for letting Jazzy in?" ZZ Top asked Christine.

"Yes," Christine said, "but that's only because Linda wasn't about to let her in without some incentive."

"Rules are rules." Linda was a dog with a bone.

"I wasn't late!" Jazzy said, feeling it all slip away.

"And then she borrowed an ingredient from me," Andi said. "I know that's not technically against the rules, but it should be. Jazzy interrupted my flow and her cookies were award-winning because of *my* ingredient and I came in second place because of her."

The third judge looked at ZZ Top around Christine's back. "With all these irregularities, we don't have any other choice but to disqualify Ms. Walker."

"But her cookies are really good." ZZ Top gave a rueful shake of his shaggy head.

"Still. The accusations are numerous, and a

judge has been compromised." The third judge lowered his voice and leaned in. "And this is all on camera. We have to do right by Twilight."

Jazzy wanted to keep fighting, to defend her win, but she had to accept responsibility. She hadn't gotten here at the appointed time and despite being certain she had restocked the butter, apparently, she had not. And Andi's coconut oil had been the thing that put the recipe over the top. She couldn't deny it. She had no one to blame but herself.

Unpinning the blue ribbon from her shirt, she passed it to Andi. "Congratulations."

Preening, Andi pinned the ribbon to her own lapel. "Thank you for conceding so graciously."

Tears clogging her throat, Jazzy turned, desperate to escape, and bumped into one of the camera crew.

"Sorry," she mumbled and stumbled off.

Only to find herself swept into Roan's strong arms. "C'mon," he said. "Let's get out of here."

Ten minutes later, Roan dropped her off at her house. He left Trinity in the truck for a second while he walked her to the door.

"I wish I could take you to my house so you didn't have to be alone," Roan said. "But I promised Trinity I'd take her to the North Pole Village. You're welcome to come along with us of course, but I have a feeling you want to nurse your wounds."

"I do," she said. "Thank you for understanding that I'm not up for company."

"It's crappy what happened," Roan said. "The cookies were damn good and don't you forget it."

"Go have fun with Trinity. We'll talk later."

"You worked hard, and you put up a good fight. You have nothing to be ashamed of."

"I'll keep that in mind as I drown my sorrows in a pint of mint chocolate chip."

Roan leaned in and kissed her lightly. "You're a champion in my book, Jazzy Walker."

"Thanks for your support. It means the world."

He kissed her again and then sprinted back to Trinity and his truck. With a honk and a wave, he was gone. Leaving Jazzy to deal with her crushing defeat all on her own.

"I'll come right over after work, Lambchop."

"No, no, Charlie. I'm fine. Honestly."

"I can't believe that witch. No, I take that back, I can believe it. Andi can't stand not being in the spotlight."

"My fault. I was stupid to think I could ever win against her."

"The cookie challenge is the talk of the hospital today. FYI, everyone is on your side."

"I shouldn't feel this disappointed. It was just a silly baking contest."

"Which you won. Know that in your heart."

"Honestly, I did use her coconut oil and that's what put the recipe over the top."

"You give her too much credit. Know what? I'm buying you a blue ribbon."

"Don't do that."

"Yes, I am. You're a blue-ribbon best friend. Maybe you don't have a lot of trophies and ribbons, but people *love* you, Jazzy. You've got that special *something* that Andi will never have, no matter how many competitions she wins. Why do you think she enjoys hurting you so much? She never really wanted Danny. She just didn't want you to have him."

"Do you really think she's that calculating?"

"We've known her since grade school. Has she ever been any different?"

"She was kinder once, before her parents divorced."

"Fifteen years ago. Cry me a river. We all have baggage. You don't act like a jerk because your mom abandoned you and you were sick with the wrong diagnosis for years."

"I'm not making excuses for her," Jazzy said. "It just feels like Andi is a lonely, desperate woman and I feel sorry for her."

"Save your pity, Lambchop. There're plenty of people who deserve it more."

A knock sounded on the front door. Hmm, she wasn't expecting company. Her heart gave a little hop. Maybe it was Roan, dropping by after his day at the North Pole Village with Trinity.

"Someone's at the door. Can I call you back?" Jazzy headed down the hallway.

"I'll let you go, sweetie. Talk tomorrow? My day off. Breakfast at Moe's?"

"That would be wonderful. Eight?"

"See you then."

"Night." She ended the call and slipped her phone into her pocket. The knock came again and Jazzy got a strange feeling in the pit of her stomach. It was a familiar knock. A certain *rat-a-tat-tat* that clued her in on who might be on her doorstep. Did she really want to answer it?

Jazzy walked to the door. Stood there with her hand on the knob. Closed her eyes. *Go away.*

A third knock. Louder this time.

She didn't have to look through the peephole. She knew who was there. But why was he here? She really had nothing to say to him.

"Jazzy? I know you don't want to speak to me, but could you open the door?"

How could Danny know she was standing there with her ear pressed against the door? Because she'd dated him for four years. He knew her well.

He was her first love and she'd once thought he'd be her last. So much had happened between them and she no longer believed or wanted that. But there would always be a tiny part of her that was vulnerable to him. She couldn't help that. Just as there would always be a part of Roan that would belong to Claire.

That's how love went, and she wasn't sorry she'd loved before . . . or that she'd lost. Being fearless in love enriched her life. How could she regret love? No, the only thing she regretted was holding on too long to someone who wasn't right for her.

With tenderness and compassion, she opened the door and stared into the eyes of her ex-lover.

"Hello, Danny."

CHAPTER 26

"May I come in?" Danny asked. He wore holey jeans, a thick green hoodie sweatshirt, and running shoes. His dark-eyed gaze darted around the hallway.

Jazzy had never seen a man look so forlorn. Her natural nurturing instincts made her want to throw the door open wide, even as the new boundaries she'd struggled to establish urged her to send him on his way.

Danny stepped over the threshold.

Jazzy caught her breath. Once, she'd been punch-drunk in love with this man. Now he seemed little more than a boy. Closing the door, she led the way into the living room.

"Have a seat."

Danny sank down on her couch and Jazzy took the rocking chair across from him. Sabrina popped out from under the Christmas tree and hopped in Danny's lap like she belonged there.

The little traitor.

Danny stroked the cat. The mantel clock chimed. The Christmas lights threw shadows against the wall.

They didn't speak.

Finally, Jazzy couldn't stand the suspense any longer. "What do you want?"

"I broke up with Andi."

The gasp jumped from her throat. She was truly shocked. "Why?"

He shook his head, still hidden inside the hoodie. She wanted to tell him to man up and take it off, but she didn't. "The way she behaved toward you today was unforgivable."

"She behaves that way quite often."

"I know." He sounded mournful. "I made a huge mistake."

"I'm not getting back with you, Danny."

"I know that too. You've found someone who really cares about you and I'm happy for you." He fingered Sabrina's tail as the tabby purred up a storm. The cat liked Danny. "I'm jealous too. I blew it and I have no one to blame but myself."

Jazzy folded her legs up underneath her butt and waited. If he wasn't trying to get her back, then why was he here?

"Andi cheated."

"She had an affair?" Jazzy winced. She wouldn't wish that kind of pain on anyone, but maybe it was for the best Danny learned his lesson before he actually married Andi.

"No. At least not that I know of, but Andi's Andi, so . . ." He shrugged. "She cheated at the contest. You won fair and square."

"How did she cheat?"

"For one thing, she'd already baked her cookies and then snuck them into the baking arena. She warmed them in the Dutch oven and served those to the judges."

"The same thing she accused me of doing." Jazzy knotted her fists and rested them on her knees. "Sneaky."

"Yeah. She couldn't master campfire baking and kept burning her cookies on the bottom. Andi couldn't tolerate the idea of you beating her."

"She always wins."

"I suspect she's been cheating in contests for a long time."

"You knew about the prebaked cookies?"

"I suspected, but I didn't know for sure until . . ." He stopped petting Sabrina, lowered his hoodie so she could fully see his face and met her gaze. "Andi also sabotaged you."

"In what way?"

"When you didn't show up at eight thirty, she roped Linda Godwin into closing off the pavilion early."

"Why did Linda help her?"

"Andi's got something over on her. I don't know what it is, but while Linda was keeping you out, Andi slipped over to your cooler and surreptitiously removed the butter."

"I was sure I'd replenished the butter! Did she confess to you?"

"No. I was filming your argument with Linda—"

"Why?"

"I don't know." Danny ducked his head and went

back to petting Sabrina. "You looked so beautiful standing there in the morning sun." He pressed his lips together, paused. "I just started filming you."

"Danny," she said as kindly as she could. "We're done."

"I know, I know. I screwed up." He looked so miserable, her heart ached for him, but her empathy changed nothing. They were over and honestly, had been since before he slept with Andi. "But you should see this."

Danny pulled his cell phone from his pocket, queued up the video and passed her the phone.

Jazzy reached for it and their fingers brushed. His hand was cool to the touch and she felt . . . *nothing.*

No spark. No electricity. No longing for what might have been.

She watched the video. Danny had started filming as she and Roan walked up. The camera zoomed in for a close-up on her face. She appeared frantic, hair in a messy bun, eyes wide as Linda cordoned off the pavilion.

Jazzy watched herself and Roan set the ice chest down. Then she'd gone up to square off with Linda with Roan right behind her, backing her up. She smiled now, seeing Roan put his hand on her shoulder to steady her.

People started clustering around, both inside the pavilion arena and out. She hadn't been aware at the time that they'd attracted a small crowd.

In the video, Linda was shaking her head. The camera crew came into view as they filmed the incident.

Danny's camera stayed focused on Jazzy's face. She could see her own desperation. It hit her then, how foolish she'd been. Thinking that if she could just beat Andi one time it would make some kind of difference. That she'd at last feel worthy.

That brought her up short. She wasted so much time and effort on a vain pursuit. Worse, she'd wasted Roan's time.

Then, the camera panned out and there, in the corner of the video, Jazzy saw Andi at the back of the crowd. Furtively, Andi looked around, and saw all the attention was on Jazzy, then she crouched, slipping a hand around the tape Linda had used to cordon off the pavilion. Andi pried open the lid to Jazzy's cooler, stuck her arm inside and quickly pulled out the butter.

Another quick glance around and Andi stuffed the butter into the waistband of her pants and walked to her station just as Christine Noble showed up to intervene with Linda. The video ended with a close-up of Jazzy's relief as Linda let her in.

Jazzy passed the phone back to Danny. She didn't know what to say. She was still grappling with the realization that she'd spent far too many years in a useless rivalry. There were no winners here.

"I confronted Andi as soon as I reviewed this," Danny said. "She wasn't the least bit ashamed. In fact, she bragged about how clever she was. That's when I realized how blind I'd been. How she'd manipulated me."

Blowing out her breath, Jazzy nodded. "I'm glad you've seen her for who she is, but this isn't a flattering portrait of me either. I've been telling myself

I wasn't jealous, but I was. I wanted to prove I was as good as Andi, instead, I proved the opposite. I'm as bad as she is."

"Hey, I'm right there with you. Andi convinced me that your positive attitude was harmful. That's how stupid I was, Jazzy."

"Don't beat yourself up. You and I? Well, we weren't working long before Andi. We were just too stuck on Twilight fables to admit it."

"You could take this video to the conference co-ordinator. Get Andi disqualified."

Jazzy shook her head. "It's not worth it. Let her have her ill-gotten win."

"You're a good person."

"So are you, Danny. A little misguided on occasion, but aren't we all?" She smiled at him.

"Why didn't we work, Jazzy?" His sad eyes filled with regret.

"We were just too young. We got together before we really knew who we were and what we wanted out of life."

"I was a fool."

"It's okay. Everybody plays the fool sometimes."

"You're so kind, Jazzy. I hope you get everything you want in life."

"Ditto, Danny."

"Hey." He gave a wistful grin. "Look at us. Being mature and stuff."

"We've learned a lot."

"We have."

They gazed at each other, and she could see respect and admiration for her in his eyes. She felt the same for him. It had taken a lot of courage for Danny to come here and admit his mistakes. He'd grown. They both had.

"For what it's worth, I think this Roan guy is good for you. I've never seen you as happy as you are with him."

"Nah, Roan and I are just . . ." What were she and Roan? "Having a good time."

"I'm happy for you. Maybe your relationship with Roan could be more than that?"

"Maybe." She was afraid to hope for more. "What do you plan on doing now?"

Danny shrugged. "Honestly, I'm thinking of joining the army."

"Like your dad?"

"Yeah. I almost joined when we were dating, remember?"

"Spinal meningitis and Guillain-Barré got in your way."

"You were there for me the whole time. I can never repay you."

"You don't have to repay me. We may no longer be in love, Danny, but I'll always have love for you in my heart."

"Same here, Jazz. I wish I hadn't hurt you. I didn't treat you right and I'm sorry. Can you forgive me?"

"If you can forgive me."

"You didn't do anything that needs forgiving."

"I didn't support you in the way you needed. You needed a shoulder to cry on, not a perky cheerleader trying to rah-rah you out of your doldrums."

"You loved me in your sweet Jazzy way. It was my fault for not appreciating you."

She wasn't going to lie. His validation felt good. "You'll find someone who matches you, Danny. I have full confidence in that."

"Anyway, I just needed to let you know that Andi cheated."

"Thanks."

Danny stood up. "Can I have a hug before I go?"

"Absolutely." Jazzy got up and crossed the room, enveloping her former lover in a tight embrace.

When they stepped apart, Danny's eyes were misty. Hers too.

"Come on," she said and slipped her arm around his waist. "I'll walk you to the door."

While spending the afternoon with Trinity and his parents at the North Pole Village, it occurred to Roan that his time with Jazzy had come to a natural end. They'd had a goal. Teach Jazzy to bake so she could compete in the challenge. They'd achieved that goal, even if it hadn't been the outcome Jazzy wanted.

And as for their affair?

Neither one of them had been looking for anything permanent. Foolishly, he'd started thinking that maybe they had a chance for something more, but then Charlie told him Jazzy turned down the job offer from Traveling Nurses. He couldn't be the reason she gave up on her dreams. He'd always thought she was too young to settle down. He couldn't be the thing that stood in her way.

"When's Jazzy coming over to bake cookies?"

Trinity asked from her car seat as they drove home from their outing.

"The contest is over, Doodlebug. Jazzy's not going to come by anymore."

"No Jazzy?" Trinity's little voice rose.

"I'm afraid not."

The back seat went silent and then he heard sniffles. He looked in the rearview mirror to see Trinity wiping her eyes with the back of her hand.

"Doodlebug? What's wrong?"

"No more, Jazzy," she wailed.

Aww, shit. He'd waited too long to break things off. His daughter had gotten invested in Jazzy. Damn his hide. He shouldn't have brought a temporary love affair into his home. What had he been thinking?

Answer: he hadn't been. He'd been too wrapped up in feeling good. He had to talk to her tonight.

He spun the truck around and headed for Rio's house. Five minutes later, he was knocking on his sister's door, Trinity in tow. Rio answered wearing her welding helmet pushed back on her head.

"What's up?"

"Can you watch Trinity for a couple of hours?"

"Sure, but you look . . ." Rio paused, eyed him up and down. "Wrecked."

"I've got to go break up with Jazzy." He kept his voice low for his daughter's sake.

"What'd she do?"

"Nothing. That's the problem."

Rio opened her door wide. "Come on in, Doodlebug. I have cookies in the cookie jar."

"You baked cookies?"

Rio snorted. "Oreos."

"Oreos!" Trinity cheered and went running to Rio's kitchen.

"Okay, now that the kid is out of earshot . . ." Rio glanced over her shoulder to make sure. "Why are you breaking up with a perfectly good girl-friend?"

"It was never meant to be more than temporary."

"Things change. Why can't your relationship?"

"Trinity is getting too attached to Jazzy."

"But you two really work as a couple. I like Jazzy a lot and she's good for you."

"I know all that."

"So let me get this straight. Things are going re-ally well, so you're gonna blow it up. Sounds like something I would do, but okay."

Was that what he was doing? A flicker of hope caught in his chest.

"Just can't let go of Claire, huh?" Rio asked.

"This isn't about Claire."

"It's about you being scared as hell to love again."

Was it?

"You don't know what you're talking about," Roan said.

"You're probably right." Rio raised both hands. "Have fun at your breakup. I'll be here to help you pick up the pieces."

"Thanks for watching Trinity."

"You've got it, big bro. You might be an idiot, but I'm here for you, no matter what."

CHAPTER 27

On the way to Jazzy's house, Roan practiced his breakup speech. He'd thought about texting that he was coming by, but worried she'd start anticipating something pleasant.

Pulling onto her street lit up with festive Christmas lights, his anxiety hit hyperdrive. This was going to be harder than he thought.

"It's for the best. For both of you."

Yeah? Who are you trying to convince?

Wincing, Roan parked his truck at the curb on the opposite side of the street from Jazzy's house.

There was a red SUV in her driveway. She had company.

Poor timing. He should have texted.

What now?

He was just about to restart his truck and drive away when her front door opened, and she walked out.

With Danny Garza.

Jealousy hit him like an arrow through the heart. It was stupid. It was illogical. He was on the cusp of breaking up with Jazzy, why did he care if Danny had been in her house?

Drive away. Drive away now.

Danny and Jazzy were facing each other. Jazzy went up on tiptoes to plant a kiss on Danny's cheek. It wasn't a romantic kiss. Clearly platonic, but Roan couldn't stop the heat swamping his chest. This man had hurt Jazzy deeply. He didn't deserve to be her friend.

You're about to hurt her too.

Danny waved goodbye, stepped off the porch, and headed for his SUV.

Frozen, Roan sat unmoving in his seat. Every instinct in his body screamed at him to leave before she spotted him, to regroup and reassess before he committed to ending their relationship, but he couldn't shake off the trance. He'd been insane to think they could come out of their affair unscathed.

Jazzy paused on the porch and peered out across the street.

Go, go.

He turned the key, pumped the gas. The truck didn't move because he was still in Park.

Beaming, Jazzy came running across the street toward him.

All right. Moment of truth.

He killed the engine. Straightened his spine, unbuckled his seat belt, and opened the door just as Jazzy ran up to hug him around the waist. He couldn't help soaking up the smell of her, sweet as cotton candy, and how good it felt to have her arms around him.

One last time.

A big smile swung from her luscious lips and her eyes sparkled like the light show at the North Pole Village as if Roan was Santa himself.

Aww, hell.

"I'm so glad you're here," she said. "Come in, come in."

"Jazzy . . ." He shook his head. "We need to talk."

His tone must have put her on guard. She dropped her arm and stepped back. Lights from the blinking Peanuts Christmas display on the neighbor's lawn flicked over her face in the darkness.

"Is everything all right?"

He shook his head. This was for the best. He knew it. "We . . . I . . ."

"Yes?" She looked so earnest, so vulnerable. Pressing a hand to her chest, she waited for him to continue.

"Charlie told me you turned down the job offer from Traveling Nurses. I can't let you do that. I know how much you want to travel. I can't be the one who holds you back from your dreams. You have to go."

She looked a bit dazed. "Are you breaking up with me?"

"We both knew this was temporary."

"But it doesn't have to be," she said. "We could have more. So much more and you know it."

"You're too young." He shook his head. How he wanted to agree with her. To tell her she was right, and they should jump into this relationship with both feet and damn the consequences. But he was a cautious man, and he had a daughter to raise.

He didn't have the luxury of impulsivity that best suited youth. "There's a big wide world for you to discover and take by storm."

"Why don't you let me worry about it?"

"We're moving too fast. We got caught in a riptide of great sex."

"What's wrong with that?"

"This isn't going to work, Jazzy. I'm sorry, but that's how I feel."

"You don't want to be with me anymore?"

"No, and that's the problem. I want to be with you more than I want to breathe. But I can't load you down with my responsibilities. I have a kid to raise. I'm not footloose and fancy-free. I've had my chance. It's time for you to seize yours."

"Can we stay friends? Can I hold on to hope that maybe you'll have a change of heart? Can I—"

"No." He heard the pain in his voice, rough and husky. "Clean break. It's the only way."

She staggered back, palm to her heart. "It's over? Just like that?"

"We accomplished our goal. There's nothing left to achieve."

"I . . ." Her bottom lip trembled as she struggled not to cry.

"I care about you, Jazzy. I always will, but it's time to let go. We had a blast and made great memories and—"

"Shh." She shook her head violently. "Don't say anything more."

"Jazz—"

"I get it. You have no desire to build a life with

someone you view as a kid. I don't see age between us, but you can't get past it. You're right. I should have taken the job from Traveling Nurses instead of spinning fantasies about you and me creating a family for Trinity."

Her words were a hammer to his heart.

"Please," she said. "Just go."

And she fled into her house.

Leaving Roan feeling utterly wretched for breaking her heart . . .

. . . and his own.

She'd known this was coming and still, she'd been blindsided. Following the end of her relationship with Danny, she'd believed she was immune to the romantic magic of happily-ever-after fairy tales.

Ha!

All this time, she'd been actively weaving a story about her and Roan. Her hometown was at fault. Twilight and its stupid myths and legends.

She paced her house, but where once it had seemed cozy, now it felt too small. She had to get out of here. Had to clear her head and try to make some sense of her situation with Roan.

Unable to stand herself, she put on her coat and headed toward Sweetheart Park. Stuffing her hands into her pockets, she bent her head against the wind. It was getting late and the stores on the square were closing. A few people lingered on the streets. Shoppers laden with bags scuttled to their vehicles. Couples strolled, holding hands. One duo stopped to smooch beneath the mistletoe hung from the quaint street lantern. Christmas music still played from the speakers on the courthouse. It would shut off via timer at ten.

Twilight was a beautiful little town. She couldn't deny that. It was the kind of place others dreamed of living in and she'd been lucky enough to be born here. Could there be a young woman in Paris with posters of Twilight on her wall? Longing for something that was missing from her life, just like Jazzy.

She walked past the windows advertising last chance sales. Tomorrow was Christmas Eve. Roan and Trinity wouldn't be coming over to spend time with her and get their Christmas stockings.

A tear formed on her cheek.

Angrily, she swiped it away. None of that stuff.

All the decorations in Sweetheart Park were lit up and she followed the path, trying to find the joy she usually felt at Christmas. But her natural glee and effervescence had disappeared along with Roan.

The wind gusted. She tugged her collar higher and hunched lower, the cold stinging the top of her ears, and she hurried past the stone archway leading into the park. A few more people were here than on the square, mostly lovers from the looks of it, out on a late evening stroll arm in arm. Heads resting on shoulders, they stopped to admire the lights.

She and Roan could have been one of those couples. They hadn't had much time for anything beyond baking. A fresh sense of loss washed over her.

The quickening breeze urged people home and one by one, the couples filed from the park as Jazzy trudged deeper into it. Twilight was a safe town, but did she really want to be in the park this late by herself?

Truth? She didn't want to be anywhere except with Roan and his daughter.

An idea hit her like a punch.

She wanted to be around Roan, but he didn't want her around. He might say it was because she was too young, but it was something else. Something deeper holding him back from loving her.

He was still in love with Claire.

That's where she'd been dumb. Believing she could replace his beloved wife. If she stayed with Roan she'd always pale in the shadow of Claire the Wonder Wife. She already had enough problems with competitiveness. She didn't need his mess.

Or Danny's.

What was happening to her? She'd lost the most essential part of herself.

Her joy.

Oh, this was bad. She shouldn't indulge her dark mood. She should go home. Go to bed. Get some sleep. Things would look brighter tomorrow.

Christmas Eve.

Normally, her favorite day of the year. She lived for Christmas Eve. Loved everything about it. The lights, the decorations, the food, the cheer, the family gatherings.

Ugh. She had to go over to Dad and Sarah's tomorrow.

That thought pulled a gasp from her throat. She'd never viewed being with her family as a burden or a chore. They were her support system and her cheering section, and she loved them with all her heart.

But right now the idea of making small talk around the Christmas tree felt like torture.

She startled. Oh man, she'd lost her Christmas mojo.

Her Jazzy joy was gone.

She hit the end of the park and turned around in the darkness. She tried skipping to boost her spirits.

It didn't work.

She just felt stupid even though there was no one left around to see her. She walked by the Sweetheart Tree where Roan first kissed her—kissed her right under the knothole with *Claire loves Roan 4 Life* carved into it. She paused, consumed by the ache in her heart growing deeper as memory claimed her.

Snap out of it. Go home.

Jazzy was turning away when she heard a sniffling. Was someone crying? Her tender heart wouldn't let her ignore it.

Stretching wide, Jazzy leaned across the ancient pecan tree, and peered around to see who was on the other side.

There, on the park bench, sat Andi, who stared at Jazzy red-eyed, a blue tissue wadded in her fist.

"What do *you* want?" Andi barked.

"To see if you're okay."

"Right. I bet you just came to gloat."

Slowly, Jazzy shook her head. She didn't enjoy seeing her former friend like this, no matter the unpleasantness between them.

"May I sit?" Jazzy asked.

Andi glowered. "Free country. Do what you want."

Jazzy edged over.

Andi scooted to give her more room.

They sat there for several minutes, not speaking. It was really too cold to sit outside, but Jazzy could feel Andi was on the verge of saying something.

"Remember that time I beat you in the Girl Scout cookie challenge," Andi said.

"Uh-huh."

"My mother cheated and bought two hundred boxes of cookies. She even bought a freezer to store them in. We ate Girl Scout cookies for a year. I still hate them."

"Why did your mother do that?"

"'No daughter of mine is going to lose a lame-ass cookie contest,'" Andi said, affecting her mother's voice. She sounded so much like Sandy Browning it was eerie.

"Win at all costs, huh?"

"Yep." Andi rocked back on the bench.

"Take no prisoners?"

"What would be the point of prisoners? You have to feed and house them."

"Every day was a battlefield, wasn't it?" Jazzy asked.

"Damn straight." Andi's voice shook and her eyes misted. "Every single day. Still is to be honest. My mother texts or calls several times a day to tell me how worthless I am. Unless I'm winning, I'm nothing."

"That's why you cheat. If you lose, your mother won't love you."

"She doesn't love me anyway." Andi sighed.

"And yet you keep trying to earn her love."

"Did Danny show you the video?"

"He did." Jazzy tilted her head and gave Andi a sidelong glance. "Your mistake was giving me the coconut oil."

"Duh." Andi rolled her eyes. "I thought the coconut would overwhelm your recipe. Apparently it enhanced it."

"Why did you give me anything at all?" Jazzy asked. "You didn't have to. No one else did."

"What kind of contest would it be if you weren't in it," Andi said.

"You mean that?"

"Sherlock is nothing without Moriarty."

"Just for clarity, you're Moriarty."

"No, *you're* Moriarty."

"Well, either way, both characters are smart."

"So smart."

"Like Sherlock was such a saint," Jazzy said.

"There you go. A heroin addict hero. What's that all about?"

"Remember that Arthur Conan Doyle reading challenge in fifth grade?"

"Why do you think I brought up Sherlock and Moriarty."

"Did you cheat on that too?"

Andi gave her a look. "I have to win. You get that, right?"

They fell silent. The Christmas music from the courthouse stopped. It was after ten. Jazzy was about to suggest they walk out together when Andi said, "I shouldn't have slept with Danny."

Bowled over by an apology, Jazzy sucked in her breath. She wanted to encourage Andi to stay open and honest. "Danny and I were taking a break. I should have been more mature."

"It was shitty of me."

"It was," Jazzy agreed.

Andi rubbed her gloved hands together. "I've always been jealous of you."

"Me?" Stunned, Jazzy stared at her. "I was jealous of you. You had all the cute clothes and high-tech toys. You won everything . . ."

"Which you now know involved considerable cheating."

"Why were you jealous of me? I was a sickly kid. I didn't get to go run and play like the other children."

"Everyone adored you," Andi said in a long-suffering voice. "Everyone made concessions for you because you were sickly. You had a good dad who showed up for every event. Then he married Sarah and you had the coolest stepmom ever. I felt like I came up short around you."

"Andi, you were healthy, and your parents had money."

"And I was a pawn in their acrimonious divorce. They didn't care about me. All they cared about was getting back at each other and I was their instrument of torture."

"I'm sorry your parents weren't there for you."

"Is that what people from normal families do? Say nice and encouraging things to each other?"

"Normal is a setting on a dryer, Andi."

"You really are a happy person, aren't you. It's not bullshit."

"I try to stay positive, but I have my moments. I get down in the dumps like everyone else."

"I'm sorry I said your positivity was toxic. It wasn't you. I just said it because I couldn't find anything else about you to bad-mouth."

"No, you're right. Sometimes I have trouble reading a room and I'm inappropriately optimistic."

"There're worse traits." Andi snorted a laugh. "Far worse."

"Like whacking your best friend in the nose with a mike stand because you're way too competitive?"

Andi smiled. "Yeah. Like that."

The lights from the town square went off.

"Turn out the lights, the party's over," Jazzy said, but neither one of them made a move to get up.

"Do you think we could ever be friends again?"

"I don't know," Jazzy answered honestly. "There's a lot of stuff you do that doesn't feel healthy to me."

"Fair point."

"But maybe we don't have to be enemies anymore."

They exhaled in unison.

"Did you take Danny back?" Andi said.

"He didn't ask me to."

"He still loves you."

"He loves the idea of me, not the reality. But it doesn't matter. I'm in love with someone else."

"Roan."

"Yes."

"How's that going?"

"I'm here with you, aren't I."

"That bad, huh?"

"It's complicated."

"So, simplify it. Tell the guy how you feel."

"It's not that easy."

"We better get out of here before they douse *all* the lights and we're stumbling around in the dark."

"Good idea."

They got up and headed for the exit.

"Have you ever considered leaving Twilight?" Jazzy asked. "Get out of the shadow of your mother?"

"You've got something in mind?"

"I do. Traveling Nurses is desperate for pediatric staff and with your drive and determination, you'd be a shoo-in."

CHAPTER 28

"Brother, you are acting like a dud. Slumping around. Sighing constantly." Rio cornered him in the kitchen at his parents' house on Christmas Eve while everyone else was in the living room getting ready to open presents. "I know your rebound booty call has ended, but—"

"Don't," Roan spoke so harshly his sister jumped back. Wincing, he gentled his voice. "Please don't talk about Jazzy that way. Yes, we might be broken up, but she means a lot to me."

"I was just being flippant to lighten the mood. Boy, did that go off the rails. I think Jazzy's great. Truly I do. You're right. I shouldn't have said that."

"Kids," their mom called from the other room. "Are you two arguing?"

"No, Mom," they called back in unison.

That broke the tension.

"Look . . ." They spoke at the same time and started laughing.

"You go first," he said.

"No, you."

"This is hard for me, Rio. Jazzy's the first woman since Claire. But the timing wasn't right. We got involved too fast. I brought her into our family too soon—"

"My turn," Rio said. "You're talking nonsense. It's never the wrong time for love."

"It's just not that simple."

"Only because you're making it hard."

"Daddy!" Trinity said from the doorway. "Hurry up! We're 'bout ta open presents."

"I'll be right there, Doodlebug."

"Now please?" Trinity twisted the hem of her Christmas pajama top around an index finger and sent him a beguiling smile.

Laughing, Roan took his daughter's hand and led her to the living room. His dad played Santa Claus, passing out the presents and in a flurry of papers, oohs and aahs and thank yous, they exchanged gifts. Trinity getting the bulk of them.

While his daughter played on the rug with her new toys, he and Rio started picking up the wrappings and bows and putting them away. His mom went into the kitchen to make hot chocolate and popcorn, a Sullivan family Christmas Eve tradition.

"Daddy?" Trinity said.

"Uh-huh?" Roan asked, leaning over to stick a bow on his daughter's head. "You're the best present of all."

Trinity leaned back her head and beamed up at him, fingering the bow on her head. The foil made a crinkling sound. "Is Jazzy coming over tonight?"

"No, sweetheart."

"When *is* she coming over?"

"Jazzy's not going to visit anymore."

"Why?"

Roan shrugged. "She's got other kids to take care of."

"She doesn't like me?"

Dammit! Kids always blamed themselves. "Jazzy adores you."

Trinity's little lip trembled. "Then why won't she come see me?"

Look what you started.

Roan glanced over at Rio who held out the recycle box for Roan to put the paper he'd wadded up in his hand.

"Yeah, Daddy," Rio mouthed silently. "Why won't she?"

Roan felt awful, but what would giving in do? Sooner or later he and Jazzy would break up. Better to end it now before they all truly fell in love with her.

"Hey," Roan asked Trinity. "Who wants to go outside and look for reindeer tracks?"

While Roan was opening packages with his family, Jazzy and Charlie were at the Twilight Playhouse, dressed in their holiday best as they waited in line for drinks during intermission. After the performance, they were headed over to her family's Christmas Eve party.

"Let me get this straight," Charlie said. "Andi, as in *our* Andi Browning, told you she was sorry for sleeping with Danny?"

"She did."

"I never thought this day would come. Wow, maybe there are such things as Christmas miracles."

"Andi's had a far tougher life than I've realized," Jazzy said. "I think she's ready to change."

Charlie raised his eyebrows and pulled his mouth over to one side. "That remains to be seen."

"I'm pulling for her."

"Of course, you are, Jasmine. It's your nature."

"Not always. I can't say I've never been a jerk."

"Sooo . . ." Charlie looked at her pointedly. "Do you want to talk about the elephant in the lobby?"

"I do not."

"Gotcha." He patted her shoulder. "Just know you can cry here anytime, Lambchop."

"I appreciate you so much."

Charlie ordered their drinks, something called a Snowball, and they slipped to the staircase out of the way from the crowd.

"Roan's right," Jazzy said.

"Oh," Charlie said. "There's the elephant. Well, hello. Care to elaborate."

"Three weeks wasn't nearly long enough to know if you truly loved someone. Infatuation, yes. Lust, yes. Real love takes time."

"You sound like a diamond commercial."

"Maybe that's what Roan's trying to teach me. That we just need more time before moving forward."

"Is that what he said?"

"Not in so many words?"

Charlie grimaced. "Can I be honest?"

"Please."

"Don't wait around for someone to decide if they love you or not. Live your life, Jazzy. Right now. Plan for your future. Don't build castles in the sky."

"So, I should just accept that we were each other's rebound and that's all we were ever meant to be?"

"Just stopgaps on the way to emotional healing." Charlie nodded.

"I care about him and respect him. I love him with all my heart, even if I can't be with him. Even if he doesn't love me back."

And she *did* love him. Three weeks be damned. Her feelings weren't bound by time and space. Would the feelings fade? Maybe. But they could grow too. No one could predict the future. What was wrong with just loving in the moment?

Why couldn't she and Roan just have *now*?

She knew the answer.

Trinity.

He couldn't be rash or foolish. He was a single dad. His daughter had to come first.

"Love him, sure," Charlie said. "But don't attach any outcome to that feeling. Don't let it stop you from moving on."

"Should I take the Traveling Nurses job?"

"Do what you want. Stay. Go. Just stop twisting yourself into knots over things you can't control."

"Play's about to begin." Jazzy nodded to the crowd coming toward them. "You've given me a lot to think about."

Christmas Eve at her dad and Sarah's house was lively. Members of the True Love Cookie Club, of which her stepmother was a member, were there for a cookie swap. Cookies of every variety—except for chocolate chip, they weren't allowed in cookie club—lined numerous cookie tins. Sarah's ubiquitous kismet cookie featured prominently. Guests came and went. They exchanged gifts and holiday cheer, played games, and reminisced about Christmases past. The holiday with her family was wonderful as always. Jazzy wasn't fully present for the event. Her mind hung on Roan and Trinity.

By ten everyone but family had gone, including Charlie.

She sat cross-legged on the floor in front of the coffee table in the cocktail dress she'd worn to the play, watching her younger siblings decorate the live tree. Decorating a live tree on Christmas Eve that Dad cut down himself had become a tradition in the house once Jazzy's asthma issues had resolved. Dad sat on the hearth so he could lean over and feed an oak log into the fire whenever it burned low. He'd done the same thing every year since he and Sarah married. Keeping the home fires burning while everyone else decorated the tree.

"Off to bed," Sarah said, shooing her kids down the hallway once the decorating was done. "Or Santa won't come."

Jazzy waved goodnight to her siblings and pried herself off the floor to hug her dad and stepmom goodbye.

"Why don't you just spend the night?" Sarah invited. "You'll be right back here in the morning."

"Sabrina hates it when I leave her alone too long," Jazzy said.

"At least take some cookies with you." Sarah thrust a tin of kismet cookies at her. "Maybe it's time you slept with one of these under your pillow."

"I don't believe in the legend."

"You don't have to. Although, your father and I *are* proof it works." Sarah moved to wrap her arm around Dad's waist.

"Anecdotal," Jazzy said.

"Maybe," Sarah said. "You're missing that Jazzy sparkle. You look as if you could use some Christmas magic and these cookies come pretty close."

"Thanks." Jazzy tucked the tin under her arm. She had no intention of sleeping with a kismet cookie.

"It'll work out with Roan the way it's supposed to," her dad reassured her. "Whatever happens, we're behind you one hundred percent."

She had the best family in the world.

When she got home, Sabrina sniffed the tin. It was almost midnight. Soon it would be Christmas Day. But Jazzy felt amped up, unable to sleep. She brewed herself a cup of chamomile tea. She wouldn't sleep with the cookie underneath her pillow, but she'd certainly have one with her tea.

Mulling over her evening and the conversations she'd had with Charlie and her folks about Roan, Jazzy took her tea to the bedroom. She and Sabrina curled up in bed as she thumbed through social media, responding to, and sending out holiday good wishes.

She sipped tea and nibbled the cookie. The kismet cookie was a delicious recipe if you ignored the silly legend. Her vision blurred and she yawned big.

Dozed.

Dreamed.

In the dream she was at Slope Ridge Ranch looking for Trinity, but she couldn't find her. Smoke rolled in like during the fire, but this smoke smelled like lemon drops and didn't make her cough. In fact, it wasn't smoke, but rather a heavy mist hovering over the land. She wore a gauzy, white ankle-length dress and she was barefoot, which was totally illogical on a ranch, but hey, it was a dream. "Trinity," she called, running, and searching for the child. "Trinity where are you?"

The girl giggled.

"Oh," Jazzy said. "Are we playing hide and seek?"

A flash of a child's leg in the mist. Another giggle.

Jazzy followed, going deeper and deeper into the fog, except it wasn't fog anymore but white tulle stretched out like wedding veil trains. The material parted and Jazzy found herself in a spring meadow. Weird because it was Christmas. She could hear the music drawing her further into the dream. And then there was Trinity standing right in front of her, looking like a flower girl with a basket of roses. She threw fistfuls of petals before Jazzy, guiding her way.

"Where are we going?" she asked Trinity.

But the girl just laughed and scampered off.

The rose petals led to a wedding arch and there, with his back to her, stood a tall man in a Texas tuxedo.

Suddenly, it was snowing in the meadow and she heard the sound of sleigh bells jingling. Heart in her throat as she walked closer. Was this her true love? The man she was to marry? All she had to do was call out to him. He'd turn to her and she'd see his face and she'd know he was her soul mate.

In waking life, she eschewed fated love, but in the dream, it felt so real.

It felt like destiny.

He turned.

She could see his profile. Her pulse quickened and the air stalled in her body.

He was facing her now, palm held out to her.

Roan!

She ran to him. Laughing, he caught her in his arms and spun her around and kissed her and . . .

Jazzy woke up in a bed filled with kismet cookie crumbs.

CHAPTER 29

Christmas morning at Roan's house was bedlam as Trinity woke at the crack of dawn, eager to tear into her presents. He told her she had to wait until her grandparents showed up. While he was in the kitchen making breakfast, the little scamp got his phone and called his folks.

They showed up a short time later, along with Rio. The ranch hands joined them for breakfast before going on to visit their families and the Christmas festivities began in earnest. Throughout it all, Roan longed for Jazzy.

Feeling at loose ends, he picked up his phone and almost texted Jazzy a cheery Merry Christmas greeting, but stopped himself in the nick of time. If he was breaking things off, he couldn't communicate with her.

But he had so much to tell her. It seemed months since he'd seen her, and it had only been two days. How long before he stopped feeling this bone deep ache? Committed to getting over her, he blocked her number, not trusting himself.

How could someone he'd only known for three weeks have made such a big impact on his life?

By noon his parents were snoozing in the lounge chairs and Rio had taken off to go hang with her friends. Trinity was playing with her new toys and Roan had finished washing the dishes and straightening up.

Trinity had a meltdown over a toy that broke. Her wailing woke his folks who decided it was time to head home. In the meantime, he put Trinity down for a nap and then the house got really quiet.

All he could hear was the ticking of the mantel clock.

He'd almost fallen asleep on the couch when he heard a faint knock at the door. He wasn't expecting any more guests, although later that afternoon, he and Trinity were having an early dinner with Claire's family.

Without even looking through the peephole to see who was there, he opened the door.

And found Jazzy standing on his porch, holding the two stockings from her fireplace with his and Trinity's names on them.

"Hey," she said, offering up that dazzling Jazzy smile. If he'd broken her heart, she hid it well. "I hope I'm not interrupting, but I wanted to give you these."

"Do you want to come in?"

"Do you want me to come in?"

"You're here."

"Okay," she said, still sunny and sweet.

He stepped aside, waving her over the threshold. "May I take your coat?"

She shook her head. "I won't be here that long."

They looked at each other and he saw the same longing in her eyes that he felt in the pit of his stomach. His pulse was a cutting horse, racing to herd a cow to the pen.

"Jazz—"

"Roan—"

"You go first," he said.

"No, please, you."

He wanted to tell her what a fool he'd been, but the problems they had were still there. He was settled, rooted. She yearned for travel and life on the road. "I'd like to hear what you have to say first."

"Why did you block my phone number? I mean I get why you broke up with me, but I don't understand why you blocked me. What did I do that was so bad?"

"I didn't block you," he said. "I blocked *me* so I wouldn't be tempted to text you. I can't get over you if I'm in contact with you."

"Seriously?" Jazzy's smile fell away, and there was a sudden fire in her eyes as she sank her hands on her hips and glowered at him. "That's your excuse?"

Roan raised his palms, stepped back. "Whoa."

He'd never seen her fired up like this. Didn't even know she had a temper. Actually, he was glad to see it. She wasn't taking his rude treatment lying down. *Damn woman, do you know how hot you look right now?*

"Whoa? Whoa?" She poked a finger at his chest. "*Whoa?*"

"Hey." He stepped away from her. "It was for the best that we go our separate ways."

"I never took you for a coward, Roan Sullivan."

"Wh-what?"

"I haven't texted you once. I haven't called you. It's not like I was stalking you or anything. Why did you block me?"

"Jazzy, I—"

"No, I don't want excuses. It hurts, Roan. Why?"

He studied her for a long minute, feeling like a jerk. The passion in her eyes was hot and shiny. "You're right. I was wrong to block you. That was extreme. I was just afraid you might text me and then I'd text back, and we'd be in a relationship again."

"I can take no for an answer. You don't want me. Okay. I accept that. But that doesn't mean Trinity has to suffer. I had already bought the stockings before you ended things. That's all I wanted. To give Trinity her stocking."

"I have no excuse," he said. "I'm floundering since I broke up with you."

His apology cooled her anger. "I am too."

They inhaled at the same time, deep and long. He wanted to hold her, kiss her, tell her that despite his best efforts not to, he'd fallen for her.

"I missed you," he said.

"I slept with a kismet cookie."

"Oh." He studied her. "Did you have any dreams?"

"I did." A faint smile played over her lips.

"And . . . ?" He held his breath. He didn't be-

lieve in fated love based on cookies, but he did believe in Jazzy.

"I dreamed of you."

His chest hitched. "Really?"

She nodded and bit her bottom lip, her eyes
misty. "We were getting married in a meadow and
Trinity was the flower girl."

"Ah, Rainbow." He couldn't help himself. He
had to touch her. Reaching for her, he held his
arms wide.

She was back in Roan's arms and nothing had ever
felt so right.

But he'd blocked her phone number. Even as he
was hugging her physically, metaphorically, he was
holding her at arms' length. Still too afraid to take
a chance on love. Jazzy got it, she was scared too,
but if that cookie dream revealed anything it was
that her subconscious mind knew something she
didn't.

The cookies weren't magic. There was nothing
prophetic about sleeping on a bed of kismet cookie
crumbs on Christmas Eve. The magic was in her
love for Roan.

She'd come here for one reason and it wasn't to
deliver stockings. That was a ready excuse.

Jazzy stepped back from his embrace. They were
standing in front of the fireplace. She turned to the
mantel and hung the stockings from the hooks already there. Swiveling back to him, she cleared her
throat.

His gaze was on her face, his eyes intense.

"Danny came to see me the night of the cookie challenge," she said.

"I know," Roan said. "I saw him there."

"He broke up with Andi."

"I see." Roan cleared his throat. "Are you getting back together?"

"Why would I?"

"Because you're still hung up on him?"

"Did you miss the part about my kismet cookie dream? You were the one I dreamed of, Roan Sullivan. Not Danny Garza."

"Danny was your high school sweetheart."

"And you are my cookie cowboy. I'm not hung up on Danny. He's ancient history. I don't live in the past the way you do."

He quirked an eyebrow at her. "No?"

"No."

"Then why are you always competing against Andi? Just because she beat you out for the lead in your fourth-grade play doesn't mean you have to keep playing into this dynamic. It's unhealthy."

Ouch! Roan scored solid blows.

Her rivalry with Andi had become unhealthy. She agreed. "Andi and I mended fences."

Roan looked surprised.

"My competitive days are over. After what happened at the cookie challenge I realized that no amount of competition wins would ever be enough. If I didn't stop that behavior, I was going to turn into Andi and start pushing people away. That's why I can't compete with a ghost, Roan. You're the one who's hung up over Claire and until you admit that, you're never going to be free to love again."

"Jazzy—"

"I love you, Roan Sullivan. I know what I feel and it's real. Just because I'm young doesn't make my feelings any less valid. You can block me all you want. You can never speak to me again. It doesn't matter. I still love you. That doesn't mean I'll sit around and wait on you. That doesn't mean I'll spend my days pining over your unrequited love. It just means I'll always treasure the time we shared, and I'll always and forever want the best for you." She paused. "I hope you find the peace you're looking for. Please give Trinity my love."

With that, she left his house, and he didn't even try to stop her.

The Recovery Room was surprisingly busy for Christmas night. Apparently, she wasn't the only one trying to escape herself. Charlie had worked that day and he came strolling in to join her at 7:35.

"Candy cane martinis?" he asked.

"I'm just having a beer."

"You seem sad, Lambchop."

She told him what had transpired with Roan. "I'll be all right. I always am."

"Nothing keeps our Jazzy down long," he said. "That's what we love most about you."

"While I will be all right, tonight, I want to wallow."

"You got it. Wallow away. Excuse me a minute. I'll be right back."

Sighing, she watched her friend trot off to the restroom and wished she hadn't called him. Right now, all she wanted was to go home, curl up in the bed with Sabrina and pretend the whole month of December hadn't even happened. Her competitiveness had landed her in this fix. If she could turn back time, she'd return to the karaoke competition and leave when Charlie prodded her to. If she'd done that, she wouldn't have entered the baking contest. Wouldn't have coaxed Roan into helping her.

Wouldn't have fallen in love.

Wouldn't have gotten her heart broken.

But if not for that, look at all she would have missed out on. Getting to know Trinity and Roan. Learning to make campfires and bake cookies. Having magnificent orgasms.

Oh damn, she was going to miss those orgasms.

Charlie had been gone awhile. What was keeping him? She thought about telling Nan to let Charlie know she'd gone on home when the heavy wooden door creaked open, bringing a blast of chilly December air.

Jazzy turned to see a lanky cowboy mosey in. Her pulse spiked and her breath stilled.

The cowboy did not go to the takeout counter. Instead, Roan came straight toward her. Just as he got to her table, Charlie came bebopping across the bar, his phone held in his hand as he headed for the door.

"Lambchop, you can thank me later." Then Charlie disappeared, leaving her all alone with Roan.

"Hey," he said.

"Hey yourself."

"This seat taken?"

"Not anymore."

He pulled out the chair and settled in beside her. "Charlie texted you?"

Roan took out his phone. Showed her the text from Charlie. U R a dumbass, Roan Sullivan. There's a beautiful girl at the Recovery Room pining for U. If U care about her at all, be a man. Show up.

"He oversteps sometimes."

"He's right. I am a dumbass. I'm trying to throw away the best thing I've ever had besides my daughter."

"What about Claire? Wasn't she the love of your life?"

"The love of your life changes from sixteen to thirty-three. Why do you think I believe you're too young to know your own feelings about love?"

"I'm not you, Roan. Just because you don't know how you feel about me doesn't mean I don't know how I feel about you."

"I know how I feel about you."

"Yeah, scared."

"You're right. I was running scared." He reached across the table and placed his hand over hers. "Terrified that if I let myself love you, I'll lose you."

"So, you dump me before you ever give us a chance."

"I did."

"I know I'm not Claire, but we could have something almost as good as what you had with her, Roan, if you just dare to let it happen."

"Look," he said. "We weren't the perfect couple. Claire and I. We made it look that way for YouTube. I loved her and she loved me, at one point. But we'd drifted apart. I was caught up in contesting, and

Claire? Well, my wife was never a woman who did well without constant masculine attention."

"She had an affair?"

Roan barely nodded. "When your wife dies young and leaves behind a baby, she's sainted. She stops being a real person with flaws and she's hoisted upon a pedestal. You can't speak the truth about her then. She's dead. She's left behind a baby daughter. I canonized her too. Lied to myself about how good our marriage was."

"Oh wow."

"I didn't even realize how much I'd been denying it until I was with you. Jazzy, you brought me back to myself."

"And to thank me, you dumped me."

"I was trying to protect you. I didn't want you to get caught up in my mess."

"But isn't that what couples do? Work as a team? You and Claire sure had that part down."

"Don't get me wrong. Claire and I had great times and we made good memories and created Trinity together, but I'm not hung up on her like you accused and I'm not here to talk about my late wife."

"Why are you here?"

"To grovel."

"Oh?" Grinning, Jazzy raised her eyebrows. "I'm listening."

"Maybe three weeks isn't a long enough period of time to know if you're really in love, but it is long enough to know if you stand a fighting chance for lasting love and I think we do."

"What are you saying?"

"I'm falling in love with you, Jazzy. I can see a bright future ahead for us, but you need to be sure this is the path you want. You're young. I know you don't think it matters, and maybe to you it doesn't. But what about your dreams of traveling? You deserve to live out those dreams."

"Roan," she said. "I didn't turn down Traveling Nurses for you or Danny. Or anyone. I turned them down because I realized I *love* my hometown. There's nowhere else I'd rather live. Sure, I want to travel someday, but I always want to come back home after the trip. I thought about being on the road without Sabrina or Charlie or my family and just didn't want to do it. I was only leaving because Andi had gotten engaged to my ex-boyfriend and I was too chicken to stick around and watch it play out. Being scared is never a good reason not to face something."

"Words of wisdom," he said. "How did you get so smart so young?"

"Probably having a childhood illness," she said. "It tends to put things into perspective."

"I apologize for breaking up with you. It was half-baked and I did it out of fear. I also apologize for blocking you. Same reason. You're unblocked by the way."

"Oh yeah?" She met his grin.

"Yeah."

She picked up her phone and texted him. How's Trinity?

Roan texted back. She's fine. She's with Claire's mom.

JAZZY: All night?
ROAN: All night.
JAZZY: Then why are we sitting here in a bar?

"Good question," he said. "Want to get out of here?"

"Cowboy, let's go home and bake some cookies."

"Is that a euphemism for something else?"

"Yes," she said. "Yes, it is."

And then Roan took her home where they made love all night long.

EPILOGUE

One year later

"Ready?" Jazzy asked Trinity who was dressed in an elf costume. Jazzy herself was dressed as Mrs. Claus.

"Ready!" Trinity sang out.

"Santa, get over here." Jazzy motioned for Roan to join them as the camera crew prepared for filming.

"Ho, ho, ho." Roan laughed and strolled over to the outdoor kitchen. Behind them, the firepit was stoked and ready for baking.

Jazzy's new husband looked oh-so-jolly in his Santa outfit. The change in him from the previous Christmas was miraculous. He'd gone from a worried dad to a relaxed husband and father and all it had taken was a little holiday magic, and a whole lot of emotional healing. She'd known all along that behind Roan's grief and heartache there was a man worth loving. They'd had their ups and downs, but moments like these were pure gold and Jazzy soaked up every minute of it.

The camera man raised a palm and counted off

the seconds before they started recording. "Five, four, three, two . . . one."

Jazzy beamed at the camera. "Hello subscribers and welcome back to the Sullivan Family Christmas. Today, our daughter, Trinity, is helping out in the kitchen as we bake our award-winning Chocolate-Gingermint Roanies! Once you've tried our recipe, we're certain they'll quickly become your holiday favorite too."

Roan patted his belly and ho-ho-hoed for the viewers.

For the next thirty minutes they baked for the camera and their five hundred thousand YouTube followers. They'd quickly amassed loyal fans after Roan had gone public about his grief following the loss of his wife and how he'd found love again with Jazzy. Since their wedding, they'd started filming a weekly campfire cooking show that had grown beyond their wildest dreams. And just last week they'd been contacted by the Food Network about the possibility of doing a show for them. They cited Jazzy's bubbly personality as the main reason they wanted the show.

Roan was a rancher through and through, and Jazzy loved being a pediatric nurse, so they probably wouldn't take the Food Network up on the offer, but it was fun being asked. What they really wanted was to grow their family and live a rewarding life right here on the ranch. After their troubles a year ago, Jazzy would never have believed such happiness was possible, but now they were living a dream come true.

Don't miss Lori Wilde's

THE WEDDING AT MOONGLOW BAY

Coming in trade paperback
from Avon Books, March 2023!

CHAPTER 1

"When I saw you, I fell in love and you smiled because you knew."

—WILLIAM SHAKESPEARE

The first time Samantha Riley married into the Ginelli family, her fanciful in-laws called it the *Lightning Strike*.

In reverential tones, Marcella and Tino Ginelli told romantic tales of legendary ancestors who'd been hit by metaphorical love-lightning. Generations of Ginellis had fallen madly in love at first sight and ended up in solid, long-lasting marriages and they had the genealogical records to back it up.

There wasn't a single story of the *Lightning Strike* gone awry. Legend had it, once you got walloped by the one-two punch of predestined love, in Ginelli-land you were mated for a happily ever-after life.

Samantha met Nick on the first day of her high school junior year.

Her foster family, the Dellaneys, had just moved

from Houston. A month before, her foster father, Heath, had taken a gig working with the Moonglow Cove Chamber of Commerce. After years in a high-pressure corporate job, he was ready for the slower pace of a small beachside tourist town.

Piper, Samantha's foster sister and best friend in the entire world, declared the town b-o-r-i-n-g and she was in a pout as they walked into Moonglow Cove High School together, unsure of where the offices were or how to find their classrooms.

"Hey, look. What a cute mascot," Samantha said, trying to cheer up her pal, and pointed to a chubby-cheeked chipmunk painted on the wall. Chipmunk Charlie had his head thrown back in raucous laughter.

"Seriously? A ground squirrel? That is so lame." Piper touched her cheeks that she bemoaned as her "chipmunk pouches."

"But look at his beautiful grin." Samantha widened her own smile in effigy.

"Chipmunk Charlie would be amuse-bouche for Ivan." Piper studied her fingernails chipped of chartreuse polish.

In Houston, their mascot had been a tiger nicknamed Ivan the Terrible, and their class song had been Katy Perry's "Roar". Cheesy? Oh yes, but Piper was right. Fierce Ivan would make short work of cheerful Charlie.

"A school the size of Moonglow Cove would never play our old high school."

"God, don't be so literal." Piper rolled her eyes.

A twinge of shame twisted Samantha's chest. Piper was just teasing, she knew that, but Samantha couldn't help thinking she'd done something wrong.

"Let me guess." Piper seemed blithely unaware she'd stirred Samantha's anxiety. "Their class song has to be that silly Chipmunk song." In a voice that sounded like she'd been inhaling helium, Piper sang a few bars of the Christmas tune by Alvin and the Chipmunks.

"Please try to like this place . . . for me?"

"Okay, sure." Laughing, Piper slipped her arm through Samantha and pulled her into a skip, and they bounced jauntily down the hallway.

"We're really doing this on the first day?" Samantha asked, feeling self-conscious.

"Yeah, baby. Let our freak flags fly. Put that in your Zig-Zags and smoke it, Moonglow High."

People turned to stare as they skipped past. Boldly, Piper stuck out her tongue and Samantha's face heated. They rounded the corner and a thick stream of students pouring in through the side door forced them to halt.

Piper blinked. "Okay, Miss Spreadsheet, where do we go from here?"

"Out of the traffic flow."

Samantha tugged her friend to one side, pulled her cell phone from her pocket and consulted the school's app she'd downloaded the night before. "Next stop, the registrar's office."

"Why? We already registered online."

"Doesn't matter. The app says we gotta check in, regardless."

"Ugh! What was the point of registering online?"

"Come on." Samantha led the way to the registrar's office. "Where's your normal sunshiny self?"

"Back in Houston. Dad ruined my life dragging us to Podunk, USA."

"We're living at the beach. I've died and flown to heaven."

"You're so easily pleased. Now I feel all guilty and shit."

Someone jostled into Samantha's elbow, and she fumbled with her phone, almost dropping it.

"We're gonna get trampled. We gotta move." Piper took hold of Samantha's arm and dragged her back into the foot traffic. Samantha kept thumbing through the app as if more knowledge could save her.

"It says here that . . ." Samantha glanced up to show Piper her phone screen and watched horrified as her friend approached a folding ladder erected below Moonglow Cove High School signage. A maintenance guy stood on the top rung, tightening down the "M" with a power drill.

Terror shot adrenaline through Samantha's veins. "Piper, no! It's bad luck!"

"What?" Her bold friend stopped directly underneath the ladder and turned to look at her. She extended her arms wide, touching both side of the ladder. "It's an old wives' tale."

Samantha took a giant step forward, grabbed Piper by the wrist and yanked her from under the ladder just as the maintenance person bobbled the power drill and it fell right where Piper had been standing two second earlier.

Thunk.

"Holy shit." Piper peeked at the drill that would have conked her on the head. "You saved my life."

They stared into each other's eyes as the maintenance guy jumped from the ladder to retrieve his drill, apologizing profusely.

"I'll never mock your crazy superstitions again."

"I'm just glad you're okay." Samantha wiped sweat from her forehead, then linked her arm through Piper's again and skirted her around the ladder.

"This school is out to kill me. I told you I didn't like it here and—" Piper stopped dead in her tracks, and Samantha was two steps ahead before she realized Piper had stayed rooted.

"What is it?"

"Changed my mind. I *love* this place."

Samantha pushed her glasses up on her nose and squinted at her friend. "Huh?"

Piper nodded toward the water fountain. "Pinch me. I must be dreaming."

Samantha followed her foster sister's gaze and *bam*! It was like something from the romance novels she read in secret so Piper wouldn't tease her.

There, in the illuminating glow from the overhead skylight, stood a handsome, dark-haired guy in a letterman jacket. He was tall, around six feet, broad of shoulders and narrow of waist. His teeth were straight and white. Dude coulda modeled for a dental commercial. In his left cheek, a dimple grew with his expanding grin. He wore tight jeans, Converse sneakers and a tight black T-shirt. His skin was beach-bum tan, the color of cinnamon-soaked peaches. His nose crooked slightly, as if it had been broken, as if he wasn't afraid of a fight.

His good looks had a Mediterranean vibe. What

was his ancestry? Italian? Greek? Spanish? She studied him, intrigued.

Italian, she decided before she ever found out his last name.

Inside her chest, her heart did a crazy bump and grind, stalling her breath in her lungs. Her hormones gripped her in a sultry heat that blistered a trail from her cheeks, down her nape, and around her spine to lodge squarely in her gut before spreading electric shock waves straight to her girly parts.

She met his dark brown mischievous eyes and welcoming grin, and Samantha was a goner.

Mine, she thought greedily. This one was heaven sent just for her. *This* was what she'd waited for her entire life.

Her nerve endings tingled, and her brain locked up as saliva filled her mouth. She hopped right onto the highspeed train to Sexy Danger Town and never looked back.

Piper poked her in the ribcage, and she didn't even notice. With his stare latched tightly onto hers, the Italian Stallion sauntered toward Samantha.

"Oh, my gawd, oh, my gawd, oh, my gawd." Panting, Piper fanned herself. "He's coming over."

Samantha stood frozen to the spot, unable to move or speak. Finally, she understood what people meant when they said someone was caught like a deer in the headlights. Her—doe. Him—eighteen-wheeler.

Everything evaporated except *this* guy.

Gone were the other students milling around them.

Poof.

The pressure of her backpack.

Vanished.

Piper.

Bye-Bye.

She couldn't have run if there'd been a zombie apocalypse. Illogical words exploded in her brain. *Fate. Destiny. Kismet*.

Her foster sister extended a palm toward the handsome guy and grinned like a loon. "Hello, my name's Piper, what's yours?"

He never broke eye contact with Samantha, just peered right over Piper's head. "That was really intuitive of you. Pulling your friend to safety just before the janitor dropped his drill."

"You saw that?"

"You've got keen survival instincts."

His words sent a heated flush over her cheeks.

"It's more that my foster sister is superstitious as all get-out than anything else," Piper said. "Me? I don't have a superstitious bone in my body. I'll walk under ladders all day long if it leads to you."

He slanted Piper a look, then to Samantha he said, "Hi, I'm Nick Ginelli."

"Sa . . . Sa . . . Sa . . ."

"SaSaSa?" he teased. "Unusual name."

"I . . . um . . . Samantha. My name is Samantha Riley."

"You're new here."

"I am."

Lightly, he nudged Piper to one side with his elbow and came closer.

Piper frowned and sank her hands on her hips. "Hey, hey. I'm not the invisible woman here."

"Excuse me." Nick didn't even glance at her foster sister.

His focused attention sent a sweet shiver through Samantha's solar plexus. Intoxicating stuff for a girl who'd spent a lifetime moving from foster home to foster home. Her self-esteem was still a little shaky, although her three years with the Dellaneys helped.

"Huh, maybe I *am* invisible?" Piper patted herself.

Samantha's heart pumped hard, thrilled that Nick had come to her instead of Piper.

Boys swarmed her friend like honeybees to flowers. Pretty, perky, and profane, Piper possessed qualities boys seemed to enjoy.

Guys were rarely interested in bespectacled, overly organized, A-student bookworms. Unless they were begging her to write their term paper. It was nice, for a change, to be the object of desire.

Nick extended his hand.

Nervous, Samantha pushed her glasses up on the bridge of her nose and caught a whiff of his fragrance. He smelled like tomato sauce, garlic, and onions. Both terrified and thrilled, she took his hand.

His touch was electric, and she lost her breath completely.

"You heard it too, didn't you," he said. Statement, not a question.

"Wh-what?"

He didn't let go of her hand, kept his gaze locked onto hers. "That unmistakable *click*."

Oh yeah, she had heard the snap inside her brain like the missing piece of life's puzzle clicking into place and her fantasies filled with romantic *what-if* scenarios revolving around her future and this boy.

But she wouldn't admit that to him.

Far too scary.

"You felt it." He paused, still holding her hand, and staring deeply into her eyes.

"Mm . . . um . . ."

"Like a cobalt blue lightning bolt jumping from the sky and shooting straight through your heart."

"Y-yes," she said. "How did you know?"

"I felt the same thing. When you know, you know."

Know what? She wanted to ask, but her tongue wasn't working.

"When the lightning strikes, the lightning strikes, and there's nothing you can do but climb aboard the ride."

Mixing metaphors, but okay. *Sign me up!*

The hallway thinned out. Soon it was just her, Piper and Nick left standing and the maintenance guy folding up his ladder.

Piper elbowed Samantha. "C'mon. We're gonna be late for class."

Lateness. It was a terrifying thought for a good-girl people-pleaser. But Piper's warning didn't even make a dent in her brain gone all mushy from Nick's warm touch.

"Go on without me."

"Oh, hells to the no, cupcake. No woman left behind. We're a team. You're here. I'm here. All for one and one for all."

On the whole, Samantha appreciated Piper's loyalty and friendship, but not today. Today, she ached to tell Piper to buzz off. Which wasn't like her. What had this guy done to her in under five minutes? It was both terrifying and enthralling.

"Goodbye now, Mr. Ginelli, we gotta go." Piper tugged on Samantha's sweater.

A lone student came running down the corridor, shouldering a heavy backpack, wide-eyed and panic-stricken, chanting, "I'm late, I'm late," as if he was *Alice in Wonderland*'s White Rabbit.

Bookish Samantha couldn't resist mentally adding *for a very important date*.

Except she wasn't late. Her very important date was standing right in front of her, looking at her as if she'd hand painted the Milky Way in oils on velvet cloth.

Nick's hand was still hot on hers. His eyes aglow like twin flames burning just for her. "We're fated, Samantha Riley. You and me. I know it. You know it. And the Lightning Strike knows it."

From anyone else, at any other time in her life, this might have sounded super corny, and maybe even a little creepy. But at sixteen, eager for adventure and yearning for her first boyfriend, it was the coolest thing she'd ever heard.

In her head, she heard Kylie Minogue singing, "Love at First Sight" and just like that, Samantha was lovestruck.

And from that moment forward, there was no one else for her but Nick Ginelli until the day he died.